Bl

"Rowen jumps from paranormal romance to paranormal mystery without skipping a beat. . . . Here's hoping Sarah will have many more adventures in her new series."

—*RT Book Reviews*

"Her writing is sharp, witty, and does not disappoint. The ending will delight both old and new fans, and leave you thirsting for the next installment."

—Night Owl Reviews

"An engaging paranormal mystery."

—Genre Go Round Reviews

"Readers will believe in vampires and slayers. . . . Filled with romance and high-stakes suspense; fans will appreciate the return of Sarah Dearly and Thierry de Bennicoeur in an exciting, dark whodunit." —Gumshoe

Praise for Other Novels
by Michelle Rowen

"I've been bitten and smitten by Michelle Rowen."

—*New York Times* bestselling author Sherrilyn Kenyon

"What a charming, hilarious book! Frankly, I'm insanely jealous I didn't write it."

—*New York Times* bestselling author MaryJanice Davidson

continued . . .

"Rowen's foray into a new dark, gritty world is a brilliant success . . . [and] an adrenaline rush!"

—*New York Times* bestselling author Larissa Ione

"Should leave readers breathless." —*Kirkus Reviews*

"Michelle Rowen's books never fail to thrill."

—Bitten by Books

"Sassy and exhilarating . . . epic and thrilling."

—Fresh Fiction

"I have never read a Michelle Rowen book that I did not adore." —Enchanted by Books

Also by Michelle Rowen

Immortality Bites Mysteries

BLOOD BATH & BEYOND

Berkley Sensation Titles

THE DEMON IN ME

SOMETHING WICKED

THAT OLD BLACK MAGIC

NIGHTSHADE

BLOODLUST

Anthologies

PRIMAL

(with Lora Leigh, Jory Strong, and Ava Gray)

BLED & BREAKFAST

MICHELLE ROWEN

OBSIDIAN
Published by the Penguin Group
Penguin Group (USA) Inc., 375 Hudson Street,
New York, New York 10014, USA

USA | Canada | UK | Ireland | Australia | New Zealand | India | South Africa | China

Penguin Books Ltd., Registered Offices: 80 Strand, London WC2R 0RL, England
For more information about the Penguin Group visit penguin.com.

First published by Obsidian, an imprint of New American Library,
a division of Penguin Group (USA) Inc.

First Printing, June 2013
10 9 8 7 6 5 4 3 2 1

ISBN 978-0-451-23996-9

Printed in the United States of America

To every reader who's been along for
the ride since the very first bite.

ACKNOWLEDGMENTS

Thank you to Bonnie Staring, who kindly beta-read this novel for me. Many friends might be afraid to tell you what they *really* think—the bad stuff, anyway. Bonnie isn't one of them. She is the invaluable blond and female Simon Cowell in my writing world and my books are stronger and my characters are smarter (sometimes) because of her.

Thank you to my editor Leis Pederson and the entire team at Obsidian. I love writing in this genre. It's seriously the most fun I've ever had in my life. Writing-wise, anyway.

Thank you to my brilliant and hilarious agent, Jim McCarthy, who's been a Sarah fan since day one. And day one is feeling like a loooong time ago! You are the bestest!

Chapter 1

Crystal balls have a lot in common with eyeballs. They both have the power to reveal hidden truths—that is, if you're brave enough to look deeply.

This occurred to me as I sat in a quaint fortune-telling café in Salem, Massachusetts, across the table from two sets of eyes and one crystal ball.

The first pair of eyes was clear blue and smiling, set into the pleasant face of a woman in her late fifties. She wore the expected outfit of a fortune-teller—colorful blue and green robes embroidered with gold stars and moons, as well as a jade green turban that mostly encased her dark hair. With a glance into her eyes, I could tell that she was both friendly and earnest.

She believed she could tell my future while I waited for my coffee order.

"You're new in town," the fortune-teller said as she gazed into the crystal ball in the middle of the small round table covered by a red tablecloth. The conversations of others in the busy café buzzed all around, and coffee, tea, and freshly baked cinnamon pastries scented the air.

"Just arrived," I confirmed.

"And you're here . . . not purely for a vacation, but for business."

"That's right."

A small frown creased between her penciled-in eyebrows as she gazed into the crystal ball. "However, you do hope this trip will serve two purposes—business *and* pleasure. This is also your honeymoon. Am I right?"

I sent a sidelong glance toward the other pair of eyes watching this reading with interest. These eyes were the gray of a winter sky. At first glance, they were cold. At second glance, colder.

At third glance . . . I didn't think they were cold at all.

To say I was fond of these particular wintery eyes would be an understatement.

"A resort in Hawaii would have been our first choice," Thierry said, giving me a wry look. "But a hotel room in Salem will suffice."

"Palm trees and hula dancers," I said with a shrug. "Who needs 'em?"

Only a day and a half after we'd gotten married in Las Vegas in a whirlwind ceremony that included an Elvis impersonator and some really cheesy but fabulous vows, Thierry had been notified of his next assignment. That call put us on a flight from Vegas to Boston. From there, we rented a car, which brought us the rest of the way to Salem—and *bam*. Here we were.

No rest for the wicked. And really, with so many airplanes in my future now that I'd happily committed myself body and soul to being both Thierry's wife and his assistant in his job as a consultant for the Ring—the official vampire council—I'd have to figure out a way to get over my fear of flying.

Since we were currently in Salem, maybe I'd learn how to ride a broomstick.

I wondered how this woman knew about the honeymoon thing. Was she a witch?

It was easy enough to figure out her supernatural insight on us. I'd noticed Thierry fiddling with his plain wedding band—which he'd insisted on wearing even though he never wore any other jewelry. You can't teach an old dog new tricks. Master vampires . . . Well, they were very much the same thing. That he was willing to try to adjust to *anything* outside his comfort zone made his fledgling vampire wife extremely happy.

"Giddy" might be a better word for it, actually.

But the fiddling was a definite tell that the fortune-teller had picked up on. Newlyweds, table for two.

She looked deeply into the crystal ball. "I see wonderful things for your future. Every day you spend together will be filled with adventure and romance."

I tried not to smile too widely at that. "That's good to know."

Thierry gave me another glance as I slid my hand over his. "Enjoying your complimentary fortune so far, Sarah?"

I nodded. "Any fortune that isn't one of doom and gloom is much appreciated."

The woman raised her eyebrows. "I don't give bad fortunes. Who wants unhappy news—especially at such an exciting time with your young and handsome husband?"

Handsome, most definitely—Thierry was tall and broad shouldered, with dark hair and those piercing gray eyes. But, young? It was a good sign that this fortune-teller wasn't quite as universally insightful as she wanted us to believe. Thierry might physically look to be in his mid-thirties, but tack on another six centuries and you'd be in the right ballpark. This particular ballpark had been around since medieval times—and I'm not talking about the theme restaurant with jousting actors and wenches delivering ale and turkey drumsticks.

Compared to Thierry, at twenty-eight I was practically an amoeba when it came to life and experience. But, as they say, opposites attract. And there weren't too many couples—fanged or otherwise—more opposite than the two of us.

I was about to reply to the fortune-teller when I felt something strange—a sensation of cold fingers trailing down my spine. I tightened my grip on Thierry's hand and turned slowly in my chair to glance over my shoulder.

Someone was watching me from the archway leading into the gift shop area. A man with black hair and black eyes. His attention was focused on me like a laser beam. His gaze was cold, hard, and endlessly unpleasant.

"Who's that guy?" I whispered, turning back around.

"Who do you mean?" the woman asked.

"The tall, pale man standing over there with cheekbones sharp enough to cut glass. He's giving me the creeps."

She frowned, glancing over in the direction I nodded. "There's no one there."

I turned again to see that she was right. "Where did he go?"

"There was no one there to begin with." Thierry's brow furrowed. He didn't say it like he doubted I saw anything. More like he was confused by why he *hadn't.*

"Hmm. Could be you caught a glimpse of our infamous local ghost," the fortune-teller said lightly. "Lucky you. He doesn't make an appearance for just anyone."

My gaze shot to hers. "There are ghosts here?"

"No—*ghost.* Singular. While there are many ghosts spotted in Salem, this is the only one that's ever really been of any lasting importance." She smiled. "Exciting, isn't it?"

"Yeah," I agreed halfheartedly. "Hooray."

We really should have gone to Hawaii.

"Spirits lose their ties to the world of the living three days after death," Thierry said. "How long has this one been here?"

"There have been sightings of Malik for over three hundred years. Not just in this café, either. All over Salem."

"Malik?" I repeated the name. It didn't sound nearly as friendly as Casper.

"Jonathan Malik, to be precise. He was a witch hunter." The woman's expression turned grave, but by the sparkle in her eyes, it was clear that she loved sharing information on this subject. "Murdered by a witch following the trials. She trapped his spirit here forevermore as punishment."

"Forevermore?" I repeated. Not exactly a word you heard every day. But it did add some drama.

"And then some." She sighed. "I've never been lucky enough to see him, although I'm told he's very handsome. Then again, we don't know for sure that's who you saw, do we? It could simply have been a customer who slipped into the next room."

She did have a point there.

After wishing us a pleasant visit to town, she picked up her crystal ball and excused herself so she could go give another table a free and pleasant—but quick and generic—fortune while they waited for their order.

The waitress brought over our mugs of coffee a moment later.

I glanced at Thierry as I stirred two teaspoons of sugar into my hazelnut blend. "The ghost of a witch hunter named Malik may have been giving me the hairy eyeball from across the room a minute ago. Should I freak out now or save it for later?"

He raised a dark eyebrow. "Better than a vampire hunter."

"I appreciate your taking this seriously."

A smile played at his lips as he gave me a slight shrug. "If that is indeed who you saw, you must remember that a ghost's effect on the living is negligible at best. Even if the rumor's true and you did see this particular witch hunter, it's nothing to concern yourself with. He can't do you—or any living being—any harm."

I took a sip of my coffee, successfully calmed by his calmness. "I'm surprised you didn't see him, too. If it's really a ghost, that is."

"Me too."

Thierry and I might be opposites in many ways, but we did share a special skill that only a small percentage of vampires possessed. We could see ghosts and also sense the departing spirit of someone after death. But ghosts weren't exactly commonplace, especially those who'd died so long ago. Either something would have to trap them here on earth or they'd have to be summoned by a psychic with very strong skills—and finding a psychic like that was as rare as finding a nun in a string bikini.

Bottom line, ghosts weren't lurking on every street corner. Thankfully.

"Here he is," Thierry said, rising from the table. Any amusement on his face from earlier faded. "Let me do the talking, Sarah. Owen is not someone I want you to have much contact with."

Well, *that* was rather ominous. "Noted. I'll play the part of the mute brunette."

We'd been asked to meet with a vampire named Owen Harper, whom Thierry knew from years ago, immediately upon our arrival. Owen was to give us an overview of the problem Thierry (and I) had been sent to check out.

That was the job of a consultant. Quite simple, really. If there was a vampire-related issue that drew the Ring's attention, they sent someone like Thierry to consult on it and assess the situation. From what I'd deduced, it seemed as if the Ring was mostly interested in keeping the existence of vampires a big secret from humans—worldwide. Anything that risked that secret needed attention and a swift resolution.

The Ring also had their own police force, called enforcers. Or, perhaps *assassins* would be a better descriptor. They were vampires who were also vampire *hunters*. They took care of problems if and when they escalated.

Just because vampires didn't automatically become evil fiends after sprouting fangs and developing a thirst for blood, it didn't mean we were all good, either. I'd met a bad one recently—a serial killer who'd nearly added Thierry and me to his list of victims. But he'd been stopped. Permanently.

Sarah Dearly lives to bite another day.

That was just a joke, of course. I rarely do more than nibble.

I'd met a few people from Thierry's very long and—at times—notorious past. So far, they were mostly horrible people who disliked him due to some lingering grudge. My hope that Owen would be different was modest at best.

"Thierry de Bennicoeur . . . ," Owen began as I tensely watched him approach the table from the corner of my eye. "It's been a hell of a long time, dude."

I blinked. *Dude?*

I turned fully to get a look at him as he clasped Thierry's hand and shook it vigorously.

"Good to see you again, Owen," Thierry said.

Owen Harper looked a whole lot like a male model crossed with an A-list actor. Blond hair, flashing green eyes, at least six-three, and he had the muscled physique of a personal trainer. Standing next to my already extremely GQ-esque husband . . . well, it was quite a sight.

Holy hotness, Batman. Times two.

I didn't know why this surprised me. I'd met my share of good-looking vampires since I was sired into a life of fangs, blood, and nonreflection by the ultimate blind date from hell last year. This was par for the course, really.

"And this"—Owen flashed me a killer smile that revealed the small but pointy tips to his fangs—"must be Sarah Dearly."

"However did you guess?" said the previously mute brunette.

"Thierry told me over the phone that you were drop-dead gorgeous. Call it a hunch."

I glanced at Thierry with surprise. "You actually used the words 'drop-dead gorgeous' to describe me?"

He was the only one of us who wasn't smiling. "I certainly could have. However, Owen has always tended to make things up to be amusing. This is one of those times."

It wasn't said with fondness.

Call me crazy, but I had a pretty good idea why Thierry didn't want me to have much to do with Owen. The guy was a serious lady-killer. However, that leering edge to his gaze didn't make me want to start swooning over his good looks.

I think I was the only woman in a thirty-foot radius who wasn't drooling. Still, I'd reserve my judgment for when I'd known this guy for more than two minutes. First impressions could sometimes be deceiving.

Thierry gestured for Owen to take a seat. "Why don't we get to the point?"

Owen slid into a chair. "No small talk for an old pal? Thierry, you haven't changed at all over the years, have you?"

"I've changed," he replied. "More than I ever would have thought possible, actually."

Owen's gaze flicked to me again. "Maybe you're right. And what a wonderful change it is. Tell me, Sarah, how on earth do you put up with Monsieur de Bennicoeur's dour ways? You must feel as if you've married a high school principal."

I shrugged. "Guess that's my type. The dourer the better, I say."

"I'm not dour," Thierry said dourly.

Owen grinned. "Congratulations on your nuptials, by the way. I think it's fantastic."

"Do you?" Thierry gave him a skeptical look before it finally eased. "Well, thank you. I appreciate that."

"Can't believe you also committed yourself to the Ring, though. They must have had some serious duress involved to get you back into the fold. When I finished my term with them I was happy to finally be free. But good luck to you."

Thierry didn't reply to this and I wasn't going to touch the subject with a ten-foot wooden stake. In a nutshell, the Ring—while a necessary entity—was a shadowy and mysterious organization that did shadowy and mysterious things. Thierry had been an original founder but left a century ago to pursue other interests. Very recently—like, less than a week ago—he'd taken the job as consultant, a job that required him to sign on the dotted line. In blood.

It was part of a blood magic spell that bound him to the Ring for the next fifty years.

I believed he'd done it because they'd threatened to kill me if he didn't. So, yeah, "duress" was a good word. He had yet to admit this to me in so many words, but I knew it was the truth. He'd sacrificed his own future to save my life and he'd never wanted me to know.

My heart swelled every time I thought about it. I would love him forevermore for that. *For-ever-more.*

And I didn't trust the Ring as far as I could throw them. I had a very good memory, and this matter, as far as I was concerned, was nowhere near resolved.

"So . . . ," I said after silence fell at the table. "What's happening in Salem? You're the guy with all the answers, apparently."

Owen gestured for an eager waitress to bring him a cup of coffee. "Not all the answers, I'm afraid."

"All I was told was that there have been some disappearances," Thierry said. "Tell us more."

Owen nodded. "Three vampires have gone missing while visiting town. Nobody would have thought anything strange about it, but they've disappeared in less than a month. One of these vampires is the mistress of a Ring elder, thus the quick response."

"Do you suspect vampire hunters?" Thierry asked.

"No. At least, I don't think so. Hunters steer clear of Salem. That's why I like it here so much."

I frowned. "Why do they stay away from here? They seem to gather everywhere else to make our lives difficult."

"Likely, the threat of witches." Thierry caught my surprised reaction. "Hunters are a superstitious lot. Witches are bad luck for them. Also, crossing paths with a witch hunter would be dangerous for everyone involved."

I thought it through, still disturbed by the idea of witches or witch hunters, let alone regular hunters. "So it would be like turf wars—*West Side Story* without the singing."

"Something like that. Or, at least, that's what they try to avoid. Other towns that are rumored to be the home to covens are treated much the same way. The world of witches and the world of vampires rarely cross paths."

"So there *are* witches in Salem," I said. For this I looked at Owen for the answer. After all, he lived here.

"Some," he agreed. "But no alphas."

At my confused look, Thierry took over. "An alpha is the term used for a very powerful witch who can do magic without a grimoire, a book of spells. These witches are rare."

"And luckily, none are currently living in Salem," Owen added. "Just the harmless ones who like to do simple spells and cook up magical recipes. There are many peaceful Wiccans here, too. And, of course, there are the ones who only *think* they're witches. They usually wear the pointy hats."

When I thought of Salem, of course I thought of witches. My knowledge of witches as a kid involved watching reruns of *Bewitched*—and I had the nose twitch down pat. This town was ready, willing, and able to appeal to that particular tourist expectation. There was even a bronze statue of Elizabeth Montgomery herself seated on her broom in Lappin Park, close to this café.

But *alpha* witch? Like an alpha werewolf, I figured—the leader, the most powerful one. Only . . . minus the hairballs.

"You said one of the missing vampires is the mistress of a Ring elder," Thierry said, helping to get us back on topic.

Owen nodded. "That's right."

"If there aren't any hunters in town, maybe nothing bad happened to her," I reasoned. "Maybe she was tired of being his mistress and took off with someone else."

"Maybe." Owen cleared his throat. He wasn't looking directly at us anymore; instead he was staring over at the coffee bar with its glass display of baked goods.

Thierry watched him carefully, his arms crossed over his chest. "Let me guess. You were romantically involved with her."

"I'm not really sure I'd say that one night constitutes *involved.* There's a popular karaoke bar that I go to all the time, and let's just say that Monique knew how to sing Beyoncé like nobody's business." He shrugged. "I had to have her."

"You slept with the mistress of a Ring elder." I put it into words so there was no misunderstanding here.

He didn't look the least bit guilty about it. "What can I say? For a three-hundred-year-old woman she was unbelievably hot. Like *porn star* hot, you know?"

He seemed to consider this to be an asset.

"But she's gone, just disappeared," he finished.

"And the other two?" Thierry asked.

"A regular vamp couple passing through town with no specific Ring affiliation. I had dinner with them. Nice." He cleared his throat again. "Really nice."

Something about the way he said it . . .

"How well did you know them?" I asked.

"Uh . . . let's just say that some couples like to experiment when they're on vacation. And if they happen to suggest that I join them, what am I supposed to say? No?"

I could safely say I'd now known him long enough to have a non-first-impression impression. Owen Harper—a vampire of amazing looks and indeterminate age—was the town slut.

"So three vampires have gone missing while traveling through Salem," Thierry said evenly, "and all three had spent a night with you."

Owen took the mug of coffee from the passing waitress's tray, throwing a couple bucks in its place, and gave her a flirtatious grin before she moved on. "Basically. And just for the record, I had nothing to do with their disappearances."

There was no accusation in Thierry's gaze toward Owen at these revelations. Nor was there any surprise. None at all.

"Does the Ring know this?" I asked. "That you were, um, *intimately* involved with them?"

"Are you kidding?" He gave me a stunned look, then turned to Thierry. "If Franklin found out about me and Monique . . . he'd probably have me staked. And it was *nothing*. The briefest of flings."

Thierry let out a humorless snort. "You're right. He wouldn't be pleased. If I'm not mistaken, you also had a 'brief fling' with his second wife during the Civil War."

Owen took another sip of his coffee. "Whatever. It's not like it's relevant. Three vamps are missing without a trace. That's all I know. Now it's your job to find out what happened to them."

"And you?" I asked. "What are you going to do?"

"Whatever I like. As usual." He gave me another friendly grin. "I can show you around town if Thierry's too busy. It would be my pleasure to get to know you better."

"I don't think so. You're not nearly dour enough for me to spend more than a few minutes with. No offense."

I heard another snort from Thierry's direction. This one held much more humor than the last.

If he'd even been the least bit concerned that I'd be taken in by this shiny but vapid vampire, then he needed to think again. I mean, please.

"We need a suggestion for a hotel," Thierry said. "Can you help?"

Owen had brushed off my dismissal without an ounce of ill will, which I had to respect. His smile hadn't even wavered. "Of course. But you don't want a hotel. I know a great bed-and-breakfast that would be perfect for you."

A bed-and-breakfast sounded wonderful, actually. I'd never stayed in one before. And Salem—witches or not—seemed like the perfect spot for a casual but fun honeymoon, even if we had to take care of some business as well.

"Lead the way," I said.

Just before I followed Owen and Thierry through the swinging glass door, I had that strange shivery feeling again. I stopped and turned to look.

The pale, dark-haired man was back, and he stood a dozen feet away, staring at me. I met his black eyes directly and felt frozen in place by the coldness in his gaze.

"Soon," he said, his voice deep and scary and as icy as his eyes. Then the corner of his mouth turned up into a sinister smile.

The next moment he disappeared into thin air.

I shuddered.

Yeah. That was definitely a ghost. And one that nobody else seemed able to see.

Lucky me.

Chapter 2

The Booberry Inn was a Georgian colonial painted shades of gray, with a purple front door and a well-tended flower garden—very colorful under the hot, bright sun of this mid-June day.

Many might expect that vampires never ventured out in the sunlight. Well, they'd be wrong. We were fine during daylight hours and slept at night—just like regular humans. However, the sun *did* feel way brighter than it had before I was sired, and it worked to quickly zap my energy. My remedy for this was a nice pair of dark sunglasses and giving up my need to maintain a tan. Problem solved.

"Booberry?" I said as we walked up the front path, glancing at the hand-painted sign.

"Ghost joke," Owen replied with a smirk.

"Is the rumor of an infamous witch hunter's ghost haunting Salem true or just a story the locals like to tell?" Thierry asked.

Owen shrugged. "Who cares? Ghosts are so meaningless in the grand scheme of things."

"True enough."

That ghost in the café hadn't seemed so meaningless to me. Especially with that cryptically whispered "soon," which still sent a chill racing through me. In other words, I'd been successfully spooked by a spook.

Still, Thierry and Owen were right. Ghosts didn't have much effect on the living other than being mostly weird and sometimes scary entities trapped at the periphery of certain places. Just because I could see this Malik guy didn't mean he had any influence over me. If I saw him again I'd just ignore him, since giving him the "You're freaking me out!" look was only feeding the troll.

Owen knocked on the front door, and it opened a minute later to a young redheaded woman whose eyes widened at the sight of him. "Owen, wow. Hi. I didn't expect to see you today."

"Yet here I am." He gave her a devastating grin. "With friends who need a spot to stay. Of course, the first place I thought of was yours."

She beamed. "Thank you. We actually don't have anyone else registered right now, so this is great!"

"Heather McKinley, this is Thierry and Sarah de Bennicoeur. They're newlyweds."

Thierry and I exchanged a look, his amused, mine surprised. *Mr. and Mrs. de Bennicoeur.* It was the first time anyone had referred to us in that way.

I hadn't even considered going by his name full-time. As the last Dearly in my family line, I'd assumed I'd hang on to the name indefinitely.

"Mrs. de Bennicoeur" sounded like the name of a much, much older woman. For example, Thierry's ex-wife, Veronique, who was even older than he was (and, happily, far out of the picture and—fingers crossed—not likely to cause us problems anytime soon). But I suppose there was no reason why I couldn't go by both when the occasion called for it.

Sarah de Bennicoeur.

It sounded so . . . worldly.

"Oh, how wonderful!" Heather grinned at us. "Congratulations."

I smiled back at her. "Thanks. Great bed-and-breakfast, by the way. And the Booberry Inn is such a cute name."

"Heather does cute really well," Owen said.

She flinched at this. I didn't think he'd meant it as an insult, but she didn't seem pleased with the thought of being "cute" to the town gigolo.

Uh-oh. I suddenly recognized that look she'd been giving him from the moment she opened the door. Heather had a crush on Owen. A big one.

"Please come in." Heather opened the door wider.

"Well, look who it is," an unfriendly voice called from the sidewalk. "Thought I'd get home without having to see *you.*"

Heather cringed again but then fixed a stiff but pleasant smile on her face. She looked over my shoulder in the direction of the voice. "Hi, Miranda."

"Friends of yours visiting?" Miranda said thinly, then let out a dry chuckle. "How adorable. At least you have some friends in town, even if you can't get any regular customers."

I turned to look at the blonde on the sidewalk, who was giving Heather a hostile glare.

"Actually," I said, bristling at the thought of anyone being mocked or intimidated who seemed too timid to immediately throw it back, "Heather and I are *best* friends. So back off, or I'd be happy to wipe that miserable look off your face."

Miranda sent a pinched look at me, appraising me from head to foot. "Whatever."

"Nice comeback."

Her narrowed gaze moved to Owen. "And *you*. What are you doing here? You told me you'd be out of town this week."

"I'm sorry," Owen said, fighting a grin. "Do I know you?"

She let out a sharp bark of a laugh that held no humor. "You are such a jerk, you know that? Everybody knows it, too. Everybody. You think you can sleep around and I wouldn't find out about it?"

He lifted a shoulder. "Wasn't a secret. If you thought what we had was more than it was, you were fooling yourself." He said it blandly, as if he couldn't care less what she thought of him.

I wasn't sure who to root for in this particular standoff, although I did lean toward Owen. He had the fangs.

Miranda glared at him. "You should leave town before something bad happens to you."

"Is that a warning or a threat, Miranda?"

"Take it however you like, *Owen*." She said the name like it tasted bad.

"Will you conjure up a voodoo doll and stick it with pins?" He laughed mockingly. "I could use a little acupuncture."

With a reddening face, Miranda finally glanced at Thierry. Her eyebrow arched with fresh interest. "Now, *you* can stay. You should come find me at Mulligan's later. I'd be happy to get to know you better, handsome."

Thierry crossed his arms over his chest and regarded her silently. He wasn't exactly the type to throw out a snarky retort. His displeased glower, however, spoke volumes.

Her expression soured. "Whatever."

Then she gave him—and the rest of us—the finger before moving on down the sidewalk.

I turned to Heather, who looked pale and unhappy. "So . . . she seems nice."

She gave me a weak grin. "Ignore her. She's been like that since high school. Thought ten years would change her. Guess what?"

"It didn't?"

"Nope."

We followed Heather into the warm and well-furnished interior of the Booberry Inn. She still seemed shaken, but I had to give her credit for trying to pull herself together and appear professional. She moved to a small antique wooden desk in an adjoining room and sat down behind it.

Uneasily, I followed, moving out of the way of the mirror on the wall near the entrance. One myth about vampires that was true—no reflections. Don't even get me started on how inconvenient it was. Just don't.

Heather pulled out a leather-bound ledger. "How long do you think you'll be staying with us?"

"Good question." I looked at Thierry.

"Let's say three days for now," he said. "It might be more depending on how things go."

She nodded and scribbled the information down.

"Is there somebody here?" An old woman appeared at the room entrance. She was small but round, with white hair in that neat style that looked as if she'd had the same hairdo since the 1950s. She wore a purple jogging suit, white socks, and black sandals. "Oh my, there *is* somebody here. How lovely."

Heather's smile was back. "Grandma, we have guests. Sarah, Thierry, this is my grandmother Rose McKinley."

She shuffled forward, giving us a big grin. "Wonderful. As I always say, vampires are more than welcome at the Booberry Inn."

My hand froze in midextension toward her. "Excuse me?"

She frowned. "You *are* a vampire, aren't you?"

Owen laughed, breaking through my knee-jerk reaction of horror at someone discovering our little secret. "It's okay. Heather and Rose know about me. Rose assumes anyone I introduce to them lately is also a vampire, which is sometimes true, sometimes not. Rose, this is Sarah and Thierry."

"Oh, I'm very sorry." Rose pressed her hands to her cheeks. "Am I wrong? Is it rude to assume these things?"

"Not at all," Thierry said. "You're very insightful, Rose. It's a pleasure to meet you."

She glowed. "You too. Don't worry—I like vampires. I remember Bela Lugosi as Dracula. You are much better-looking than he was."

"I . . . appreciate that, Rose."

Call me crazy, but I think the old lady was flirting with my husband. It was kind of sweet.

Kind of.

Heather's eyes had widened a little as she processed this new info. "Okay, then." She jotted something down in her ledger. "In that case, I'll put you in the Batberry Suite. It has some special features, including extra-thick blinds."

Batberry? "You have a special suite for vampires?"

"I like to cater to my guests. Whoever they may be."

"So you're not freaked out at the possibility that . . . you know. We are?"

Her initial surprise had faded and her friendly look

returned. "I've known Owen long enough to realize that vampires aren't the stuff of nightmares."

Right. And by the look on her face, I was guessing that she thought Owen was the Edward to her Bella—and I didn't mean Lugosi. The drama outside with Miranda calling Owen out as a cheater hadn't seemed to diminish her crush in the slightest.

"There's a toad on your desk," Thierry said to Heather.

I glanced over, surprised to see he was right. A small brown toad sat next to the register. Since it had been so still, I'd previously thought it was a paperweight.

"This"—Heather patted its head absently—"is Hoppy. My pet toad."

"Her *familiar*," Rose corrected, nodding. "Witches need familiars."

My eyebrows shot up. "You're a witch?"

Heather had the grace to look embarrassed. She ran her fingers over the antique-looking gold locket she wore on a chain around her neck. "Hardly. I mean, I try to do a little magic every now and then. But doesn't everyone?"

"No," I said firmly. "Not everyone."

"The other girls won't let her in their coven," Rose said. "They're mean to my Heather, especially that nasty Miranda Collins."

"Grandma," Heather growled under her breath, her cheeks reddening.

"Miranda's part of a coven?" Thierry asked. "So you were baiting a real witch, Owen? Doesn't seem very wise to me."

"She's harmless." Owen shrugged, absently studying his fingernails. "She wouldn't try to hurt me. She's crazy about me."

"You're sure about that?"

Owen regarded him with a bored but patient expression. "Women adore me. Miranda included, despite her momentary hissy fit. To hurt me would be to hurt any chance she ever has of being with me again."

"What a tragedy," I said under my breath.

"Nobody understands Owen," Heather said, standing up. "He's wonderful, really."

Hoppy let out a low croak.

Heather glanced at the toad. "Owen helped me find Hoppy. Two months ago I broke up with my boyfriend at the time—then he took off without a word. Owen tried to cheer me up with an afternoon at the beach . . . and there Hoppy was, in the middle of a spring rainstorm on the shore. I brought him home, gave him a box to sleep in. He's been with me ever since."

Rose nodded. "Familiars choose their witches."

Heather sighed. "Hoppy is not my familiar, Grandma."

"Not with a silly name like that he isn't! When I practiced, I had a lovely black cat named Sheba."

"You're a witch, too?" I asked, surprised. It was witches galore around here.

Rose stroked her white hair to neaten it. "This is Salem, dear. Everybody's either a witch or they *want* to be a witch."

"Not me."

"Of course not. You're a vampire."

A vampire who sincerely hoped for a minifridge in her room.

Since Salem wasn't a hotbed of vampiric activity, except for Owen and the occasional missing person, and didn't have any blood banks—businesses that sold the red stuff by the ounce to paying fanged customers—we'd gone the BYOB route.

The last *B* didn't stand for booze.

Or actually, I should say that *I'd* gone that route. At his age, Thierry didn't need to drink blood regularly to survive.

Heather showed us the room on the second floor. It was small but quaint, with a double bed, a vanity, and an en suite bathroom. Every fabric, quilt, and afghan in the room appeared to be homemade.

"You weren't kidding about the special features." I stared at my reflection, which included both vampires standing behind me as well as Heather. Rose had temporarily excused herself to put away her gardening supplies while we checked out the room.

While we couldn't see ourselves in regular mirrors, luckily there were *special* mirrors manufactured for the vampire population. Problem was, they were very expensive, so not everybody could afford one.

"I've never understood why we don't have reflections," I said. "It's just so bizarre, isn't it?"

"It's a witch thing," Owen offered.

I glanced at him. "A witch thing?"

"I've heard this rumor over the years," Thierry said. "Legend has it that there was once a witch who loved a vampire, one who was very vain about his appearance. One who was loved by many, be they witch, vampire, or human."

"Was his name Owen?" Heather joked.

"Very funny," Owen said, then frowned. "Wait, was it?"

"No, not Owen. The legend goes that the vampire betrayed this powerful witch, but since it was a matter of the heart, she couldn't bring herself to kill him. Still, she wanted him to suffer. She cast a spell on him so powerful that it, in turn, cursed all vampires from that day forward to never again see themselves in a mirror, a spell that survived even after the witch's death."

I stared at my rare reflection, at my shoulder-length brown hair and my hazel eyes with hastily applied mascara. "Witches," I said under my breath. "Total troublemakers." Then I sent a glance at Heather. "Present company excepted, of course."

"Heather," Thierry said, "do you know anything about the vampires who've gone missing in town lately?"

"Only what Owen's told me about it."

"Any idea what might be behind their disappearances?"

"None. Sorry."

Thierry frowned. "Owen, you said that Monique was over three hundred. How about the other two?"

"I think they were up there as well." Owen nodded.

"Hmm. All master vampires."

A little Vampire 101: vampires were considered fledglings for their first fifty years, regular vampires till they were three hundred. After that, they'd earned the title of "master."

"If these vampires didn't just go missing, but were murdered, none of them would have left any body behind," I said. Only vampires less than a century in age left a body when they were killed. Older ones disintegrated into a gooey mess. Trust me—it wasn't pretty. "Therefore, there'd be no clues to find out who did it."

"Correct," Thierry replied.

"So basically, the Ring's handed you a case that's pretty much impossible to figure out."

He held my gaze. "Essentially."

"A test," Owen said after a moment. "The Ring loves handing out tests to determine a consultant's worth in his first few assignments."

"I don't like the sound of that," I said. "What if we fail?"

Thierry's lips thinned. "Let me worry about that, Sarah."

"Just your saying 'Let me worry about that' makes me worry. About that."

"Don't. It'll be fine. I know how to handle them."

"Yeah," Owen breathed. "Good luck with that. Sarah, have you ever met any of the current Ring elders?"

I grimaced. "Haven't had the pleasure."

"Keep it that way."

Yeah. That was really comforting.

We unloaded our small amount of luggage in the room, then went back downstairs with Heather and Owen. It was well after eight o'clock by now, and the sun was starting to set. Rose had come back inside and was dusting the table near the front door.

"Where are you off to now?" she asked Owen as he made for the door.

He gave her a wink. "Places to go, Rose, my love. People to see. Life is good."

Heather picked up Hoppy from the desktop and cradled the toad in her arms like a tiny dog. Hoppy seemed perfectly content there.

"Anyway, Thierry, if you need any help"—Owen raked his hand through his blond hair—"you have my number."

Thierry nodded. "We'll take a look around town tomorrow when everything's open."

Owen paused at the doorway. He pressed his hand against his forehead, his brows drawing together.

"Something wrong?" Heather asked with concern.

"No, it's just . . . a headache. I'm sure it'll pass."

"Maybe Miranda got one of those voodoo dolls after all," I said. "And she's stabbing its forehead with an ice pick as we speak."

He laughed. "Yeah, maybe. Anyway, it's nothing. Talk to you later."

He pushed open the front door and took two steps onto the porch.

A weird chill shivered down my arms, which was odd since it wasn't the least bit cold outside.

"Owen," Thierry began, "what's wrong?"

Owen pressed his hands to either side of his head.

"It's weird. I just get the strange feeling that—" He gasped. "What's happening to me?"

Without another word, he stopped talking, turned away, and started to run. He got halfway down the driveway before he dropped to his knees.

And then, as if somebody had just shoved a wooden stake through his heart, he disintegrated like the Wicked Witch of the West right before our eyes.

One moment he was there.

The next . . . he was dead.

Chapter 3

Since he'd been a vampire for more than a hundred years, Owen left no body behind, only a gruesome black stain on the interlocking brick of the B and B's driveway.

Stunned and sickened, I clutched the sleeve of Thierry's black jacket. "What happened?"

Heather began to shriek in horror and was about to run out to where Owen's remains were, but Rose held her back.

"Owen!" she wailed.

"Oh no!" Rose's eyes were also wide with shock as she pulled her granddaughter into a comforting embrace. "Honey, it's horrible. But . . . he's gone. We can't help him now."

"I'll take a look around," Thierry said, a grim look on his face.

"Take a look around?" I blurted out. "Are you crazy? The same thing could happen to you!"

"I need to check."

"No. You need to stay here with me."

He touched my face. "You stay here. Look after Heather and Rose. I'll be right back. I promise."

"Thierry!"

Before I could stay anything else, he slipped out of my grasp and headed down the driveway. I watched him, frightened that he was about to vanish right before my eyes.

I don't think I actually breathed for three minutes after he left my view. Finally, he returned and met my angry but relieved glare.

"You scared me!" I exhaled shakily. "Did you find anything?"

"Nothing," he told me. "Nobody. And there are no weapons near the place he expired."

"Then what happened?"

"A spell," Heather said, her voice garbled and hard to understand. Tears streamed down her cheeks. "Someone did a spell to kill him from a distance. It had to be Miranda. Oh, my God. Owen. Owen's gone!"

She let go of her grandmother and clung to me. I didn't let go of her. I felt horrible for this girl I'd only just met, who'd lost someone who meant something to her—so suddenly, so unexpectedly.

Miranda Collins had threatened Owen in front of all of us, but did I think she was the one responsible for this? She wasn't a nice person by any means, but I didn't think she was that stupid.

"I'm sorry," I whispered as Heather's tears soaked into my shirt. "I know you cared about him."

"I didn't just care about him. I loved him." She pulled back and stared into my eyes. "I *loved* him. And I never told him."

My heart wrenched. "I'm so sorry."

"Oh, Owen." She ran her hand under her nose, but there was now a resolution in her gaze pushing past the pain and grief. "I need to tell him how I felt. And I'm going to find out who did this to him—and if it's Miranda, then she's going to pay."

I frowned at her. "How are you going to tell him how you felt? He's . . . I'm sorry, but he's gone."

"His spirit isn't gone. Not yet. A séance," she said firmly. "I'll do one at midnight. It's when the magic is the strongest. I can summon his spirit."

I shook my head. "I don't know if that's a good idea."

"Sure it is," Thierry said.

I looked at him with surprise. "Excuse me?"

He regarded Heather very seriously. "Do you honestly believe you have the power to summon Owen's spirit?"

The weak girl I'd met earlier was fading away, leaving behind one much more determined. "I can damn well try."

"Then do it. Sarah and I will be there, too."

"You will?"

"We will?" I raised an eyebrow.

His jaw was set. "Yes. Because whatever happened to Owen may be the exact same thing that happened to the other three missing vampires. And if that's true, then it means something very important—and very dangerous—about Salem."

"What?"

"That there is an alpha witch in town. One capable of death magic, one who can kill from a distance. One who is specifically targeting vampires. The Ring will want to know about a threat like this and take steps to deal with it."

"How many alphas are still around?" I asked. "Is this something that anybody would know?"

"There's none," Rose said. "There aren't any of those witches left—not in this country, anyway."

"None?" I repeated with shock. "Why not?"

"Witch hunters," Thierry said simply. "They've been very adept at their jobs over the years. But if an alpha escaped their attention and is killing vampires, then it's a problem."

I swallowed hard. "I'll say. But if anyone finds out what we are . . ."

"Your secret is safe with me," Heather assured us, taking small, shaky breaths. Her eyes were red and shiny with tears.

"Me, too," Rose agreed. "I won't tell anyone. I swear it."

My mouth was dry. If vampires were being killed in Salem—just for being vampires—then we were in serious trouble from somebody able to kill from a distance.

Adventure and romance, that fortune-teller had promised earlier. I really wished she'd been a bit more specific.

Thierry and I went up to the room alone and I closed the door behind us. I sat down on the edge of the bed and clasped my hands together, trying my best to calm down. I caught his expression in the mirror—it was grim. Then again, grim was a typical look for him.

Since I wasn't a mind reader, I decided to go ahead and ask. "Is it safe for us to stay here?"

"I don't know." He didn't seem happy about that at all. "But I'm not ready to leave. Not yet. Nobody knows who we are—*what* we are. I want to explore Salem tomorrow and see if we can find anything useful."

"And if we don't?"

"Then we leave."

"What about the Ring? Are you going to call them?"

"No. Not yet, anyway. Letting them know Owen's fate before we know any further details would raise an alarm.

They could overcompensate, and we really don't want that."

"Understood." I didn't really, but I wasn't sure I wanted to. "I noticed you didn't suggest I hightail it out of here and leave you to check things out by yourself."

His lips curved even though his gray eyes remained serious. "I know you well enough by now to presume that would be a futile suggestion."

"Smart guy." I sighed and moved toward the window to look outside. From where I stood I could see the exact spot where Owen had met his Maker, since there was a black stain there now, kind of like a small, gory oil slick of death. I shuddered. "You didn't like him."

"You don't think so?"

"I felt a definite vibe of dislike."

Thierry managed a small laugh at that. "I didn't dislike Owen. However, his lifestyle choices leaned toward the hedonistic and frivolous, often to the detriment of anyone who relied on him. I suppose I found him selfish more than anything else. But I never would have wished him dead."

I was glad to hear that. Somebody could be a scummy person in a whole lot of ways, but that didn't mean they were evil down deep. "Heather saw the good in him."

"There was good in him."

"I think there's good in just about everyone. It's simply a question of whether it's enough to outweigh the bad."

"Exactly." He met my gaze. "You look surprised that I agree with you."

"Not surprised, exactly. You're just all . . . optimistic and positive today. Nearly shiny, really."

He raised an eyebrow. "Now, let's not get carried away."

I almost laughed out loud at that. My cell phone suddenly let out a buzzing sound. I pulled it out of my bag and looked down at the screen.

CALL ME AS SOON AS YOU CAN. SAY NOTHING TO THIERRY.—MR

I swallowed hard.

"Something important?" Thierry asked.

"No, it's just . . . Amy," I lied. It was the name of my best friend from back home. "She wants me to call her back and it can't wait." I laughed nervously. "You know Amy."

I escaped from the room without any more lies spilling from my lips and hurried downstairs to a far corner of the bed-and-breakfast. My hands were now sweating.

I couldn't delay getting back to him. Markus Reed, the Ring's most accomplished and deadly enforcer, wouldn't be too happy about that.

He picked up on the second ring.

"Sarah," he said. "How are you finding Salem?"

"Witchtastic, thanks." I forced myself to sound calm. "What do you want, Markus?"

Unless he was psychic, there was no way he knew what had happened to Owen. And since Thierry wasn't planning to contact the Ring with that information—at least not yet—I wasn't going to say a thing.

"I know it hasn't been very long at all since our deal, but I'm thinking you're in a prime spot to find out more information."

A shiver went down my spine.

A "deal" made it sound so innocent. Like I was buying a used car through Craigslist. Only this was the kind that came with a body in the trunk.

Here's the thing. Despite Markus being a deadly kind of guy, he wasn't a villain. He was actually extremely good at his job, the kind of scary grim-reaper type you'd want on your side if faced with adversity, but terrifying if you crossed him.

Markus had done a favor for me in Vegas by retrieving my stolen engagement ring from an underground-dwelling street kid vamp. In return, he wanted information.

Information about Thierry's past.

"I don't know anything yet," I whispered. "I mean, it's been, what, a whole two days since you asked me for this? Who do you think I am, Houdini?"

"It was in Salem that Thierry was last seen before he disappeared for fifty years."

My brows shot up. "It was?"

"Yes. And it was also there where he resurfaced five decades later. Since you're there, we want you to find out more about this. The elders are very interested in this information."

My grip on the phone tightened. "Why do they care? Thierry's been around for nearly seven centuries. What do fifty unaccounted years matter in the grand scheme of things?"

"It's not for me to say, but they want to know. Right now, the only one who would know the answer to this is your husband himself."

"Then you should ask him yourself instead of sending me cryptic messages."

"I thought you were going to be helpful, Sarah. Don't you want to make sure Thierry's term with the Ring runs smoothly?"

Of course I did. There was no question about it. They

had a bat in their bonnet about where he'd gone during those fifty years, during which nobody had seen or heard from him. Frankly, I was curious, too.

"I'll see what I can find out," I said halfheartedly. "But I can't promise anything."

"I know you'll do your best."

"Oh really? And how do you know that?"

"Because I'm certain you don't want anything bad to happen to your new husband."

The line clicked.

"Yeah, well," I spoke into the phone, furious now, "why don't you stick your passive-aggressive threats right up your—"

"I'm still here, Sarah."

My stomach sank. "I thought you hung up."

"Obviously. Bottom line, Sarah, it's in your best interest to get me this information as soon as possible. Do you understand me?"

My mouth was nearly too dry to form words. "I'll do my best."

"I know you will."

This time *I* ended the call.

I slowly made my way back up to the room while my thoughts raced. Thierry had "disappeared" here in Salem in the seventeenth century and hadn't been seen or heard from until fifty years later. It sounded like something that had a simple answer, although I couldn't think what it could possibly be.

The Ring wanted to know the truth.

I hated keeping secrets from Thierry—from anybody, really. I was terrible at it, always had been. Friends had rarely trusted me more than once or twice with any of their intimate details, usually because when I was younger

I'd end up blurting it to my next friend before I even realized what I'd done. My mouth had always lacked a filter.

But this wasn't an innocent secret. And I'd do whatever I could to help Thierry and keep him safe from the Ring, whom I had no doubt would go to extremely unpleasant lengths to get what they wanted, whatever it might be.

Thierry was on his laptop computer when I entered the small room. I went directly to the vanity and sat down in front of it, digging into my purse for a brush. I began to violently brush the tangles out of my hair.

"How's Amy?" Thierry asked.

"She's, um, just peachy."

"Right." There was a long pause. "Who were you really speaking to just now, Sarah?"

My brush froze in midstroke. I caught his gaze in the reflection of the special mirror. "What do you mean? I was talking to Amy."

"I don't believe you."

My throat was tight. "You think I'm lying to you?"

He nodded. "Lying is not one of your strongest talents. I can tell every time you attempt it."

"I resent that."

"Resent it all you like. It's still true."

I pointed my brush at him. "I'm a very good liar."

"Perhaps. But still, you're lying right now about who you spoke to. And I would like to know why."

The man had a talent for pinning me with those intense gray eyes of his, like a brunette butterfly he'd collected on an afternoon walk. I couldn't look away even if I wanted to.

I stood up and began pacing the small room. "How can you sound so calm right now?"

He cocked his head. "Should I be otherwise?"

"Oh, I don't know. Owen just got killed by a witch's death spell and is splattered all over Heather's driveway. We're stuck in a town that has a murderous alpha witch lurking somewhere. A witch hunter's ghost was giving me the evil eye earlier. And now I'm lying to you about who I spoke to on the phone."

"So now you're admitting it."

I hissed out a breath. "Fine. It was Markus Reed."

His gray eyes widened a fraction as he took this in. "Interesting."

"I tell you the Ring's favorite enforcer is contacting me out of the blue and you think it's *interesting*?"

"You seem rather distressed about this."

I wrung my hands. "You could say that."

"Tell me." His expression turned serious and he got up from his seat by the window. He touched my chin to raise my gaze to lock with his. "What does he want from you?"

With Thierry it was really hard to tell what he was thinking if you went only by his expression. He'd had a long time to perfect the ability to appear unreadable.

But there it was—that edge of something dangerous, something barely restrained. It wasn't directed toward me, though. It was toward Markus.

"Has he threatened you?" He said the words simply, but there was a thick layer of underlying darkness there. If I said yes, I had no doubt that Thierry would immediately go to find Markus, and it wouldn't be to make small talk about the weather.

"No, no threats. Well, not toward me, anyway." I hissed out a breath. "He wants me to find out some things. About you."

His brow lifted. "About *me*?"

"Yeah. Namely, about another time you were here in Salem."

"Is that so?"

"So why don't we just get it all out into the open." I took a deep breath and let it out slowly. "Apparently you went missing for fifty years and the Ring is dying to know where you went. Care to share with the class?"

He studied me for several drawn-out moments as if trying to figure out the riddle in my eyes. Then something very unpleasant flashed across his face. "How dare they use you to try to get this information. If Markus wanted to know so badly, why didn't he simply confront me about it face-to-face?"

"Would you have told him anything?"

"Of course not."

I nodded. "Then that's very likely why."

Thierry pulled his BlackBerry out of his inner jacket pocket. "I'm calling him right now."

I snatched the device away from him before he'd even attempted to scroll through his address book. "No, you are most certainly *not* going to call him right now."

"Sarah," he growled, "let me handle this. You don't have to be any part of it."

"I guess you misunderstood the part in Vegas when we said the 'for better or for worse' thing?"

"You're paraphrasing. Our vows were not that traditional due to the Elvis impersonator you thought would be—how did you put it? *Super fun?*"

"Yeah, well, the better or worse thing was implied." When he reached for the phone, I hid it behind my back. "Nuh-uh. No way, vampire. You're not getting your hands on this. Markus didn't want me to tell you anything about this."

"And I wonder why that is. Because he wouldn't want me to know that he threatened you. I will not let anyone bully you. Not today, not ever."

"Markus isn't bullying me. He's just doing his job."

His lips thinned. "So now you're defending him, are you?"

"What happened back then, Thierry? Where did you go? We can make something up to tell him if it's really bad—if it's dangerous information. But I want to know. I *need* to know."

He searched my face. "Why?"

"Because . . . I should know your deepest, darkest secrets. Especially if they're weighing heavily on you. I might be able to help."

He shook his head, bemused. "You really mean that, don't you?"

"Of course I do."

He turned from me and went to the window to look down at the street outside, his shoulders tense. "As heroic as you might wish to believe I was, I've done some unsavory things in my life, Sarah. Existence, especially one as long as mine, is an evolutionary process."

"And this means what exactly? You're actually a dinosaur in hiding?"

He turned to face me again, his expression shadowed. "All I'm saying is that you wouldn't have liked me back then."

I watched him steadily, refusing to be swayed by his cryptic Tales from the Darkside. "You're wrong. I'm sure I would have. I love you—I always would have loved you."

"Don't be so sure about that. If you saw me, who I was,

especially leading up to my missing years . . ." He trailed off. "It wasn't the most heroic time of my life."

I crossed the room and reached down to take his hand. "It's more than three hundred years ago. And I totally believe the whole evolutionary process. So, okay, you think you were a caveman back then, but you're more evolved now. So don't sweat it."

He raised an eyebrow. "I'm not sweating."

I smiled. "I promise there's no judgment here. None at all. Now, tell me what the Ring is so curious about."

Finally, just when I thought he wouldn't tell me anything, he spoke. "The truth is, Sarah, that I don't remember the years that I was allegedly missing. One moment I was here in Salem at its bleakest hour during the witch trials. I'd arrived by ship from overseas that very day. The next moment it was fifty years later." His jaw tightened. "What happened in the interim is not something I retained."

I stared at him with shock. "You don't remember. Seriously?"

"Seriously. I've tried to put it behind me, but this blank spot is more worrying to me than any memory I do possess."

"Why?"

"Because I don't know what I might have done during those years. Or who I might have harmed."

That was a chilling thought. "Maybe you didn't do anything at all. Maybe you were in a coma. Or hibernating, like a fanged groundhog."

His lips twitched. "Perhaps. However, I don't believe the answer is quite so cut-and-dried. It was a long time ago. I returned to my regular life, found those whom I had known before. No one questioned me too deeply about what happened, where I'd been—not even Veronique. It became a nonissue. But now I see that the Ring has been attempting to compile my full biography. They must have a great deal of time on their hands."

"Apparently they have a file on you. Three inches thick."

His expression darkened. "Must make for interesting reading for someone."

"Epic, I'm sure."

"Do you want access to this file?"

I took a deep breath and let it out slowly. "No."

He gave me a wary but surprised look. "Really?"

"Really. Anything that you don't tell me yourself, I don't need to know. And, quite honestly, there are some things I know you'd rather me not know. I've made my peace with that."

He searched my face. "I think you honestly mean that."

"You said yourself I'm a terrible liar."

"True. But I actually consider that a strength, not a weakness."

He would. I nearly laughed at the thought before I sobered. "What about you? Are you a good liar?"

"An excellent one. But not with you. I don't lie to you, Sarah. You're the only one I feel I can be completely truthful with. That means more to me than you will ever know." He leaned forward and brushed his lips against mine.

I kissed him back. "Although . . . you did just admit to being a pro at lying, so, really, you could be lying right now."

He gave me the barest edge of a smile. "Touché."

I had my answer, but I wasn't sure it would do us much good. "So what happens with the Ring? Will they be okay finding out that you don't remember anything?"

His expression darkened again. "We should get ready for the séance."

My throat thickened. "I'll take that as a no. What will they do?"

"Let me worry about that."

"You should have a T-shirt made with that slogan. You use it a lot." I nervously twisted a finger into my hair. "Seriously, though, is this something to be worried about?"

He regarded me, raising an eyebrow. He was used to my tenacious nature—which was a nice way of saying that if I was a dog, it would take a great deal of effort to pull away a bone I'd been chewing on. "The Ring sees most difficulties in black or white terms."

"And . . . I'll take that as a yes to the worrying. You were with the Ring before—I mean, *you* created it in the first place. Is that how you see things, too? Black or white? Right or wrong? No shades of gray? And I'm not talking about the naughty book."

"Once I was like that. Lately, though, many things have changed. My outlook on life is one of those things." A new smile tugged at his lips. "All thanks to you."

My heart warmed. "Such a good answer, Monsieur de Bennicoeur. Gold star."

"It's the truth." He slid his hand around to the small of my back to draw me closer. "For some reason, the Ring's curiosity has been piqued about my history. I won't lie. It could become an issue, but it's not something we need to worry about today. Let's deal with Heather's séance and get to the bottom of Owen's murder without further delay. All right?"

Owen. Poor Owen.

"Heather loved that guy, you know," I said, my throat tightening again. "Even though he was an unredemptive womanizer who seemed shadier than a black umbrella, even though the writing was on the wall that he would have broken her heart into a million pieces on the heels of her last boyfriend leaving town, she still loved him."

"She's young. She'll recover and be better off without him in her life."

"Promise?" I asked.

He nodded. "Promise."

I really hoped he was right. It was both challenging and wonderful being in love with a living vampire.

A dead one wouldn't be any fun at all.

Chapter 4

Midnight was the best time to summon the recently departed spirit of a vampire sex machine—or, apparently, any other spirit. Solemnly, we gathered in a small room downstairs around a circular table—Thierry to my left, Heather to my right, and Rose across from me. Heather had lit many candles, which lent the only light other than that from the moon streaming through the bay window in the adjoining living room. Hoppy the toad sat on the table next to Heather, as still and silent as a toad-like rock.

"Have you ever done this before?" Thierry asked.

She grimaced as if embarrassed by the question. "Once or twice. But I'm not very good at it."

Rose took hold of her hand and squeezed it. "Heather's mother was an incredibly talented witch. I still believe Heather's greater powers are to come. It's why I gave her the locket."

Heather touched the gold locket at her throat. "It's a family heirloom. Grandma says it was worn by all the strongest witches in our family line, including my mother. She gave it to me on my fourteenth birthday, just after my parents died."

Rose patted her hand. “It’s good that we’ve had each other over the years.”

Heather looked at her fondly. “I don’t know what I would have done without you.”

“You would have been just fine, sweetheart. I, on the other hand, likely would have ended up at Salem Acres.” She glanced at me. “The old-age home on the west side of town. Old, warty witches live there. Stuck in their silly memories of long-lost loves. I prefer to live in the present and look toward the future.”

Heather drew in a shaky breath. “I can’t believe Owen’s gone.”

“Not that I’d ever wish that end on anyone,” Rose said, “but he was a man who got around. Every girl in town knew what he looked like with his clothes off.”

“*I* didn’t,” Heather said with a sigh.

Hoppy let out a low croak.

I felt Heather’s pain at losing Owen, but I had to agree with Rose. *Anyone* could have killed him—and my guess was a jilted lover had.

“Shall we get started?” Thierry asked gently.

“Yes, of course.” Heather wiped away her tears. “I’m sorry.”

“Please, don’t apologize,” he said. “Owen and I never got along that well, but I am sorry for your loss. I know you felt close to him.”

“Yes, but this is your honeymoon,” Heather said. “I don’t want to take time away from that.”

“It’s a rather small bed in the Batberry Suite,” Rose noted. “If you need an extra cot, we can have one brought up for you.”

I almost laughed. “I think we’ll be okay.”

A small bed on one’s honeymoon certainly wasn’t a

bad thing, in my opinion. I'd bought some sexy lingerie before leaving Las Vegas that I hoped would see the light of day—or the dark of night—before we left Salem.

"Yes," Thierry agreed. "But thank you for the kind offer, Rose."

I gave him a sidelong look to see that he was now repressing a smile. The old woman seemed to amuse him. It was a talent both she and I shared.

"Here. Take my hand." Heather reached out toward me and I took her hand. Then I took Thierry's and he took Rose's, until we formed a ring around the table.

"You can do this," Rose soothed. "I know you can."

Heather's expression tensed. "I hope you're right."

Then I had a scary thought. "Just try not to summon the spirit of that Malik guy."

"Malik?" Rose said with surprise. "You've heard of him?"

"Saw him," I confirmed. "At a café before we came here. Seemed like a very unpleasant ghost."

"Why? What did he do?"

I shifted in my seat. "Well, he was just generally creepy. That was more than enough for me to get a bad vibe."

"I'm sure," Heather murmured. "Jonathan Malik allegedly killed a dozen witches with his bare hands—those who aren't even in the history books or who weren't given a trial first. He played judge, jury, and executioner. Or so the story goes. I hope I don't summon him by mistake, either. Yuck."

A chill went through me at hearing about Malik's crimes. It was even worse than I'd imagined. "Then my vibe was right on the money. Evil spirits are not invited to this séance. But how do you home in on the exact spirit you're searching for?"

"I have a lock of Owen's hair." From her pocket, Heather pulled out the dark blond hair, which was tied with a thin red ribbon, and placed it in front of her next to Hoppy.

Was that weird or was it just me?

Thierry eyed the hair skeptically. "May I ask *why* you have a lock of Owen's hair?"

Maybe it wasn't just me.

"I gave him a haircut last week and still had the sweepings. But, I mean, it's not like I kept some of his hair in an envelope." Heather cleared her throat. "That would be strange."

I exchanged a glance with Thierry. "Not strange at all," I said. "Nope."

Rose gave us a squeamish look. "My granddaughter was working on a love spell. Luckily for her, she doesn't have access to that level of magic."

"Grandma!" Heather's face reddened. "Anyway . . . let's get started, shall we? Close your eyes."

I closed my eyes as instructed, disturbed that this girl had considered doing a love spell.

Love couldn't be forced. It either happened or it didn't, whether with the wrong guy or not. And you could only hope the other felt the same in return—no envelope of vampire hair required.

"I'm speaking to the spirit world," Heather said. "I am searching through those who abide there. I come in peace, and I mean no harm. I seek Owen Harper. Owen? Are you there?"

There was silence at the table, so much that I could hear the tick of the grandfather clock to my right.

I cranked open one eye and glanced around. Heather was concentrating so hard that her forehead wrinkled beneath her long red side-swept bangs. Thierry's eyes were closed, his expression controlled. Rose's face was peaceful, as if she enjoyed her granddaughter's attempts to tap into her dormant witchy talents.

"Do you sense anything, dear?" Rose asked after a minute of silence.

"Not yet."

"Keep trying. You know it doesn't always work on the first attempt."

I didn't have much experience with séances. I remembered doing a few back when I was a teenager—gathered with my friends at a sleepover and pulling out the Ouija board. I will reluctantly admit to being the one who'd pushed the pointer and freaked everyone out whenever I got the chance.

Good clean fun.

I closed my eye again.

"Owen . . ." Heather's tone had turned wistful. "Please come back. We want to help you. We want to know who did this to you."

Again, she was greeted by nothing but silence.

Thierry's thumb slid across my knuckles and I opened my eyes a crack to glance at him. He shook his head once.

It was enough for me to understand what he meant.

Heather might desperately want to summon Owen's recently departed spirit back to the Booberry Inn, but it didn't look like she'd be successful.

Closure for her, and for us as well—since the Ring would want to know what happened and how it related to the other missing vampires—wouldn't happen tonight.

"It's okay, dear," Rose soothed. "It might not be the

right time. We can try again tomorrow night if you're having problems."

Heather's face was tense. "I always have problems when I'm trying to do any magic—even something relatively simple like this. I've summoned spirits before."

"Not for a long time."

"True," she allowed, glumly.

Rose brightened. "Remember when ghosts used to visit you when you were a little girl? Almost every night?"

"Vividly." She blinked. "It was . . . kind of fun."

"Ghostly visits were fun?" I found that rather difficult to believe. Some considered vampires to be scary monsters, but I'd put my money on dead people any day. I mean, *really* dead people, not just sort of *undead*. Totally different. "I guess you didn't have a lot in common with that kid in *The Sixth Sense*. He did not have fun."

"The ghosts I met haven't been scary. Although I know they were all afraid of Malik, even back when I was a kid. He's been the only ghost who's stuck around town; the others all disappeared within a few days."

Thierry took this in. "So these abilities have little to do with witchcraft. You're a medium."

"I don't know. I thought so at one time. Maybe I've got that bit of psychic edge to me, but it's nowhere near as good as being a real witch who can work with magic all the time."

"Says who?" I said. "That Miranda chick?"

It was a guess. But by the blanched look on her face at the name, probably a good one.

"Miranda won't let me join her coven," Heather said, her jaw tight. "Maybe I just need their help to access my powers."

"No," Rose insisted. "You want nothing to do with

those girls. They've been cruel to you, excluding you. Why would you want to give them a chance to be mean to you again?"

Heather deflated. "You're right. Miranda wouldn't lift a finger to help me."

"Well," I said, "she did lift a finger when she left earlier. Unfortunately, it was the middle one."

The direction of this conversation had only worked to harden Heather's expression. "Okay, let's try again. I mean, it's *Owen*. We had a connection. I swear we did. If his spirit is still around, I know he'd want to talk to me."

Despite the worries about Owen and the other missing vampires, I couldn't get my mind off my conversation with Markus about Thierry's mysterious past—or really, that missing fifty-year chunk of it. I hadn't always been the most proactive person in my life, but when somebody I loved was threatened, my claws came out. My claws could currently use a manicure, but they were still very sharp.

I'd find the answer to keep those greedy elder vamps off Thierry's back. Either that or I'd start keeping a sharp wooden stake around for protection.

Heather closed her eyes and the rest of us did the same.

"Owen Harper . . ." Heather's voice was strong and clear, more so than before. "I'm summoning your spirit to appear in my presence. Owen, hear my voice. Come to me. I want to help you."

A whisper of cool air zipped across the bare skin on my arms. I opened my eyes.

And shrieked.

There was a luminescent ghostly face staring at me, only a few inches away from my own.

Just a face. No body attached.

"Well, hello there," the face said. "And who might you be?"

I pushed back in my chair, my heart doubling its speed. "Hi. I, um, I'm Sarah."

"*Buonasera*, Sarah. Lovely to meet you."

Thierry's grip on my hand tightened. "You're not Owen."

"No, no, not Owen." The face belonged to a man, a fat man with salt-and-pepper hair. It glowed in the dim, candlelit room. "I'm Lorenzo."

"Lorenzo," I repeated.

"I owned the Italian restaurant on the corner."

I glanced at Heather from the corner of my eye. "You summoned the wrong spirit."

She looked stricken. "Oops."

"My meatballs are the best in all of New England," Lorenzo said, smiling widely. "Two-for-one spaghetti dinners on Thursdays. *Delizioso*."

Heather frowned. "Well, damn."

"Still," Rose said, "it shows that you have great talent in this, dear. Don't be too discouraged."

"But it's not Owen. Lorenzo, can you help us?"

"I don't know this Owen." Lorenzo now frowned. "Wait. Unless you mean Owen Harper."

"That's who I meant to summon," Heather said, excitement rising in her voice. "Have you seen him?"

"Seen him? After insulting my world-famous meatballs without even tasting them first, that bastard slept with both of my daughters! I'm going to kill him!" The face bounced up and down erratically.

"That might be difficult," I said, cringing. "Someone already beat you to it."

"Oh." Lorenzo came to a stop. "Well, then, good. Deserved it, too."

"No one deserves such a fate." At Thierry's intimidatingly icy glare, one of his most dangerous weapons, the ghost reared back, looking ill.

"Well, then . . ." Lorenzo cleared his nonexistent throat. "Who killed him?"

Thierry's fierce gaze didn't waver from the spirit. "That's what we're trying to determine."

"I can think of twenty men in this town who would have liked to see him dead."

"Twenty?" I repeated. "Wow. Owen really got around."

"You're a cute little thing." Lorenzo's face zoomed toward me again. "What's your favorite Italian dish? Maybe I can prepare it for you."

"Sounds great, but . . ." I grimaced. "I don't eat solid food. Sorry."

"Oh, a dieter." He nodded. "I see. No trouble at all. Anyway, was there anything else I can do for you lovely folks? It's been delightful having this chat. The mortal world is a dangerous place, but much more interesting than where I've been hanging out."

Dangerous? I would think his dangerous days were over.

"Lorenzo," Rose said, "why are you appearing to us only partially?"

"Am I?" He frowned, then turned in a full circle so I could see the bald spot on the back of his head. "Ah, you're right. I don't know. I had a body."

"It's me," Heather said, her voice catching. "I'm not powerful enough to summon his entire body. Only"—she sniffed—"a face!"

Lorenzo was fading as I watched him, like a firefly nearly out of juice. "Good night, all. I must leave. Please, tell my wife that I loved her. Even though . . ." His expression darkened. "Wait a minute. She poisoned me! Let everyone know—"

He disappeared with a soft popping sound.

"He was poisoned?" I looked around at the others, alarmed.

Rose waved a hand dismissively. "Lorenzo was always full of drama. His wife didn't poison him. He choked to death on a piece of salami the day before yesterday. It was certainly tragic, but not a crime. By the way, he wasn't kidding about the meatballs at his restaurant. Fantastic."

We'd come close to contacting Owen but, alas, no luck. Instead, we got a friendly floating head who'd choked on a piece of processed meat.

Still, it was better than a scary witch hunter with glittering black eyes and a stare even icier than Thierry's at his most intimidating.

"I can't believe this." Tears rolled down Heather's cheeks. "I failed. Owen's gone, out of my reach. I'll never see him again."

Rose pulled her chair over close enough that she could give her granddaughter a hug.

My throat thickened to witness her pain. I glanced at Thierry. "Now what?"

"Now," he said grimly, "we accept that there will be no easy answers in this particular matter."

"Are there ever?"

"That depends entirely on the question."

The answer to the question we'd asked tonight was *no.*

But tomorrow was another day.

After experiencing life as a vampire for going on eight months now, sometimes I forgot how dangerous it could be. How, lurking in the shadows, there might be someone with a pointy wooden stake, his goal to wipe me off the face of the planet. Bottom line: Vampire hunters sucked.

To think I was now in a town that had additional dangers in it—dangers that could kill a vampire from a distance when you least expected it. Well, that sucked even more.

We had to scour Salem for clues about what happened to Owen Harper—and also what happened to the missing VIP vampires—all without clueing anyone in to the fact that underneath our honeymooning exterior we were both so-called creatures of the night.

Thierry had had six hundred years to perfect his camouflage. He'd gone with the rich, untouchable businessman look to keep people from getting too close, as opposed to Owen's playboy hedonist, which only seemed to have brought people closer.

Thierry and I, at first glance, didn't exactly look like the perfect match. Him in his Hugo Boss suits, me in my jeans and T-shirts . . .

He eyed me before we left the inn, sweeping his gaze over my chosen "Let's investigate Salem!" outfit. "You look rather dazzling today."

I touched my shirt, which literally had the words "Dazzle Me" in sequins. "Got it in Vegas."

"I have no doubt."

"You like it?"

His gaze moved down the front of me, then back up to lock with mine. "Very much."

I'd earned the hint of one of those rare smiles. I considered it an excellent way to start the day.

After a quick breakfast that included three cups of

coffee and a little something from my BYOB stash in the minifridge, Thierry and I emerged from the Booberry Inn to check out the town.

I busied myself taking pictures with my cell phone—anything that looked interesting. Not tourist photos, but businesses Owen had been known to frequent. Bars, taverns, homes of rumored lovers.

Thierry and I spoke to many people during the course of the day. We showed photos of the missing vampires to shop owners and people on the street and received unhelpful responses such as, "Yeah, I think I saw her a couple weeks ago," or "Never seen him before—sorry." After a couple of hours of this, we shifted our focus to Owen.

Everybody knew Owen.

Most conversations went a little something like this:

"Owen Harper? Gorgeous, right? Friendly? Loves to hang out at Mulligan's? Yeah, he's a great guy. Everybody loves him."

"Everybody?" Thierry asked. "So he doesn't have any enemies?"

He said "doesn't" rather than "didn't" since nobody knew Owen was dead—other than us witnesses and the murderer. No body. No proof. We were pretending to be old friends visiting town concerned for his well-being.

Whomever we spoke to, male or female, would usually laugh at this and answer with something along the lines of "Oh, he had enemies. Jilted girlfriends. The jilted girlfriends' boyfriends. Yeah, that guy might be a stud, but he should sleep with one eye open."

One woman asked me, her expression pinched, "Are you one of his exes?"

I grimaced. "No."

She gave me an unfriendly head-to-toe scan, and then,

just before she walked away, threw out, "I'm surprised. You look like his type."

I really wasn't sure if I should take that as a compliment or an insult.

Needless to say, we found nothing helpful. At the end of the day, everyone we'd spoken to seemed equally innocent and guilty. Anyone could have done it.

Anyone could have been the alpha witch who just might have a death wish for all vampires who entered the town limits. And we were nowhere closer to finding him or her than we'd been yesterday.

"Maybe we should check out Mulligan's tonight," I said once we returned to the inn just before nine o'clock. It was the karaoke bar Owen liked to go to that got busier later in the evenings.

"If you like."

I checked myself in the vampire-approved mirror, tucking my hair behind my ears. "Or we can hang out here and I can show you what I bought in Vegas other than this delightful shirt."

"And what might that be?"

"Let's just say silk and lace are involved. But not very much of either." I glanced at him over my shoulder.

He raised an eyebrow. "Then my vote, most definitely, is for us to stay in this evening."

"You and me, alone in a tiny bedroom with a very sexy minifridge. Didn't seem right to experiment in honeymoon lingerie after the séance last night. Tonight, however . . ."

"You had me at the sexy minifridge."

"Then we can focus on getting to the bottom of your previous Salem visit and what could have wiped your memory."

His expression tensed. “Let’s forget about that.”

“See, I think that’s the problem. Too much forgetting. We need to figure out something to tell them.”

“I know what I’m going to tell them. I’m going to lie and hope they believe me. However, there’s a problem.”

Lying worked. Not all the time, but in this instance I’d totally allow it. “What?”

“You know the truth. And Markus, for some unacceptable reason, feels comfortable contacting you personally.”

I understood what he was trying to say. “And I’m a lousy liar.”

His tense expression eased. “I can handle the Ring. This isn’t the first problem I’ve had with them.”

I shivered and wrapped my arms around myself to warm up a little. “Who are these people, Thierry? Why are they so good at being shadowy and creepy?”

He went to the window to glance outside, past the curtain. “They only do what they must.”

“Yeah, I’m sure that’s what the friendly gazelles say about the hungry pride of lions circling their herd.”

That earned me a glance. “Last time I checked, I’m not a friendly gazelle.”

“Point taken.” I snorted. “Do you even know what they’re after? Why they’re so interested in something that happened so long ago?”

“I know exactly what they’re after.” Then he turned away again, as if he regretted saying anything at all.

Which only earned my complete attention. I crossed the room to face him, so he had no choice but to look at me directly. “What?”

He met my gaze. “An amulet. Something I sought in the late seventeenth century. I’d come here to Salem to retrieve it from a contact. But I don't remember ever having it in my possession, and I don't remember meeting that contact."

All of this boggled my mind. "They want an amulet you may or may not have had more than three centuries ago? But why?"

"The Ring enjoys collecting things. Magical things. Powerful things. The elders have a secret museum of rare artifacts. Actually, it's one I started myself when I was in charge."

I processed this as quickly as I could. "So that's what this amulet could do? Powerful magic?"

He didn't answer for a moment. "Something like that."

His evasive tactics were frustrating at the best of times. He didn't want to tell me more about this. Couldn't say I was all that surprised. "If I could do powerful magic right now, I'd get you to tell me everything."

The glint of amusement returned to his wintery gray eyes. "Sarah Dearly, able to do magic. It would make you much more dangerous than you already are."

"Don't doubt it." I moved toward the bathroom since I wanted to take a shower before dipping into the stash of expensive lingerie I'd bought to impress my wonderful yet enigmatic husband. "And you know what else I'd do? I'd do a spell to summon Owen's spirit so we could get to the bottom of all of this once and for all."

I pushed open the bathroom door.

Owen Harper stood on the other side, staring at both of us with shock.

Chapter 5

"You know," Owen said slowly, "I could have sworn I left. Yet now I'm randomly standing in your bathroom."

I just stared at him, stunned.

"Owen," Thierry said, his tone cautious. "You're . . . here."

He rubbed his head. "What happened?"

"That depends."

"On what?"

"What do you remember?"

"Not much. I mean, I was here with you two, Heather, and Rose was there, too. And that frog."

"Toad," I corrected shakily.

"And now I'm up in your room again. Weird." He frowned. "No, wait. I remember something else. I had this strange itchy feeling. It got worse by the second. And then . . ." His frown deepened. "I don't know."

"Come closer."

Owen did as Thierry asked without any further questions. I took a good look at him. He seemed perfectly fine to me, which was disturbing since I knew very well he *couldn't* be.

"What?" Owen asked.

"I need to check something." Thierry calmly reached forward to touch his shoulder, but his hand zipped right through Owen's body and the shoulder turned to swirling gray smoke. Thierry pulled back and Owen's body re-formed itself.

Owen's eyes had gone very wide. "What. The. Hell."

"You're a gh . . . ," I began, bringing my hand up to my mouth before I finished the sentence. Then I reached forward to touch him, but I felt nothing but cold air that swirled like smoke, just as it had with Thierry. "Um . . . don't panic?"

"What is going on here?" he demanded.

"I'm sorry to tell you this, Owen," Thierry began, "but you were killed yesterday by what we believe was an alpha witch's death spell."

Owen gaped at him. "No way!"

Thierry cleared his throat. "Way."

"This is impossible. Why wouldn't I remember something so major? I was *killed*? And you witnessed this?" He spun to face me as if hoping I might provide a more favorable, second opinion.

I cringed. "It's true. You were there . . . and then you weren't."

His face paled. "This can't be happening. It *can't* be."

"You don't feel any different?" Thierry asked.

"I feel . . . I don't know. I hadn't given it any thought yet. But if I'm dead—oh, my God. I'm dead!" He pressed his hand against his chest. "My heart is not beating! I'm a ghost!"

I didn't know what to say, so I said the only thing I could. "Owen, I'm so sorry."

"Why am I back? Why am I here? Why aren't I in, like, Heaven's waiting room, or something?"

"I know why." I tried to sound as calm as possible. Panicking wasn't going to help matters. "You're back to help us figure out who killed you."

Owen groaned and covered his face with his hands. "It could have been anybody!"

"I thought you wanted us to have the impression you were universally loved by every woman in town," Thierry said.

He peeked out from between his fingers. "Well, I was. Kind of. But some of those women had husbands and/or boyfriends. And some husbands and/or boyfriends can work black magic just as well as any sexy witch can." His expression was shifting from stunned to annoyed. "Oh, this is just great. I'm dead. I had a lot of things I still wanted to do in life. And it's over? Just like that? How is that even remotely fair?"

"It's not fair." Thierry shook his head. "You didn't deserve this end, Owen."

They hadn't been the best of friends, to say the least, but Thierry sounded genuinely sincere in his regret.

Owen began pacing our small room. "There has to be some way to reverse this."

"Reverse being dead?" I said. "Not that I'm aware of. Thierry?"

His serious expression grew thoughtful. "Many have tried such a thing."

"Successfully?" Owen asked with hope.

"Necromancers have been known to raise the dead with varying degrees of success."

I stared at him. "Like zombies? Like walking dead rotting corpses who want to eat brains?"

"Not exactly. However, if one gets to a body in time,

and everything lines up perfectly—both magic and strength of will—it *is* possible to raise the dead."

"Yikes." I shuddered at the thought. Some believed vampires were essentially the walking dead, but no—we had heartbeats, blood pressure, the need for oxygen. It was a completely different thing altogether. Happily so, thank you.

"So that's what I need," Owen said, now excited. "A necromancer! Where do I find one?"

"I believe, at last count, there were three in the entire world capable of this kind of sorcery. Two are in prison for life in solitary confinement. A raised corpse becomes the necromancer's slave and will be forced to do whatever is requested, no matter how violent or distasteful. Those two necromancers were allegedly not good people."

I crossed my arms tightly. "That doesn't sound too pleasant."

"Believe me"—Thierry gave me a sidelong glance—"I'm leaving out the gorier details."

My stomach turned over. "I appreciate that. What about the other one, though?"

"It's possible she might be helpful. She's located in California, although I'm not certain how to directly contact her. I know someone who might be able to, though. The raising must be attempted within seventy-two hours of death, while the spirit still has ties to the mortal world."

Owen nodded. "This sounds perfect!"

"However, there is one problem that would prevent her from being useful in resurrecting Owen's corpse even if we could get her here in time."

"What?" Owen asked breathlessly.

"You don't have a corpse."

His face fell. "Damn."

Thierry's dark brows drew together. "I am truly sorry, Owen."

The dead vampire let out a shuddery sigh. "Why? You didn't kill me." Then he frowned. "Or did you? You never liked me, Thierry."

"Trust me, Owen, if I'd had reason to want you dead"—Thierry's lips thinned—"I would have had no need for magic."

He said it with such conviction I definitely believed he was capable of it. A shiver—one more of appreciation than fear—went down my spine at the reminder that the man I'd married could be extremely dangerous to someone who crossed him.

However, Owen took this chilling explanation totally in stride, as if he expected no less. "Well, okay. I believe you. This, though . . . it's not right. I had plans, you know. Big plans. And now it's all over."

"If you're a ghost, maybe you can still do things," I offered, wanting to say something, anything, to help make this better, even if only in a small way.

He gave me a sad look. "It's not the same. I don't have solid form. I can't touch anyone. They can't touch me." As if to prove it he reached for me. When his hand went straight through my stomach, it felt like I'd just swallowed a tray of ice cubes. I took a step out of his reach.

"You're right," I said, grimacing, "it's definitely not the same. Sorry."

He groaned and stomped his foot. "This totally sucks!"

"I don't disagree," Thierry said. "But you must tell us everything you know about who might be responsible, since we believe it might have something to do with the other disappearances in Salem. And it must be now while you're still here and we can talk to you. Ghosts are rarely earthbound for more than three days unless there's strong magic involved to bind them to the mortal world."

"Is that what happened with Malik?" I asked.

"Very likely."

"Oh, hell. Malik." Owen glanced around nervously. "I don't want to meet up with that guy. *Total* douche bag, I've heard."

I shook my head. When we'd asked him about Malik before, he'd dismissed it as nothing. "Ghosts can't hurt anybody, so you shouldn't worry about him."

"Well," Thierry said, "that's not always true. Ghosts don't have any ill effect on the living, but on another ghost . . ." He looked at Owen. "Try to be vigilant. Do not seek out the spirit of this witch hunter in case he's dangerous to you. Soon you'll be free to move on to the afterlife if nothing is binding you here. I'm assuming that you're visible in the mortal world due to the séance Heather performed to draw your spirit here."

His eyes widened. "She did a séance?"

Thierry nodded. "We didn't believe it was successful last night. But you're here now. It's a sign that the results were simply delayed."

Owen scratched his forehead. "You know, I really can't believe this is happening. Maybe it's all just a big dream and I'm going to—"

And then, just like that, he disappeared into thin air.

I stared at the spot where he'd been standing. "Where did he go?"

"I don't know," Thierry answered. "Perhaps his spirit isn't strong enough to remain in the mortal world for very long."

I eyed him uneasily. "You sure know a lot about ghosts."

"Not much, really. But I know enough."

I had a horrible thought. "Heather wasn't able to see him. She couldn't tell him she loved him. This would have been the perfect opportunity for closure."

"Hopefully, if he was able to return once, he'll return again."

"Just in case, don't mention this. I don't want her to be any more upset than she already is."

"I won't say a word."

I chewed my bottom lip and tried to put our conversation with Owen out of my head, but it didn't work very well at all. "Remember that thing I said earlier about Vegas-bought lingerie and staying in this evening?"

He studied my face. "You've changed your mind."

I laughed at that. "Hardly. This *is* our honeymoon, mister, such as it is. However . . . it's still early. I think we should check out that bar—Mulligan's—tonight. One last shot to see if we can find anything to help unravel this particular mystery before we skedaddle tomorrow morning."

"You care about Owen."

"I wouldn't go that far. But I care that he got killed, that maybe other vamps met the same fate, and more in the future could, too. If there's still something we can do to find the answers, then what else can we do?"

He leaned over to kiss me. "I think it's a good idea."

I smiled against his lips. "Two hours max, promise. Then we'll come back here and get back to the honeymoon."

"An excellent plan. Shall we leave now?"

I peeked around Thierry's tall frame to catch a glimpse of myself in the mirror to see I was rather disheveled from ten hours of hoofing it around Salem. "I want to have a shower first and change into something more nightclub appropriate. That man we spoke to earlier with the cigar? He gave me cigar hair."

He nodded. "I am curious to see what you consider 'nightclub appropriate' when you wore these sequins all day."

I looked down at my shirt. "These are day sequins. Completely different thing."

"I see."

I slipped away from him and closed the bathroom door behind me, hoping Owen wouldn't make another appearance when I was in the middle of my shower.

A liberal application of shampoo, conditioner, and shower gel later—followed by a fresh layer of makeup—and I was ready for the rest of the evening.

I wrapped a soft white towel around me and emerged from the steamy bathroom. "The shower's all yours if you want it."

When I didn't get a reply, I glanced around at the room and frowned.

Thierry wasn't here.

I went to the window and looked outside, cringing when I saw Owen's stain still there on the driveway, lit by a streetlamp. The clouds were gathering thickly in the dark sky, blocking the moon. There was a chance of rain tonight. That should be enough to sweep away the rest of him.

My stomach soured thinking of it. It was a very innocuous-looking dark stain, kind of like one of those inkblots psychiatrists use to determine a patient's state of mind, or maybe a parked car leaking oil. But the thought that it was once a person . . .

I shuddered. One moment you were walking, talking, living your life, and minding your own business, and the next you were a Rorschach pattern.

I retrieved a red dress from my suitcase and slipped it on, along with a pair of heels, and waited for Thierry to return. When he wasn't back fifteen minutes later, I went downstairs to look for him.

Rose was in the living room sitting in a large easy chair, knitting. She looked up at me brightly. "Looking for that handsome husband of yours?"

"Uh, yeah. Have you seen him?"

She nodded toward the front door. "He left a little while ago."

He left? "Did he say where he was going?"

"No." She gave me a concerned look. "Did you two have a squabble? It's nothing to worry yourself about, I'm sure. All new marriages are wrought with trouble from the get-go. All you need to do is weather the storm and he'll be back."

I grimaced. "Thanks for the tip. But we actually weren't arguing. Not today, anyway."

She gave me a patient look. "If you say so, dear. I was married to my husband for thirty-five years and we had plenty of troubles. If I had it to do all over again, I would have divorced him the moment things went sour."

We were swiftly moving into a very TMI area. "I'm sorry you didn't have a happy marriage."

"Sometimes you don't find the perfect man until very late in life."

I assumed that meant Granny had a boyfriend. Well, good for her.

I texted Thierry immediately to see where he'd gone and why he'd left without me. When I didn't receive a reply right away, I decided to head out after him.

The night was warm, but there was electricity in the air. I liked that feeling, just before a storm, kind of a metrological excitement just beyond what one could see. When I was a kid, I'd sit out back of my parents' house and close my eyes, letting that charged air sink into me. At the time, I'd believed being struck by lightning would give me superpowers.

From what I'd learned about the supernatural world in less than a year, I wasn't convinced it wouldn't. Still, I was in no hurry to find out.

"Thierry, where did you run off to?" I said under my breath as my heels clicked against the sidewalk. It wasn't like him to disappear without saying anything.

Wait. Who was I kidding? It was *exactly* like him.

He'd probably headed to the nightclub to get a head start, time being of the essence and all that. However, the least he could do was reply to my text or call me.

Despite being both perplexed and annoyed at his vanishing act, a sliver of worry worked its way under my skin. He'd better not be doing anything dangerous right now that might attract the attentions of murderous alpha witches.

Luckily, it wasn't too far a walk from the inn. It was just after ten o'clock, and there were plenty of people at the club. Mulligan's was a large English pub–style bar with dartboards, lots of beer, and karaoke after dark. As I entered the establishment, the lilting sounds of those who were completely tone deaf met my ears.

I'd been encouraged to sing karaoke once at an office party when I was a personal assistant a few years ago. I'd had one too many tequila sunrises, and . . . let's just say, Christina Aguilera had no reason to feel threatened.

The lesson I learned that night: If you're going to take an embarrassing risk, try to ensure there are no video cameras present. It was the last time I allowed my inner diva free. I'd kept her locked in the basement ever since.

The bar was elbow to elbow with both locals and tourists. I scanned the many faces, searching for a sign of Thierry, but didn't spot him. My level of worry rose a few notches.

I pulled my cell phone out and texted him again.

WHERE ARE YOU???

When there was no immediate response, I shoved it back in my purse. Since I was here, I might as well have a drink and try to relax. The bartender came over when I finally made it to the bar.

"What'll it be?" he asked.

"Margarita, please," I said, after noticing that it was the special of the evening. If I couldn't get palm trees and a beach for my honeymoon, at least I'd get a vacation-worthy cocktail.

He disappeared and returned a minute later with my order. I paid him and sipped on the fruity drink.

"Nice of you to join us," a voice said to my left.

I froze. I recognized that voice. It belonged to a witch.

Slowly, I turned to see Miranda Collins standing there, giving me a dirty look.

Definitely a witch. Definitely with an ax to grind about Owen. Miranda was a woman with anger issues.

And definitely a suspect, although I doubted she'd be so blatant with her hatred just before she made him go splat.

But I could be wrong. It wouldn't be the first time.

I forced a smile on my face, one that didn't show off my fangs. At first glance, most people would immediately assume bad dental work, not vampirism, but why risk it?

I needed answers. And Miranda Collins was going to give them to me.

"I think we got off on the wrong foot yesterday. I'm Sarah Dearly. It's nice to meet you . . . Miranda, right?"

"You're best friends with Heather." She said it like it was an accusation.

"I just said that so you'd stop picking on her." My smile held, hopefully making me seem friendly and disarming. I tried not to think about the fact that this woman might have the ability to kill me with a death spell at any moment. "I only met her yesterday."

Her eyebrows shot up. "You're honest."

"To a fault, really. My husband says I'm a lousy liar, so I suppose I don't have much choice in the matter." My thoughts went immediately to Thierry. My phone hadn't sounded to alert me that he'd sent a text reply to let me know his whereabouts. Worry churned in my gut.

The VIP vampires had gone missing without a trace. Just vanished. Poof.

Thierry, where are you?

"Your husband . . . ," she began. "The tall, dark-haired, gorgeous man you were with at Heather's?"

"The very one."

Her glossy red lips thinned. "I didn't realize he was married."

"I'll forgive you for flirting this time. I don't get violent until the second offense." I followed it up with a smile so she'd know I was just joking around. Mostly.

She looked down at my ring finger to see my three-carat diamond and gave me a tentative smile. "You're a lucky woman."

"I like to think so."

Then she burst into tears.

Okay, didn't expect that. I grimaced. "What? Was it something I said?"

"No, no." She waved a hand. "I'm sorry. I don't mean to seem so weak, but sometimes it's hard to hold it together."

I patted her awkwardly on her shoulder while I downed the rest of my margarita in one icy gulp. "Anything I can do to help?"

She slowly gathered herself, wiping her face with the sleeve of her yellow blouse, succeeding in smearing her mascara. "You must think I'm a horrible person, after . . . after that scene in front of Heather's."

"I reserve total judgment until I've gotten to know all the parties. I mean, I know you had something with Owen."

She rolled her eyes. "That waste of space. You know, he'd be smart to leave Salem altogether with the number of women I know want to tear a strip off his hide."

My ears perked up. "Really. Like who?"

"Name her. Everybody's got a grievance against that jerk."

"And you?" I watched her carefully for her reaction. "You actually don't seem too upset by his reputation."

"Oh, please. It stung, of course, but that loser's meaningless to me now. Besides, I'm used to disappointment from men. Ever since high school and . . ." Her jaw clenched and she signaled to the bartender for a drink. "And that bitch, Heather McKinley."

I'd known Heather for a little over a day, and "bitch" was not a word I'd use to describe her. At all. "What did she do?"

She grabbed hold of the edge of the wooden bar so tightly I thought she might get a splinter. "Let's just say she's not as sweet and innocent as she might want you to believe. Maybe you should ask her sometime about Jacob Black."

I blinked. "The werewolf from *Twilight*?"

She snorted. "No. He was my boyfriend in senior year. Heather and him ran off on prom night, leaving me there looking like a fool."

Well, well, well. So if Miranda's trot down memory lane was true, the innocent, toad-loving innkeeper wasn't nearly as innocent as she might have me believe. At least, according to Miranda Collins, rival witch. Very interesting. Not necessarily relevant to the topic at hand, but interesting.

"People make bad choices when they're teenagers," I said with a shrug. "Believe me, I'm no exception."

"Let me guess . . ." She swept a glance over my short shirt, bare legs, and high heels. "Cheerleader, right?"

My shoulders sank. Most people, especially those who'd hated their high school years, had preconceived notions of ex-cheerleaders. I didn't exactly fit the typical mold of endlessly popular bubblehead. Well, not the endlessly popular part, anyway. "Don't judge. It was a small school. Somebody had to deal with the pom-pom situation. If it helps, I was a really sarcastic cheerleader. My cheers were only half-cheerful."

"Good to know." The bartender brought her a drink, placing it in front of her on a coaster. Since he knew what she wanted merely from a wave in the air, I assumed she was a regular here.

A glance and a sniff told me her regular drink was a double scotch on the rocks.

She downed it, then signaled for another, wiping her mouth with the back of her hand. "Owen Harper is meaningless to me. I hope that guy dies a slow, painful death."

If she was the murderer, she certainly wasn't trying to appear very innocent.

"Did you know his secret?" I asked tentatively.

"Owen had a lot of secrets." She jabbed a drunken finger at me. "You want to know his biggest one?"

"Um . . . I might already know it."

She swiveled her glass, watching the ice cubes spin around. "He read *Cosmopolitan* magazine every single month, cover to cover. He even had a subscription. He thought reading up on what women want would help him score all the better."

Seemed like it helped him, if you asked me. He wasn't my type, but there was no argument that he'd been a popular guy around town. "So he subscribed to a women's magazine. Okay. And you think that was his biggest secret?"

"Sure." She gave me a sharp look. "Why, what do you know about him?"

"Oh, nothing important, I guess."

"Unless you mean the vampire thing," she said, flicking her hand. "Like, *whatever*."

I glanced at my bare wrist. "Oh, would you look at the time. My husband should be here any minute."

I hoped he would be. Otherwise, I needed to keep looking for him. I couldn't stay here any longer. I wasn't finding out anything useful—other than Miranda's drunken apathy about Owen's vampirism.

"I should go. I came here to try to meet somebody new, but I'm not into it. I mean, I know I look good. Never looked so good in my life. I could get anybody I want." She downed her second drink even quicker than she had the first.

I had to admit, it wasn't just drunken bragging. She had a flawless complexion and perfect blond hair. She could pick somebody up—if that was what she wanted. "Well, it was nice talking to you."

She pointed at me, her eyes half-closed. "Sometimes I feel like I've been cursed, you know? Like I do everything right, I get what I want, and it's still the same crap."

Cursed. That was something a witch could do. That is, if Miranda wasn't being euphemistic. "You don't think somebody really cursed you, do you?"

She scoffed. "The only one who would try would be Heather. And that try-hard witch doesn't have enough magic in her to . . . to . . . well, she just doesn't. That's all. It's kind of pathetic, since I know her mother had serious skills."

So Heather might have the inclination but not the skills to work some dark magic. Then again, I'd had some high school rivals I would have been happy to turn into warthogs if given the option. "Is that why she isn't allowed to join your coven?"

Miranda's open expression shuttered, as if she'd just realized she'd been openly talking about magic with a stranger. The look was enough to chill me. "Did Heather tell you I was in a coven?"

I shifted uncomfortably on my bar stool. "No. I don't remember who mentioned it."

I could lie when I had to. Not everybody was an expert lie detector like Thierry.

Speaking of . . . I pulled my phone out of my purse and glanced at the screen. Still no reply.

"It's not a coven," Miranda insisted. "It's a book club."

A book club. I nodded solemnly. "Of course it is. I have no doubt."

"Covens are not allowed in Salem. There are rules, you know." She scanned the surrounding area as if fearful someone might overhear us.

"Actually, I don't know. I've met a couple independent

witches in the past, but none who are part of a . . . book club."

"Whatever." She pushed off her stool. "Treat that husband of yours right, okay? There are plenty of women who'd be happy to step in and take care of that hunk if you're not doing a good enough job."

She'd just called Thierry a hunk. How retro. "Thanks for the warning."

With a mischievous smile returning to her lips, she turned away from the bar and disappeared into the crowd.

Well, that was a waste of time. I didn't learn anything new. No new suspects, no new information.

Other than the fact that Heather might have been a boyfriend-stealing hussy ten years ago.

I quickly called Thierry's cell number, but it went directly to voice mail.

"If something bad has happened to you," I said after the tone, "I'm going to be furious."

I tossed the phone back into my purse, swallowing back the lump in my throat, and got up from my seat as the next karaoke song started. It was "Islands in the Stream."

That poor guy, whoever he was. He could not carry a tune to save his life.

I turned to look at the stage and at the man holding the microphone.

After that, all I could do was stare.

"You have got to be kidding me," I whispered.

It was Thierry. Onstage.

Singing.

Really, really badly.

Chapter 6

The lights shone on my husband, the sometimes dour and almost always serious centuries-old master vampire, as he sang into the microphone while perched upon a wooden stool. Same dark hair brushed back from his handsome face, same strong jawline, same dark slashes of eyebrows above piercing gray eyes. Same tailored black suit, Italian leather shoes, and glint of his platinum wedding band.

For three and a half minutes I stood there, stunned. My mouth literally hung open like a carnival game waiting for a little kid to try to pitch a rubber ball in to win a prize.

When the song finished, I tentatively approached the stage. He stepped down, and several people at the tables close by slapped him on his back and told him he'd done a great job.

"Thanks," he replied. "It's always been one of my favorite songs."

I drew closer. "Thierry?"

His gaze met mine. "Sarah, I'm glad you're here."

"So . . ." I began as another eager singer jumped onstage ready to rock. The intro of Gloria Gaynor's "I Will

Survive" began to swell. "You like karaoke? This is something I actually didn't know about you."

"You don't know everything about me, do you?"

"That is an understatement if ever I've heard one."

He spread his hands. "I know it might have looked a bit silly to you, but I figured when one is in Rome . . ."

"One should sing Bee Gees songs? Or was that the Kenny Rogers and Dolly Parton rendition?"

He smiled. "If you want to have a go next . . ."

"No, no. That's quite all right." I cleared my throat, eyeing him curiously. What was up with him tonight? "You left the room without telling me. Then you ignored my text and call. Not cool. You worried me."

His smile disappeared. "I wanted to come here right away and didn't know how long you'd be. I knew you'd be right behind me."

I was about to make a bigger deal of this, tell him how he couldn't be so reckless with a murderous alpha witch loose around town, but he seemed so relaxed that I began to doubt that it was as important as I'd made it out to be.

Still, I hadn't liked it at all. Communication was the cornerstone of a successful marriage. I think I'd heard that on *Dr. Phil* once. That man knew his stuff.

"Okay, let's forget it. Anyway, I talked to Miranda a minute ago," I said, hitching my purse strap higher on my shoulder. "I think she's off the list of suspects."

"Suspects . . . for Owen's murder?"

"No, for being a local fashion disaster. Of course for Owen's murder." I hooked my arm through his and gave him a cautious look. "I think we need to go back to the inn. Now. You're acting kind of strange."

Kind of strange?

"Am I?" He shrugged. "I feel fantastic."

"Once we get out of Salem tomorrow, I think everything will be better. We can reassess and regroup before contacting the Ring with a nonprogress report."

"Get out of Salem . . . right." He nodded. "Yes, I think that's a good idea. Put plenty of room between us and this place. Figure things out from a safe distance."

I looked up at him, frowning. "Exactly. So let's go."

He didn't argue or try to request another song. We left the bar and walked silently back to the Booberry Inn.

"Hey, Rose," he said as we passed by the living room toward the stairs.

"Good evening, Thierry," she responded. "Enjoying Salem's nightlife?"

She was still knitting. It looked like a warm, colorful afghan for one of the beds upstairs. I'd always wanted to be more crafty, but I'd once gotten a paper cut from my scrapbook that literally required stitches. I took it as a clear sign from the universe *not to scrapbook.*

"Love it." He put his arm around my shoulders and tugged me closer to his side. "My wife and I are retiring for the evening."

She nodded. "Sleep well."

"Sure thing," he replied as we moved up the staircase.

Sure thing?

Had I just entered Bizarroland?

Finally we were in our room. I locked the door and turned to face him. "Okay, spill. What's up with you tonight?"

He watched me carefully. "Nothing. Why are you asking me that?"

"I don't know, it's just . . . you seem—I don't even know how to put it." I wracked my brain. "Not normal."

His smile stretched. "I think you're imagining things,

Sarah. I'm the same as always. I know the karaoke might have thrown you off a little, but don't you think I might have a few whimsical quirks to my personality that you were previously unaware of?"

"No," I replied honestly. "I know you pretty well, Thierry, at least personality-wise. You don't sing. Or tell jokes. Or use excessive modern slang. Or smile even half as widely as you are right now."

He laughed and pulled me into his arms. "Maybe I'm more fun than you thought I was."

"Fun is a good word. A word I'm totally open to." Maybe the threat of the Ring coming after him for his missing memories had made him remember that life was precious and every day should be an adventure.

Nah. This was something else entirely. Call it a gut feeling.

Thierry did not have whimsical quirks. Period.

"So what's the problem?" he asked.

"I don't know." I was utterly perplexed. "Maybe I'm overreacting."

"I promise, if it bothers you that much, I swear I'll never sing again. Scout's honor." He raised two fingers. "Am I really *that* bad of a singer?"

"Yes, you really are. No offense."

This didn't make his broad smile slip even a fraction. His gray eyes actually sparkled with amusement as he raised his brow. "Now"—he moved toward the bed and picked up the black silk teddy I'd taken out of my suitcase earlier—"this looks promising."

"It's my Vegas lingerie. Ready and waiting for this honeymoon to kick into high gear."

"And here we are."

I glanced away from the scrap of lace and silk to meet his now heated gaze. "And here we are."

He approached me again, sliding his hand around to the small of my back, and pulled me closer. "You in sexy lingerie. I can't think of a single thing hotter than that."

"Okay." Something was *seriously* wrong here.

What in the world had gotten into Thierry tonight?

He smirked. "Mr. and Mrs. de Bennicoeur. The ancient and grumpy meets the young and beautiful—and sparks fly. We're like soul mates or something. Right? Kiss me, baby."

I dodged his kiss before it hit its target. "I don't believe this."

The realization that had been circling like an approaching storm slammed into me with the force of a hurricane. He hadn't been behaving like himself at all ever since I found him at that karaoke bar. I hadn't understood why, figured he was just having an off evening. He looked the same as always, but he acted totally different.

There was only one reason I could think of.

I gasped. "You're not Thierry!"

"Uh, *wrong*. I am." He sent an appreciative look toward the vanity mirror and raked a hand through his hair. "I mean, look at me, all tall, dark, and fangsome. I'm *totally* Thierry."

"No, you're not." I stared at him, stunned, until it finally hit me. My hand shot to my mouth. "You're . . . you're Owen!"

Total silence filled the room for a heavy moment.

He raised his index finger as if ready to make a valid point, but then his hand dropped to his side. "It's not going to help me very much if I keep trying to argue with you on this, right?"

I staggered back from him until I hit the wall. A framed picture of a field of daisies crashed to the floor.

"Oh, my God! Owen, what the *hell* is going on here? What are you doing? You're possessing Thierry's body!"

Thierry's normally restrained and unreadable expression turned sheepish—definitely a look I'd never seen from him before. "This seems to be the logical conclusion."

"I don't even know what to say." I pointed at the door in a furious thrusting motion. "Get out of my husband right now!"

He spread his hands. "Can't do that."

"Yes, you can!"

Now he looked at his hands, back and front. "No, I'm in here, like, pretty solidly. And just for the record, it's not as if I was even trying to do this in the first place. Before, when the three of us were talking in here, I disappeared. I went to this cold, dark place with nothing to look at. So boring! And then, shazam, I was looking out from Thierry's eyes. I had nothing to do with it. It just happened!"

I grabbed the lapels of his suit jacket and stared up into his eyes. "Thierry, are you in there?"

Owen frowned. "Nope, I don't think so. I can't hear a thing."

"And you were just going to pretend to be him? Until when? After we'd slept together?"

He grimaced. "Putting it like that makes me sound kind of sleazy."

I let out a cry of outrage. "You're disgusting!"

"What can I say? I'm a man! I have needs!"

I dug my fingernails into his arm. "Bring Thierry back and get out of his body."

"Sorry, but I don't know how to do that."

Panic twisted around me like magical vines, tightening until I could barely breathe. Somehow, some way, Owen had possessed Thierry's body. And Thierry himself was currently AWOL.

It must have happened while I was in the shower. This was why Thierry had taken off to go to the karaoke bar alone. Because he actually hadn't. *Owen* had.

Grabbing his arm, I pulled him with me out into the hallway to find Heather. I didn't know which room was hers, so I just started pounding on every door.

"Heather!" I yelled. "I need you! Right now! Where are you?"

Finally, she emerged, bleary-eyed, from the last room. She pulled her powder blue bathrobe tighter around her. "Sarah, what's wrong?"

"The séance you did last night to summon Owen's spirit," I began.

"What about it?"

"It worked."

Her eyebrows shot up. "It did?"

"This"—I yanked on Owen's borrowed sleeve—"is the result. Owen's spirit is now possessing Thierry's body."

Her eyes grew as wide as saucers. "You have got to be joking."

My heart pounded. "Nope. No joking. Not even feeling the least bit humorous right now, actually."

She looked up at Thierry's face. "Owen? Is that really you?"

He eased away from my viselike grip. "You did a séance, Heather? For me? That's so nice!"

"I can't believe this is happening."

"You and me both," I grumbled. "You need to fix this. Now."

Her face had lit up. "This is a miracle. Owen, it's really you?"

He nodded. "The one and only."

She threw her arms around him and hugged him tightly.

Normally, I might find this endearing. The girl with the crush gets her chance for closure with the vampire she's in love with. However, my patience had worn right to the breaking point in a matter of minutes. "As heartfelt as this reunion is, and I hate to sound overly bossy, but it's over. Right now."

She finally turned to me. "It is?"

"Yes! Thierry's gone." I tried very hard to calm myself. This could be fixed. It would all be put right again quicker than ordering a pizza. "Look, I don't know how possession works. I'm not even an expert on vampires, let alone ghosts and spirits. All I know is that you need to do something to get Owen out of Thierry's body and return him to normal."

Her joyous expression faded at the edges. "Oh. Um, how am I supposed to do that?"

This was not what I wanted to hear at all. "I hoped you'd know."

"I don't think Thierry would mind if I borrowed his body for a little while," Owen said, disconcertingly in Thierry's voice.

I tightly gripped the railing that looked over to the main floor. "How long's a little while?"

He shifted in his Italian leather loafers. "I'd prefer if we leave that open-ended."

I shook my head violently. "No way. I'm sorry about what happened to you, Owen. Seriously, I am. But I can't allow this. I know you would have kept pretending to be him if I hadn't figured it out."

He grimaced. "I guess I'm not very good at acting dour."

All that was needed here was a little direction and I could get this back on track. "Heather, you need to do another séance. You can summon Owen's spirit right out of this body."

I thought for a moment she might resist. After all, her dream vampire had just been resurrected into the body of another tall, handsome man. Hopefully she'd changed her vixen ways since high school. Since all I had to go on was Miranda's scotch-colored word, I was willing to give Heather the benefit of the doubt.

Finally, she nodded in agreement. "We can try."

A wave of relief splashed up, currently only ankle high. "Good."

She went to wake her grandmother, so we could all gather around the round table just as we had last time. Even Hoppy was there.

Owen, in current possession of Thierry's body, looked depressed.

"This sucks." He pouted.

I didn't like seeing a pout on Thierry's face. He might be well-known for his glower, but he never pouted. "I know. But you have to see this is wrong. Right?"

His pout deepened. "Yeah. I can't steal a body. Especially if there are witnesses."

So if there *weren't* witnesses, he would be fine and dandy with keeping a stolen body?

"If I can be the one to see the silver lining in this, it *is* a tangible sign of your burgeoning powers, Heather," Rose said excitedly. Her white hair was up in curlers, and she wore a zippered purple velour robe. "I'm proud of you, honey."

Heather wrung her hands anxiously. "Yeah, well, it didn't exactly work like I thought it would."

"Could the séance last night have done this?" I asked. "Like, on a delay since it took so long for his spirit to even show up?"

Rose nodded. "Certainly. The spirit world is a vast one. Sometimes there are issues with travel to the afterlife."

I had that problem with a travel agent once. This, however, wasn't as simple as being stuck at an airport all day after a missed connection.

Thierry, wherever you are, please be patient. I can fix this.

We all held hands.

"Do you have anything that belonged to Thierry?" Heather asked. "I thought we should check to see if his spirit is wandering loose from the rest of his body."

At my glare, Owen cringed. "Remember, this wasn't my fault."

"So you keep telling me." I tried to restrain myself from wringing his neck. "Do I have anything that belonged to Thierry? Well, his body seems like a good thing. It's sitting right next to me and you're holding his hand."

"Oh, um. Good point." Heather cleared her throat nervously. "Then I should probably get started."

She went silent and studied the smooth wooden surface of the table. Her grip on my hand grew tighter. She didn't close her eyes and she didn't say anything to start summoning spirits.

"Are we going to start?" I prompted after a full minute went by.

"Is something wrong, dear?" Rose asked, concerned.

Heather inhaled deeply. "I have something to say first. In case I don't get the chance later."

Her gaze rose to look at Thierry. Or rather, Owen.

"I'm so sorry you're gone," she said, her voice breaking.

He nodded. "That's sweet. Yeah, it's kind of sucky. Like I can't even wrap my head around all my questions. What's Heaven going to be like? Are girl angels hot? Can I still fool around? That sort of thing, you know?"

With statements like this coming out of his mouth, I was shocked it took me more than thirty seconds to figure out the truth. Honestly, I was embarrassed.

Her expression tensed and she shook her head. "Stop it. I know you're just putting on this facade and trying to be strong."

I stared at the two of them. I honestly didn't think Owen was putting on a brave front for her. I actually believed he was pondering how many hookups he might achieve in the afterlife.

Heather let out a long, shaky sigh. "Okay, I'm just going to say it."

Hoppy croaked. She stroked his head absently.

"I love you, Owen." She let out a giddy little laugh. "There. I said it. It wasn't that hard after all. *I love you.*"

Rose and I watched Owen for his reaction.

He shifted uncomfortably in his seat and cleared his throat. "That's nice. Thanks. That's . . . really sweet of you to say."

Heather's cheeks flushed. "Nice? Sweet? Doesn't it mean anything to you?"

"Of course." He nodded. "It means tons. I really appreciate that."

"That's it? That's the only reaction I get?"

Owen grimaced. "I'm sorry if I'm disappointing you, but . . . I mean, don't get me wrong. I like you. But I always got more of a sister vibe from you. I never got any romantic vibe. Anyway, I thought you were still kind of hung up on that other dude you were dating before."

She stared at him. "I've imagined this moment in my head so many times, but it always turned out way differently than this."

"Um," Owen began, "I mean, don't get me wrong, you're super cute. But it's just not like that between us."

A shiver of electricity sped down my arms and the candles began to flicker. I glanced around the room with alarm.

What was that?

"Anyway, dear," Rose said from across the table, squeezing her granddaughter's hand. "Let's get on with it, yes?"

It was enough to bring Heather back to the moment. The flickering stopped and the strange tingling feeling went away.

Heather might be a more powerful witch than she believed she was, after all. It made me both uneasy—since I wasn't sure how far I could trust the girl—and reassured. If she had more magic than I thought, then she'd be able to help fix this problem.

I mentally crossed my fingers.

"Everyone close your eyes." Heather didn't sound quite as happy and joyously in love after Owen's "I like you as a friend" admission as she had earlier. Couldn't say I entirely blamed her there.

"You know, Sarah, we can discuss this," Owen murmured. “I know Thierry was probably a bit too much of a curmudgeon for you—”

“Please stop talking,” I said tightly.

“I think I’d make a fabulous husband. We could have lots of fun together. I’m only two hundred and six. I’m a third Thierry’s age. I exude youth from my very pores. Seriously. I do.”

“You’re going to exude more than youth in a minute. Heather? Can we move this along?”

“Yes, of course.” She took a deep breath and squeezed her eyes shut. I did the same. “I’m reaching out into the spirit world to inquire if there is a Thierry de Bennicoeur there. Someone who does not belong there since it is before his time. Is he there? Thierry?”

Silence fell—a weighty silence with only the tick of the grandfather clock as its soundtrack. I waited, squeezing both Owen’s and Rose’s hands, and just tried to breathe.

There was a whisper of cool air a minute later. I opened an eye.

“Hello again!” Lorenzo’s disembodied head exclaimed merrily.

I grimaced. “Oh no. Heather!”

She opened her eyes and frowned. “Lorenzo, you’re back.”

He nodded. “I’m feeling much better than last time. Yet, alas, still no body.”

Heather’s face paled. “I see that.”

“Lorenzo,” Rose ventured, as calm as if there was nothing odd at all about this situation. “Maybe you can be of help.”

“I’d be happy to be helpful to anyone. Except my wife, that is! Did I mention that she poisoned me? She’s like a black widow spider!”

"You weren't poisoned," Rose assured him. "And Maria had nothing to do with your death, I assure you. You choked to death."

His expression turned sour. "She *made* me choke to death!"

"No, she didn't. It was an unfortunate accident."

Lorenzo frowned. "Maybe you're right. But she *wanted* to poison me. She told me so every day!"

"Lorenzo . . ." I took over. "Do you know anything about possession?"

"Certainly. What do you want to know, young lady?"

"How do you do it?"

He pursed his lips. "Oh, that's very difficult. It takes a strong spirit to possess a living body, but it is possible."

A chill zipped down my arms. "And where does the spirit of the original person go when and if another spirit is successful in possessing them?"

He shrugged. Which, since he didn't currently have shoulders, was rather impressive. "Nowhere. Possession never lasts very long. A handful of minutes at the most; then the original occupant pushes back. It's impossible to maintain a possession."

Owen glanced at me, confused. "It's not like that for me. I'm in here, like, solid. I don't feel like I'm being pushed out at all. And I don't sense Thierry."

None of this was what I wanted to hear. But it confirmed that something bad had happened, something magical, and it wasn't just a random fluke. "Lorenzo, what if the body is supernatural in some way? Would that make a difference?"

"Supernatural?"

"Like, it's a . . . vampire?"

He reared back from me in horror. "Like Dracula?"

I sighed. "I don't think he's going to be much more help."

Rose considered the ghostly face for a moment. "He doesn't know. He can't help us."

"Eyes shut," Heather commanded sharply.

I squeezed my eyes shut again, blocking out the shimmering image of the deceased Italian restaurateur's face, blocking out any doubt and fears that had taken up residence in my mind.

"Thierry, where are you?" Heather said, her voice strong. "Come to us. You are welcome here."

More silence filled the room. I counted the ticking clock all the way to sixty. I wanted this over and for life to return to normal. Or as normal as it could ever be.

Then I felt that whisper of cool air brush against my skin again.

"Sarah . . ."

My eyes popped open. There were now two Thierrys in the room with us. One seated next to me clutching my hand. The other standing to my left in the darkness. Despite wearing his familiar black suit, his form seemed to glow a little.

My breath ceased. "Thierry!"

He looked around the room slowly before his gaze fell on Owen and narrowed dangerously. "What is going on here?"

Relief mixed with dread. Good news, he seemed to be okay. Bad news, he was now doing an uncanny impression of a ghost.

"Isn't it obvious?" Owen said sullenly, as if disappointed we'd managed to successfully contact the real Thierry. "I possessed you. So sue me."

Thierry's dark brows drew together and his gray eyes glittered. "I strongly suggest you *un*possess me. Right now."

My chair squeaked as I let go of both Rose's and Owen's hands and got up from the table.

"You're here," I said. "It's going to be okay. We can fix this."

I automatically reached forward to touch him, my hand trembling, but his chest swirled like gray smoke. I stared at him in horror. I should have expected it, but it still managed to take me by surprise.

"It's all right, Sarah," he soothed, as if sensing my oncoming anxiety attack. He glanced down at himself as his body re-formed. "You're right. We *can* fix this. And we will."

My gaze shot to his. "The sooner the better."

He nodded. "I agree."

"This isn't my fault." Owen raised his hands as if warding off an expected onslaught of anger. Thierry appeared calm on the surface, but I suspected it was his growing anger that made the room feel colder than it had with Lorenzo.

"Then whose fault is it?" Thierry asked icily.

"We think it was a side effect of the séance last night," Rose said. "My granddaughter is a more powerful witch than she ever would have believed."

"You're wrong. I can't do magic like that." Heather's voice shook. "Any magic I have done in the past, aside from the odd séance, I've needed your grimoire for."

"You have a grimoire?" Thierry asked Rose. "That could help us."

A grimoire was a witch's book of spells. Most witches had one that they updated regularly with new information—kind of like a really creepy diary.

"It doesn't contain powerful magic since my magic was never powerful," Rose said regretfully. "Just some spells to help my flowers grow, some pet obedience spells, and other simple magic. Nothing that could help you, I'm afraid."

Thierry's jaw tightened. "Then we have a problem."

"What do you mean?" I asked. "Can't you just take your body back?"

When he met my gaze, his finally softened. "I'm afraid it's not that simple."

"Have you ever dealt with anything like this before?"

He shook his head. "No."

"You seem so calm right now, it's seriously freaking me out."

"I seem that way." His lips thinned. "Remember, though, I did tell you I'm a skilled liar."

"Oh, crap," I whispered.

He raised an eyebrow. "Bottom line, we need to find a solution. And it must be found in the next three days."

"Why? What happens in three days?" I asked, my voice hoarse.

Thierry glanced toward Heather, who'd gone a pale shade of green. She didn't speak. Instead, Rose took over.

"In three days," Rose said, her expression sympathetic, "a spirit loses all connections with the mortal world."

"Which means"—I inhaled sharply and met Thierry's serious gaze—"in three days I'll lose you forever."

Chapter 7

Thierry nodded grimly.

I gripped the edge of the table tightly so it would help me keep standing. Then I turned a fierce look in Heather's direction. It must have been fierce, since she literally cringed. "Then you are going to find a solution for me in the next three days."

She blanched. "I don't know if I can."

"You can. And you will." I meant every single word. "Your séance made this happen, and now you're going to fix it."

Her eyes filled with tears. "But I don't know how!"

How could she not know? She could summon spirits with a snap of her fingers. She could fill a room with a shiver of electricity when she got riled up. This girl had magic in her whether she believed it or not.

Rose looked dire as well. "I don't know, either, I'm afraid. Only the most powerful witch's grimoire could contain magic that might be able to restore a spirit to its original body." She nodded thoughtfully. "It's really quite fascinating—don't you think?"

She and I obviously had differing opinions on fascinating.

"Like I said," Owen murmured, "you and me, Sarah. It's not such a bad match when you think about it."

I shot him a withering glare.

"Excuse me?" Thierry hissed, and the room's temperature dropped a few more degrees. "What did you just say?"

Owen cleared his throat. "No offense, Thierry, but I think she'd have much more fun with me in the long run. Tell me one thing that you two have in common. It isn't karaoke; that much I know."

"You know nothing about us." Thierry's tone was pitch-black. "You're simply a fool who talks to hear himself speak, but your words hold no meaning—just as your life held no meaning other than a quest for momentary pleasures. It was always that way with you."

"Yeah," I said, nodding, thoroughly impressed by Thierry's skill at being menacing. "What he said."

"Does she know half of what you've been accused of in the past, or have you shared only the more pleasant stuff?" Owen asked, smiling darkly. "What? You don't think she could handle it?"

The room chilled a few more degrees.

"If you're trying to help your case," I said, every bit as ominously as Thierry had before, "you're failing miserably. Now, I want my husband's spirit returned to his body right this minute, and then you can feel free to continue on to find your afterlife booty call."

Owen gave me a wry look. "Oh, come on, Sarah. You didn't even know I wasn't him for a while. Almost long enough, Thierry, for her to get to know me a little better. If you know what I mean."

His controlled exterior finally shattering, Thierry attempted to grab hold of Owen's borrowed throat.

Instead, his fingers slipped right through like tendrils of smoke.

"Don't push me," Thierry growled. "I've given you far too many chances already."

Owen regarded Thierry's spirit with a sour look as he got to his feet. "Yeah, yeah. I'm so scared. Now you're the harmless ghost and I'm the one with the heartbeat. It might be stolen, but sometimes you need to take what you can get. I need a body and yours will do nicely, thanks."

Panic rose inside me as I realized Owen was going to give us a hard time and fight to keep Thierry's body. This wasn't part of the plan.

Heather stood up from the table as well, staring at Owen as if this outburst had surprised her. "You can't be serious."

"Can't I? It's probably your love and devotion to me that even made this possible. What do you say, Heather? Does this body do it for you? Want to give it a test drive later?"

Her expression fell. "You're disgusting."

He smirked. "I thought you were pledging your never-ending love to me a minute ago."

I exchanged a tense look with Thierry, only an arm's reach away from me.

"What do we do?" I asked him quietly.

"We find a solution."

"What do you suggest?"

"First and foremost, Owen *must* stay here. You can't let him leave town."

"Sorry," Owen said with an easy shrug, "but I really don't think you're in a position to stop me. I have the power now. I know you always hated my guts, Thierry. Why should I care to help you now?"

Fury flashed across Thierry's expression. "You selfish son of a—"

And then he vanished like someone had flicked a switch.

I reached forward to where he'd been standing, my eyes widening with shock. "Thierry? Where did he go? Heather! Bring him back!"

She gave me a scared look. "I don't know why he disappeared."

"Heated emotions will do it." Rose was still seated at the table. She patted Hoppy on his back absently, receiving a low croak in response. "That surge of energy makes a spirit's lightbulb pop. It'll take him a while to gather himself back together and reenter the mortal world. He'll be back. He's a fighter, that one."

Owen brushed the sleeve of Thierry's suit jacket and straightened his collar. "I should probably be on my way."

My chest tightened. "You're not going anywhere, mister."

"Wait." Heather ran out of the room and returned only a few moments later with a small, black, leather-encased book.

"Is that Rose's grimoire?" Owen said, bored. "Going to make some flowers bloom?"

"No flowers today." Her expression held no humor. "Grandma? Remember the spell for Baxter?"

"Page sixty-two," Rose replied. "Ah, yes. Baxter. The mutt who kept trying to run away and hump every lady dog in a three-mile radius. The similarity is uncanny."

Heather flipped forward through the pages.

Owen rolled his eyes. "Sarah, one last chance to come with me on an adventure of a lifetime. You, me, this body—we could have tons of fun."

He was literally going to do it. Just take Thierry's body and march right out of here like it meant nothing.

I blocked his path as he tried to leave the séance room. "You're not leaving. Even if I need to restrain you myself."

"Are you kidding? I now have the strength of a master vampire. That's major, sweetheart. A fledgling would have as much luck holding me in place as a house cat wrestling a mountain lion."

"You might be surprised how sharp my claws are."

He pushed past me and headed toward the front door, where the large wall mirror didn't show either of our reflections. I zipped in front of him and blocked the door, holding my arms out to either side of me.

I hadn't thought of him as an evil guy before—maybe a bit deluded and self-absorbed at the most—but I'd now upgraded him to aspiring villain.

"No way. You're *not* leaving here with Thierry's body. What part of this don't you understand?"

This got another eye roll. "The *not leaving* part."

Grabbing hold of my upper arms, he shoved me to the right with enough power to launch me halfway into the living room. I slammed hard into an end table and knocked a lamp to the floor, where it shattered.

His eyes widened as if he was shocked at his own strength. "Sorry about that. But stay out of my way and you won't get hurt. Okay?"

I just lay there for a moment, stunned, until Rose came over to help me back up to my feet. I knew Thierry was strong, but—well, I hadn't personally experienced it before quite like this. He was Hulk strong. Hulk Smash strong. And now Owen had every bit of that master vampire strength at his fingertips.

The front door creaked as he swung it open.

I hadn't been able to keep him here through force of will, so I'd have to try a different tactic. "Please don't go! Please, Owen, we can find another way."

"Another way? Your way means that I stay dead. I like this way better." His brows drew together. "Sorry, really, but I have no other choice here. I gotta look out for number one."

He turned toward the open door and took a step onto the porch.

Heather entered the foyer, holding the grimoire tightly in her hands. She was reciting a spell in Latin, reading it from the pages—the same short phrase over and over.

The tingling electricity from before returned to charge the air.

Owen took a shaky step backward. Then another one, and another, until he was fully back inside the house. The door swung shut behind him.

A little blood trickled from Heather's nose. She absently wiped it away.

"Be careful, honey," Rose cautioned. "You're pushing it too far."

Heather twisted her fingers into the chain of her necklace and kept reciting the spell without stopping.

Owen glanced over his shoulder. "What are you doing? That doggy spell?"

She nodded, still speaking in Latin. Never hesitating once.

I tried very hard not to pay attention to the fact that she was bleeding.

I mean, I *was* a vampire. And blood was distracting even while currently low on my list of priorities. Finally, I tore my attention away from her and focused again on Owen.

"Good luck with that." Owen opened the door and strode outside, skipping down the five steps leading toward the driveway. I was about to chase after him when Rose caught my arm.

"Don't worry," she said. "The spell will buy us some time."

Heather closed the grimoire with a snap.

That very moment, Owen smashed into something invisible that stopped him in his tracks. He held his hands up, touching the air like a mime stuck in an invisible box.

He sent a glance over his shoulder. "Cute trick."

Heather offered him a thin smile. "Doggy spell."

"Let me leave."

She shook her head. "Can't do that. This barrier works to keep you within ten paces of the house. You're not going anywhere, bad dog."

Owen groaned and his pout was back. "I thought you said you loved me. Don't you want me to be happy?"

She wiped at her bloody nose, her strong expression wavering. Then she lifted her chin. "I'm starting to think I shouldn't have let my emotions overrule my head. And here we are."

He pushed up against the invisible barrier for another few minutes before giving up and heading back inside. He didn't look as defeated as I expected, faced with two witches of varying power, a pissed-off vampire, and an oblivious toad.

"What's with the smug look?" I rubbed my arm, bruised after my airborne trip across the room into the table.

He shrugged. "You can't keep me here."

"Sure we can," Heather insisted, glancing at her grandma for backup.

"We can," Rose agreed. "And we will. You're not going anywhere, Owen."

Owen peeled off Thierry's jacket and threw it over the back of a nearby easy chair, then rolled up the sleeves of his black shirt. "Did you forget the part about me being as strong as a master vampire now? I can take this place apart brick by brick if I have to."

And, if he was so inclined, he could murder every one of us with his bare hands. Or his bare fangs.

I shivered at the thought. Was Owen Harper that dangerous?

Heather didn't seem nearly as concerned. Then again, she'd known Owen longer than I had. "I don't think you'd do that. You know how much I love this place."

"Oh really?" He moved to a table near the door and flicked off a crystal vase. It shattered on the floor.

Her expression fell. "That was a family heirloom, you jerk!"

Rose just watched their exchange with curiosity. "Feeling tired yet, Owen?"

"Tired? Why would I feel tired? I'm alive, I'm devastatingly handsome, I'm healthy, I'm . . ." He yawned and stretched his arms. "I'm so, so tired."

I exchanged a look with Heather. "Part of the spell?"

She looked just as surprised as I was. "Grandma?"

"A spell within a spell." Rose nodded. "Baxter required mandatory initial downtime to deal with his naughty behavior. Couldn't have him destroy the furniture."

"Which means?" I asked.

"It means you suck. All of you." Owen dropped to his knees. He slowly crawled toward the couch but didn't quite make it. Finally, he curled up on the area rug in the fetal position and fell asleep.

Rose studied the six feet of vampire now dozing on their living room floor. "Not sure how long it'll last on somebody who isn't a dog. Up to a day, I would think."

This did nothing to ease my mind, but it did give us a small window of time to work with. "You said before, Rose, that a powerful witch might have a grimoire with the magic to reverse what's happened to Thierry, right?"

She nodded. "I did say that."

"Then it's simple. We need to find a powerful witch."

Heather and Rose exchanged a look.

"There *is* somebody, isn't there?" I prompted. "Somebody who can help?"

Heather chewed her bottom lip nervously. "Well, I honestly don't know how powerful she is, but I've heard some rumors. She *might* be able to help us."

A powerful witch in Salem. The last time I was looking for one of those, it was to figure out who was the murderer who'd thrown a death spell in Owen's direction. Now I needed one to help me. My appreciation and use for witches seemed to be on a sliding scale. "You're not talking about Miranda, are you?"

She shook her head. "No. Miranda's coven leader."

I *knew* that scotch-swilling blonde was in a coven. "Okay, then let's go."

"It's too late." Rose glanced at the grandfather clock in the corner, which now read twelve thirty. Time sure flew when dealing with ghosts and possessions and wandering vampires. "Go see her tomorrow at noon."

"Why noon?" I was thinking the crack of dawn. Why waste time?

"That's when their coven meets so we'll know she's definitely there," Heather said without any friendliness. After all, this was the coven she wasn't invited to join.

"And Raina Wilkins, well, she's not exactly the friendliest person in town. She likes her privacy."

"But both of you think she might have a grimoire that could help us."

Heather looked thoughtful. "Raina's family has allegedly been in Salem since the *Mayflower* arrived. And there are rumors that there was a powerful witch in her family line killed during the Salem trials, but her death was never documented. And more rumors that it's this witch's grimoire that can be found somewhere in her house."

"That's a lot of rumors."

She nodded. "I'm sorry we can't be more specific."

Me too. But sometimes you had to take what you could get. Tonight I'd have to be satisfied with the promise of rumors and the hope that tomorrow would bring solid answers. "Okay, fine. Tomorrow at twelve o'clock we're going to go crash a coven meeting."

Heather looked ill at this prospect. I looked determined.

Or at least I thought I would if I could see my reflection down here.

The small room seemed even smaller without company that night, and it took me forever to go to sleep. But finally I did. I dreamed that the Ring had imprisoned Thierry, holding him in a medieval dungeon until he answered their questions.

I woke when a swarm of armor-wearing bees swept through the air.

Then I realized it was my cell phone buzzing next to me on my pillow.

YOU HAVE TODAY ONLY TO LEARN MORE OF THIERRY'S MISSING YEARS. THE ELDERS WANT ANSWERS.—MR

Heart racing, I began to type "The elders can go to hell," but then deleted it. I was crazy, but not *that* crazy.

Thanks for nothing, Markus.

After having another moment of crazy when I nearly texted Markus back to ask him for help with regard to the possession, I shoved my phone into my purse. I wasn't that desperate yet.

Soon, I was sure. But not yet.

I sat vigil next to Thierry's unconscious body in the living room all morning. I'd managed to get him onto the couch last night and thrown a knitted afghan over him.

I touched his face, stroking the dark hair off his forehead. "I got this, Thierry. Don't worry about a thing, okay?"

Sleeping Beauty did not respond.

His body stayed there, safely unconscious. His spirit did not make another appearance. I tried not to dwell on that and wonder what horrible things it could mean.

I focused on two things, witch and grimoire, while I paced back and forth, an eye on the grandfather clock.

Rose gardened with Hoppy out back in the bright sunshine. Heather skimmed every book in their library she could find on the subject of ghosts.

Finally, it was time to go.

"Will Thierry's *spirit* come back all on his own or will it take another séance?" I asked Heather as we left the inn, cringing as I spoke the words out loud.

She fumbled for her car keys. "I don't know."

I hissed out a breath. "Considering the magic you can do, I'm surprised you don't know these things."

Doubt etched into her expression. "I can't do anything."

"But you *can*. You did it all last night."

She twisted a finger into her gold chain. "I know, but

it's not like . . ." She blanched. "I can do some minor grimoire magic and séances. But, well, that's different from really powerful magic."

I eyed her pendant. "Your mom was a strong witch, right?"

"Yeah, she was amazing, actually. She and Grandma never got along so well, and they were usually arguing about me—Grandma knew I had more magic in me, but Mom never wanted to push me too hard to learn. And now, real magic . . . I don't have any control over that, not like she did."

I guess we had different ideas about "real magic." All I knew for sure was that Heather could do more magic than I could. If you didn't count that really cool card trick I knew. And that wasn't going to help us out at all right now.

We took Heather's rusty Volkswagen Beetle to a three-story house, twice the size of the Booberry Inn, with a huge wraparound veranda and a gable roof. I didn't know much about architecture, but it looked like it had been around for a long time.

"Impressive," I said. "Is this Raina woman rich?"

"I think she has some family money." Heather didn't say it pleasantly. "This is a waste of time."

I gave her a patient look when I was feeling anything but. "Don't get cold feet. We can do this. And let me do the talking."

"Okay."

Yes, I would keep holding on to this shaky rope of optimism until my hands were blistered. Without another moment's delay, I marched right to the front door, which was painted a pale shade of lavender, and rang the doorbell.

A minute later, the door opened. Miranda Collins stood there.

"Sarah! What a surprise."

"Hey there," I said with a chipper smile on my face, stopping just short of any off-putting fang reveal. "How are you today?"

She grimaced. "I have a bit of a headache." Then her gaze moved over my shoulder, landed on Heather, and soured. "Oh, you're with *her*."

A rivalry between the two didn't help my cause at all. Plus, it seemed to be due to some pretty unimportant history and hurt feelings from long ago. "I have an idea. Let's make today the start of a new chapter in your lives and forgive and forget."

"No," both Heather and Miranda said in unison.

Heather looked at me with an edge of disappointment. "You and Miranda know each other now?"

Well, I knew that Miranda had high self-esteem about her dewy good looks and a rapidly developing drinking problem. "We chatted at Mulligan's last night."

"Sarah *knows*, Heather," Miranda snarled. "I told her what a tramp you were for stealing my boyfriend in high school."

Heather looked embarrassed before her gaze hardened. "I didn't steal him. I was helping him escape."

Ouch.

The next moment, electricity crackled in the air. I looked at Miranda to see her eyes had turned red.

Eyeballs—they really could reveal hidden truths.

Vampire eyes turned pitch black when we were famished and needed to feed (it was just as fearsome as it sounded). From previous experience with a troublesome witch, I knew their eyes turned red when getting their witch on. Although, come to think of it, Heather's hadn't changed color during the séance or the spell she did on Owen—her nose just bled.

"So . . ." My voice was strained, but I tried to keep the smile steady on my face. "Is Raina here?"

"Maybe." Miranda, still upset about the walk down memory lane, shot me an unfriendly look. Maybe we wouldn't become buddies after all.

"I'd like to speak to her. Pretty please."

I expected her to yell and scream and tell us to go to hell, but instead, her eyes shifted back to their normal shade of green.

"She's here. Come in."

She opened the door wider and I tentatively stepped inside. Vampires didn't actually need an invitation to enter a private home, but polite people did. I had about ten more minutes of polite left.

Heather silently trailed behind me as we were ushered into the large house. A chandelier that looked like it had been there for hundreds of years hung from the high ceiling. To the left was a staircase to the second floor with an iron banister. Oil portraits of stern men and women watched our journey down the long hallway.

"We're meeting in the salon," Miranda said. "Follow me."

"Let me guess. Book club, right?" I refrained from making sarcastic air quotes.

"You got it."

Yeah, right.

Heather stayed silent, but I sensed her uneasiness. It was hard to be shunned from a group—I knew that from personal experience. Women tended to be cliquey, be it in high school or beyond. Those who were in were in. Those who were out were out. Now I realized that most of the groups that hadn't wanted me weren't worth being in anyway.

We were led into an adjoining room that held two women. One was blond, like Miranda, the other dark, both attractive women who appeared to be in their late twenties to early thirties.

In front of them on the coffee table were mugs, a plate of cookies, and minimuffins. Copies of *To Kill a Mockingbird* were opened on the shiny mahogany.

I did a double take at that.

What do you know? This actually *was* a book club.

"Raina," Miranda began, "this is Sarah. She wants to speak with you. You already know Heather." She didn't even try to hide her contempt for the redhead next to me.

I held out my hand to the raven-haired woman and gave her a fang-hiding smile. "It's nice to meet you, Raina."

She shook my hand, holding my gaze. Her eyes were blue—a vivid sapphire shade—and held no suspicion, only curiosity. I could work with that. "Are you new to town, Sarah?"

"Just visiting, actually."

"Welcome." Raina had jet-black hair she wore in long layers past her shoulders. Her skin was pale and her makeup applied perfectly. Her outfit at a glance was expensive but not overly showy. Other than a small solitaire diamond necklace and a charm bracelet, she wore no jewelry. The woman had money, but she didn't flaunt it. "You already know Miranda. This is Casey."

"Hi there." I shook the other pretty blonde's hand and forced another smile. My cheeks had started to ache. I was glad the coven was only a trio.

"Gorgeous ring," Casey said, gazing down with appreciation at my engagement ring.

"Thank you. I couldn't agree more." And thank you so much for the reminder of my marriage, currently in dire jeopardy of not lasting more than a week before I lost my husband forever to the spirit world. Yeah, thanks, Casey.

"You wanted to speak with me?" Raina asked, her gaze moving between me and Heather. "About what?"

"I need help," I said bluntly, heart pounding. Why mince words? Plus, I wasn't that great at small talk, and I had to admit, I'd read only the cheat notes on *To Kill a Mockingbird* back in high school. "I'm currently dealing with a problem involving a ghost and a stolen body. There's a rumor that you might be in possession—no pun intended—of a powerful witch's grimoire that might be helpful in righting what's wrong. So I'm here to ask you if we might borrow this grimoire."

Raina studied me, blinking a few times as if trying to follow along but having difficulty. "I'm not sure I understand. A grimoire? What's a grimoire?"

Doubt nudged me with its pointy elbow. "It's a witch's spell book."

She cocked her head to the side. "My goodness, I don't have anything like that. You must be one of those people who thinks that everyone in Salem is a witch. I'm sorry to tell you that's not true."

Sure. And the red-eye reception I'd received at the front door had only been due to Miranda's need for Visine.

She was lying. Still, I knew I had to tread softly right now. I hadn't forgotten for a minute that Owen's murderer was somewhere in town, and she or he was a powerful witch. Cross one of them by accident, or reveal that I was a vampire, and I didn't think this story would have a happy ending. I liked happy endings. In fact, I insisted on them.

"Trust me, Raina," I said, "I'm not trying to get in your business. I think everyone is more than entitled to keep their individual skeletons tightly locked in their private closets. However, I'm quickly running out of both options and time."

"And I would love to help you, but I don't have this spell book you're looking for." She gave me a sympathetic look that didn't push away an ounce of my uncertainty. "If you've happened to tread upon some supernatural unpleasantness here in Salem, I'm sorry. If I could help you, I would. But I can't."

I looked into her blue eyes, attempting to see deception there. All I saw was vague confusion and patience. The expression reminded me of a teacher I'd had in third grade. After I'd fallen off the jungle gym three times and literally broken my arm in two places, I kept trying to get back on it. The teacher didn't understand why. But I knew mistakes would inevitably lead to success. And bones healed eventually.

Although, I had to admit, I'd prefer not to have any broken today.

"I'm really sorry to hear that," I said under my breath, then swept a glance around the room. "So isn't this a coven?"

Raina's jaw tensed. "It's a book club."

The proof of this was on the coffee table. I couldn't exactly argue with her even though I wanted to. I couldn't see any bubbling cauldrons or broomsticks.

"What happens in book club stays in book club," I said, flicking a glance at the woman again.

I couldn't read her face. Her gaze was steady as she took my hand in hers and squeezed it. "Don't worry, Sarah. Most problems work themselves out. Like a ball of wool with some knots. What looks like a tangle can be sorted through in time, and it's no reason to overreact. Go now, with Heather. You will find your answer somewhere else. Everything will be okay very soon."

With that, we were ushered back to the front door. A soothing sense of calm now emanated from the center of my being. She was right. Everything was going to be okay very soon.

"Everything's going to be okay." Heather echoed my thoughts on the drive back to her house.

"Yes, of course it is," I agreed. "These sorts of things work themselves out. Like wool. Or whatever she said."

"Tangles. Tangles work themselves out."

"Exactly." I frowned. "Wait. What am I saying? This isn't going to work itself out. What was that?"

Heather nodded. "Patience solves many problems."

Why did I feel so calm? I wasn't calm. Thierry was currently in mortal jeopardy. And he was supposed to be immortal!

"Stop the car," I commanded. "Heather, stop the car! Right now!"

Heather slammed on the brakes and then pulled off to the side of the road. My mind raced. My former sense of serenity had suddenly been torn away like a wax strip on a hairy leg.

I stared at Heather, stunned. "That witch put a spell on us!"

Chapter 8

Witches freaked me out.

I mean, vampires I understood. Mostly. We were what we were, and there wasn't too much hidden from plain sight. We had pointy canines that some filed down to appear more human, but the moment that we felt that bloodlust come upon us—which, let's face it, happened more often than I'd like to admit—they re-formed like tiny switchblades. So having them filed down, in my opinion, was a big waste of money.

We drank blood to survive. On paper, it seemed pretty gross, but it was a fact of life. We were allegedly immortal, since the transition to vampire meant that our ages froze at the point we were sired. I couldn't get sick like a human—so no more head colds or flus. We were still killable, though, which was what vampire hunters preyed upon.

But we couldn't do magic. We couldn't snap our fingers and summon an object out of thin air. And we couldn't make somebody explode with the power of our minds.

Yeah, witches freaked me out. And I kept forgetting, despite any arguments to the contrary, that I was currently in the middle of a town overflowing with them.

As soon as I convinced Heather that we'd somehow

been bespelled to leave Raina's house, she drove back and parked two blocks away. We got out of the car and approached the house on foot. The area was all white picket fences, green yards, and colorful flower gardens.

I'd started off angry that Raina had used magic on me to make me turn tail and get out of her hair, but now I'd settled into a simmering certainty that there was only one answer available to me today.

"I don't know why we're even back here," Heather said, eyeing the house with uncertainty. "She's not going to talk to us again."

"No, you're right. She isn't."

"So what do we do?"

I pressed up against the side of the house, the brickwork rough against my hands. Before I could say anything to the redhead, the lavender front door creaked open. I pressed my index finger to my lips to tell Heather to be quiet, and I peered around the corner of the house to see the trio emerge onto the veranda. A pot of red geraniums partially blocked my view.

After saying their good-byes, both Casey and Miranda got into separate cars and drove away.

Book club my butt. This was definitely a coven of witches. The only question was, how witchy were they?

Two minutes later, Raina also left the house, locking the front door behind her, and after getting into her Lexus sports car, pulled out of the driveway. I pressed so firmly against the wall as she drove down the street, I was certain I'd have the permanent impression of a brick facade etched onto my skin.

"Is Raina married?" I asked. "Kids?"

"No. She's single. No kids. Not even a cat."

"Good."

"Why?"

I looked at her. "Because we're going to break into her house and steal her grimoire."

Heather gasped. "That's illegal."

"Desperate times, Heather. Raina had her chance to help me. I'm going to have to help myself."

"If she catches us . . ."

I grimaced. "Yeah, well, let's try to think positively. I'm thinking after our next talk I might start clucking like a chicken. And I don't want that. Nobody wants to cluck like a chicken."

I swept my gaze over the light purple door once we got there. "Do you know how to pick a lock?"

"Afraid not."

"Can you do a spell to open this up?"

"I can't do spells without a grimoire. I already told you that."

I hissed out a breath. "I am starting to think that you seriously underestimate yourself, Heather. I mean, just the séances alone . . . can you imagine how much easier it would be if the police had a séance division? They could just summon everybody who ever got murdered and ask them who did it."

"Doesn't work that way. Murder victims never remember the exact moment of their death. It's blocked out."

"Like a memory wipe?" I kept wanting to find clues to unlock Thierry's missing memories to get the Ring off our backs, but that wasn't the same as this. He hadn't been murdered.

She shrugged, shifting her feet. "All I know is it doesn't work. Besides, if witches started coming forth and volunteering their time to the local police force, witch hunters would have a field day."

Just like vampire hunters. I shuddered at the thought. Let's just say that I was extremely lucky to still be breathing, given my history with the wooden stake carriers. Hunters killed without interest in determining who deserved to die. Evil, good, tall, short, blond, brunette, whoever—stake to the heart, one and all. Sounded like witch hunters were exactly the same.

I glanced over my shoulder toward the street to watch for Raina's return. I had no idea where she'd gone or when she'd be back. We had to make this quick.

"So how are we going to get in?" Heather asked.

At least she wasn't trying to talk me out of this. I surveyed the door.

"I hope this works." I grasped the door handle tightly, turned it as far as it could go. Then turned it a little more, putting some of my extra vampire strength into it.

The sound of the lock splintering the wood wasn't pleasant, but it was rather satisfying.

I made a mental note to leave an envelope of money later to pay for the repairs. It was the least I could do. I'd drop it off with the returned grimoire once we were done with it.

But first we had to find it.

Raina's house was big—six or seven thousand square feet at least. After scouring the living room where the book club meeting had been, including the bookshelves, which were filled with hardcover novels both new and old, I started to worry about how long this was taking.

What would Thierry do? He wouldn't have let himself be bespelled in the first place. Plus, when he was determined to get something done, it got done. He'd probably have the grimoire in one hand and Raina eating out of the other.

Or he'd be dead from pushing the witch too far.

I shuddered.

"We need to split up," I announced.

Heather gave me a strained look. "You sure?"

"I need that grimoire. If it's here, then we have to find it. You keep looking down here, and I'll check upstairs. Okay?"

She nodded. "Okay."

I couldn't believe I'd ever doubted her sincerity for a moment, especially considering what success would ultimately mean for the man she once loved. "Thank you for helping me, Heather. I know that if we get the grimoire, if we get the right spell, it means that Owen will not be able to stick around."

"I know." Her expression turned solemn. "But I already made my peace with that when I did the Baxter spell."

"Which you did really amazingly well."

She gave me a shaky smile. "Thanks. Okay, I'll look down here. Holler if you need me to come up."

"Ditto."

I headed up the staircase to the second floor as she continued to check the bookcase in the main living room. The stairs creaked with each step I took. I was a little surprised that Raina lived in this big house all by herself. I expected to find a pit bull or a sleepy rugrat lying in wait. But there was nothing but silence.

On the second floor there were six rooms, a bathroom and five bedrooms. I opened the door to each one and quickly checked inside. The second bedroom held another wall-sized bookcase, which I quickly scanned. These were more pulp fiction: many dime-store paperbacks, and mysteries from the fifties. The room had a musty smell.

But no grimoires.

What I expected to find was a large, leather-bound,

dusty tome with parchment scrawled with writing and illustrations, but I kept my eyes peeled for something smaller, like Rose's. All I knew was that it wouldn't be a dime-store paperback with a heaving-bosomed woman on the cover.

In the last room, I peered out from the window to the driveway, praying I wouldn't see Raina's car pulling back into it. We'd searched for more than a half hour, but we hadn't been as thorough as I would have liked. This would have been so much easier if Raina had been willing to help. If somebody had come to me asking for help, I'd like to think I would have done what I could, even if I didn't know them. Unless something was stopping me. The question was—what was stopping Raina?

Something legit? Or maybe she was just a coldhearted, selfish witch. And I didn't mean the magical kind.

At the end of the hall were the stairs to the third floor, which was almost a clone of the second floor, except that up here there were only four bedrooms. I checked the bathroom, the clawed tub, the pedestal sink. This house was like a museum, its fixtures right out of an episode of *Antiques Roadshow.* Other than a scattering of creepy oil paintings, I found no photos or anything overly personal.

The history here seeped into my bones. The house felt alive; it squeaked and made other noises that would freak me out at night if I lived here.

I picked up my pace, checking the first bedroom, quickly peeking under the bed. I tested the squeaky floorboards to see if there were any hidden compartments.

A chill suddenly brushed down my bare arms. It was a sensation I remembered from the previous night.

"Thierry?" I whispered.

"Looking for something?" The voice was as cold as the room had become. And it was *not* Thierry's.

I swiveled slowly to face him. I already had a good idea who it was since I'd heard him say one word to me before. One ominous, scary-ass word: "Soon."

Soon had become *now*.

Jonathan Malik, the witch hunter, watched me from the corner of the dark room. I willed myself to stay calm and tried to remember what little I knew about ghosts.

They couldn't hurt a human. Or a vampire. Or anything living. All they really were was a projection, not quite of this world, stuck somewhere between the living and the dead.

Bottom line, he couldn't hurt me. All he could do was creep me out.

"Yes, I am looking for something." I forced my voice to remain steady. "Maybe you can help me find it."

His black eyes glittered. "This isn't your house."

Fear shivered through me. "No, it isn't. Do you haunt this place often?"

The rest of him was slightly luminescent, just as Thierry's and Owen's ghostly forms were. His hair was long, to his shoulders, and he had a short, neat beard. He wore clothes circa three centuries ago, all black. I was used to that color scheme, since it was Thierry's daily choice as well. I *had* bought him a blue shirt recently that would look fantastic on him, but he refused to wear it.

But I digress.

This man was certainly attractive, in a Dark Pilgrim kind of way, but there was something in his eyes I couldn't ignore. Something cold and hard and unpleasant.

"This is one of my haunts," he replied. "Among others."

"You're Jonathan Malik, right?"

"Malik is fine." His gaze lit with interest. "You know my name."

"Were you trying to give me a message in the café the other day?"

"Not really. I simply like to make my presence known to those capable of seeing the spirit world."

"My husband couldn't see you."

"I don't make my presence known to everyone."

"Why haven't you moved on to the afterlife?"

"Why do you care?"

I considered my reply as a cool line of perspiration slid down my spine, betraying my nerves. Thierry was now a ghost, threatened with eviction from the mortal world in two days. This guy had stuck around for three hundred years.

"I'm just curious," I said, my throat tight.

He drew a little closer and I tried not to take a step back. The cold in the room intensified the nearer he got to me.

He's harmless, I reminded myself over and over. *He can't hurt you. He can't hurt anyone.*

The ghost drew closer to me so he was only a couple of feet away. He was well over six feet tall.

"You're a vampire, aren't you?" he said again, his lip curving downward with disdain. "I don't like vampires. But they do serve their purpose from time to time."

My stomach soured. I would hate to learn what he considered a vampire's purpose. "Not sure what difference it would make to you, Casper. You were a witch hunter, not a vamp hunter."

"True."

"Now that you've been trapped in Salem for over three hundred years, have you seen that witches are not always bad? Not always deserving of death?"

His lips stretched. I almost expected him to have razor-sharp teeth to go along with his nightmarish reputation, but no, they were regular teeth. And a regular, if cold, smile. “Do you think vampires go to Heaven or Hell?”

“Depends on the vampire.” I suddenly wondered how I’d gotten stuck in this conversation. I cast a fearful look toward the window and the driveway beyond. Still no sign of Raina.

He searched my face, as if fascinated by whatever expression I now wore. “You’re different from the other vampires that have come to Salem recently. None of them could see me.”

My breath caught. A ghost would be the best watchdog—invisible, silent, able to spy on unsuspecting witch activity. “Do you know what happened to them? Any of them? A vampire was killed the other day remotely by a witch’s death spell.”

“You want me to help you?” He laughed. The sound slithered unpleasantly. “Are you sure this is what you want my help with?”

He was playing with me now. I wasn’t a fan of being an amusing toy. “What witch did you piss off to get stuck in this town forever, Malik? She must have been really badass if you’re still here.”

His amusement vanished and the room grew colder. “You know my name, vampire. It’s only fair that I know yours.”

“Sure,” I said. “My name is Bite Me. Now, why don’t you make like a good ghost and disappear?”

“Very well.” His cold smile returned. “By the way, what you’re looking for isn’t on this floor. Follow me if you want to find it.”

He turned and walked straight through the bookcase behind him.

I surveyed the shelves of books I'd already looked at, but I looked at them again, trying to see if the grimoire was hidden among them. But no, there was nothing here that hadn't been printed by a publisher at some time in the last hundred years.

Grimoires—I knew this much for sure—were handwritten. Like scary, hocus-pocus scrapbooking projects. And due to the paper cut from hell, I was not a fan of scrapbooking projects.

"Sorry, Malik," I mumbled. "But I can't exactly follow you through a solid bookcase."

Or could I?

There were fewer rooms on this third floor than on the second, but this last room wasn't any larger to make up the difference. So what happened to all that extra space?

I felt around on the bookcase, pulling out books as I searched. I felt along the frame, along the top. My hands came away dusty, and I swear I touched a big, furry spider.

"Are you just messing with me some more, ghost boy?" I said under my breath. "I'm going to call 1-800-EXORCIST. See how you like that."

This wasn't working. I had to go back to the inn and come up with a Plan B. I should have guessed Plan A wouldn't work. It never did. Luckily there were twenty-five other letters in the alphabet.

But then I leaned against the bookcase.

And it moved.

I jumped back and looked at it warily for a moment. I'd been looking for a hidden lever. This was just as good. I pressed my hands against the edge of the bookshelf and pushed. The entire unit began to swivel like a revolving door.

One that led to another staircase in a hidden fifth room.

I hesitated for a full minute before moving another inch. I'd been given this particular tip by the ghost of a malevolent witch hunter. Unfortunately, I didn't have enough time to be choosy about my informants.

The stairs led to another door, which I pushed open.

It was the attic, full of boxes and books. And also a glowing ghost with an extremely devilish look on his face.

"You can find the grimoire up here," he said, then nodded to the left. "Over there, actually."

I didn't take another step. "Why are you helping me?"

"Do you always question those who wish to lend assistance?"

"Usually."

"Not the trusting type?"

"Unfortunately, I've trusted too many people who don't deserve it. Have the scorch marks to prove it from the times I've been burned. Kind of like the witches you tied to the stake and set on fire."

His amused expression didn't flicker. "You're thinking of England. We didn't torch witches here in Salem. We hanged them."

I shuddered. "Thanks for the history lesson."

"It's in the box with the red lid. Use it well, vampire." And then he disappeared into thin air.

I spotted the box easily. It was the only one that didn't have a thick coating of dust on it. I had two choices. Leave now or check out the box, which could very well have a larger version of the bookcase spider lying in wait inside it, ready to chew off my hand.

I went directly toward the box and opened it up. No spiders. Instead, there was a large black book covered in worn leather, with parchment pages filled with writing and illustrations. I flipped through it quickly, my eyes widening with every page.

Raina's ancestor's grimoire. This was it. Thank you, evil dead witch hunter!

I thundered down the stairs with it clutched against my chest. Out of the corner of my eye, through a window on the second floor, I saw Raina's car pulling into the driveway.

The witch was back. And if she found me here attempting to steal her property, I had no doubt clucking like a chicken would be the very least of my problems.

Chapter 9

I thundered down the rest of the stairs until I landed on the first floor.

"Heather!" I yelled.

Heather appeared. Her face was smudged as if she'd been searching in dirty places. "What?"

"Raina's back. We need to get out of here. Now!"

Her eyes went very large. Then she grabbed my sleeve and we hurried through the kitchen toward the back door. She flicked the lock and we burst out into a fenced-in backyard.

"You have the grimoire!" she said, amazed. "How did you find it?"

"I'd say it was divine intervention, but I think that might be giving the credit to the wrong place." I clutched the large, heavy book tightly to my chest. "Malik's ghost helped me out."

Heather gaped at me. "Malik, the witch hunter?"

"Is there another one around town?"

"Not that I know of."

"Then yeah, Malik, the witch hunter. He's extremely helpful, if seriously creepy."

We climbed over the back fence and swiftly made our way back to the car. My heart pounded hard, but I tried to focus on the future—not the past. And not the fact that I'd just stolen a grimoire from a witch's attic.

My mind raced, making plans. "We get this book back to the inn. We go through it and hopefully find a spell to fix Thierry. Then I'll come back and return it and give her some cash for the damages." I nodded, going over every Choose Your Own Adventure outcome in my head. "Simple, right? My karmic scoreboard of shame will be wiped clean."

She nodded. "Sounds good to me."

We got in the car and Heather wasted no time in peeling away from the curb. I checked the rearview mirror and relaxed a fraction to see there was no raven-haired witch chasing after us shaking her magic wand and yelling "*avada kedavra*."

My knowledge of magical spells extended only as far as Hogwarts.

"Even if Raina knows it was us who broke in," Heather said after a moment, as if she too had been frantically imagining the outcomes of our actions, "there's a protection spell on the inn meant to keep away anyone with dark intentions. She won't be able to enter if she's . . . uh, really upset with us."

I looked at her with surprise. "I don't care what you say, you are *seriously* witchy. And I meant that in a good way."

She twisted her necklace. "My grandma helped with that one. And—I mean, I don't even know if it works."

I sighed. "Can you at least *try* to be confident here, Heather? Just a little?"

She grimaced. "Sorry."

Five minutes later, Heather pulled into the Booberry Inn's driveway and we hurriedly went inside. My heart twisted to see the unconscious Owen-possessed Thierry still sleeping on the couch.

"Welcome back, girls!" Rose sat in a rocking chair nearby, knitting.

"So," I began, "any reason why there's a toad sitting on his forehead?"

Rose put her knitting down as Heather sat on the arm of the large chair next to her. "Hoppy is being a good little guardian toad, watching over the sleeping vampire. Aren't you, Hoppy?"

Hoppy let out a small croak, as if in agreement.

"Good boy," Heather said fondly.

I shifted the grimoire in my arms and tensely studied my amphibian-laden, possessed husband. "Do me a favor and don't get him all slimy," I told Hoppy, while I shivered a little from how chilly it suddenly seemed in this room. "I'm very fond of that forehead."

"I'm glad to hear that."

"Thierry!" I spun around to see him standing in the corner.

The fear I'd felt since the moment he'd disappeared last night vanished like . . . well, a ghost. I hadn't let myself dwell on it, but deep down I'd been afraid he was gone forever.

Whatever he saw on my face made pain slide through his gray eyes. He was at my side a moment later, reaching for me, before his hand dropped as if he'd suddenly remembered he couldn't touch me. "Sarah, don't cry."

"I'm not crying," I insisted, wiping at my cheeks. Despite my stinging eyes, I couldn't help but smile from ear to ear. "I'm glad you're back. When you disappeared . . ." Another chill went through me that wasn't caused by the ghostly presence in the room.

His dark brows drew together. "I now see I must better control my emotions if I want to remain in the mortal world." His gaze lowered to the grimoire in my arms. "What is this?"

I looked down at the spell book that currently held the promise of an answer between its leather-bound covers. "A grimoire we stole from a local, book-clubbing coven leader named Raina Wilkins. It allegedly belonged to a very powerful witch once upon a time, so I'm hoping rather desperately there's a spell in here that can help us."

The truth seemed the best story to tell—warts and all.

His expression tightened. "May I speak to you in private?"

Uh-oh. "I broke laws for you, Thierry. No reason to get upset."

"I'm not upset. If I was, I'd probably disappear again. Our room. Please, Sarah."

"Okay, fine." I handed the grimoire to Heather, reluctant to let it out of my sight. "Start looking for a spell, okay? I'll be back in a minute."

"Will do." She gave the cover of the spell book a wary glance.

"Now that you're back from your quest, Heather," Rose said, "I'm going to do some more gardening. Please keep an eye on the vampire and holler if he starts to wake up. Come on, Hoppy." She picked up the toad from his current perch.

"Stay close to the house," Heather warned.

"Why?" Then Rose grimaced. "Oh dear. The protection spell? Well, better safe than sorry, I suppose."

Better safe than sorry. Yup, that pretty much summed it up.

With a last glance over my shoulder as Heather settled into the armchair near the slumbering Owen and Rose headed toward the backyard, I followed Thierry up the stairs to our room. He watched me, his arms crossed, from the side with the window. The sunlight brushed across his handsome but stern, ghostly features.

"I didn't only steal her grimoire," I said, feeling the need to confess everything, "but I went all Chuck Norris on her front door, too."

"I see."

"You *will* see. That grimoire is going to help us . . . *if* Heather can find a good spell in it. It wasn't easy, you know. It's not like Raina just had it lying out on the coffee table. It was hidden up in her attic in a box." I didn't know why I felt so defensive—breaking, entering, stolen property. Oh, right. That was why.

But I'd gladly break more laws if it meant we could fix this mess. Just watch me.

Thierry cocked his head. "Then how did you know where to find it?"

"Malik showed up. We had a little tête-à-tête at the witch's house. I think it's one of his daily haunts."

His expression grew strained. "The witch hunter."

"The *dead* witch hunter." That ghost still gave me the heebie-jeebies. "No idea why he helped me, though. It's not like he's a stand-up sort of guy. But he's harmless—a scary barking dog with no teeth. Anyway, why did you want to talk to me? Are you mad about me stealing the grimoire?"

"You don't know how powerful this Raina woman is."

I raised my chin. "I can deal with her."

"I'm sure." This feigned confidence had coaxed a half smile to his lips before it faded. "However, we need to discuss what happens next if we can't fix this in time."

I held up a hand. "I'm going to stop you right there. Because we're *not* going to fail. We will figure this out."

He met my gaze full on. His had turned stormy. "I know you mean well, Sarah."

"I mean very well. The wellest. The grimoire plan—"

"Might not work. And very soon what's happened to me will become a permanent—"

"Stop it, right now." I glared at him. "Did you eat your pessimistic cornflakes today? That won't happen because I won't let it happen. Got it? You're not escaping me mere days after we get married. It's just not going to happen. And if you're even suggesting that I stay with Owen and see if we have a love connection—"

"Never," he growled. The room grew as cold as a meat locker in seconds.

I couldn't help but grin. "Just testing you. Glad to see you're still in the game."

His shoulders relaxed and he shook his head, bemused. "I want to find a solution to this as much as you do."

"Good," I said, satisfied. "Then along with checking out the grimoire, we need to contact Markus Reed and ask for his help—and the Ring's help, too. I know you have issues with them, but I'm sure they must have faced something like this before. They have files, right? A history of crazy paranormal wackiness to draw from?"

He regarded me as if what I'd said had taken him aback. "We're not contacting them."

I'd expected opposition, but I had to make him realize we needed a Plan B here. "Why not? They hired you to be their consultant. Do you think they'd want to lose you so quickly? Especially with their sudden interest in finding out about your hidden history. No way. They'll do whatever it takes to keep you around."

He shook his head, studying me as if, despite his reservations, he found my frenetic plan making fascinating.

Kind of like a scientist watching a brunette microbe pinging wildly off the edges of a glass slide. "I'm sure there's another answer."

"Oh, *now* there is, huh? A minute ago you were about ready to recite your last will and testament to me."

Despite the fierceness on his face, the hint of a smile returned to his lips. "You're rather incorrigible—you know that?"

My heart lightened by a few ounces. "I choose to take that as a compliment."

Our gazes locked. "Just when I begin to think hope is fading, you appear with it exuding from your very essence."

"Which sounds kind of gross." But I was happy he was ready to fight this battle with me. I'd accept no less. "Do you want to find a way to fix this, Thierry? Or do you want to go gentle into that good night?"

He raised a dark eyebrow. "Dylan Thomas."

"I might be a beach-read girl now, but I did take English lit in college. I can quote with the best of them."

"I don't doubt it."

I reached for him then without thinking, but instead of touching him, all I felt was coldness as his chest turned to that swirling gray smoke. It was like sticking my hand into a freezer. I drew back from him with alarm.

He looked down at himself as his chest re-formed, before his tense gaze met mine again.

"You don't want me to call Markus," I said flatly. "Fine. Then you better come up with another plan. Right now."

He moved back toward the window to look outside. "I don't want anyone else brought into this situation, Sarah. Period."

I put my hands on my hips as I studied him, wondering

for a moment why my throat felt tight. Then I realized I was angry.

"You're something, aren't you?"

He flicked a look toward me. "Excuse me?"

"I usually put you in a different category from all other men. A *better* category, actually. Thus the whole 'I do' thing from a few days ago."

He regarded me with an edge of caution now. "You *usually* do."

I started pacing the small room, needing to somehow expend my built up energy. I gestured wildly in his direction. "Yeah, *usually*. Because right now you're pissing me off. You *are* just like other men, Thierry. This is the proof. This is your 'I'm lost but I'm not asking for any directions since it will make me feel like less of a man' thing. That's not cool."

"Far be it from me to not be cool."

"Are you going to help me find a way to save your butt, or what? I already stole a witch's grimoire for you—"

"A reckless and dangerous thing to do." But before I could defend my actions again, his hard expression softened. "That I know you did for a selfless reason."

"No. It was a very selfish reason." I took a deep breath in and let it out slowly. "Look, Thierry, I know you don't trust anyone . . ."

"Wrong. I trust you."

The fight went out of me at that. "Promise me, Thierry, when this is over, and everything's okay again, that we'll go on a *real* honeymoon. Somewhere with palm trees."

He nodded slowly. "Turquoise seas, warm breeze."

"Being an excellent rhymer isn't going to cheer me up right now."

"Once we deal with this, I promise, the world is yours."

I finally smiled. "*That's* what I like to hear. Now, let's go fix this mess."

Downstairs, Heather was poring through the grimoire, scanning each page before flipping to the next. She looked up as we entered the room.

"This is so fascinating," she said. "All this history and magic at my fingertips."

Thierry eyed the grimoire. "Did you find anything, Heather?"

I held my breath and waited for her answer.

"The good news is that I found lots of amazing spells in here." Heather turned her attention back to the book. She raked her fingers through her long, messy red hair. "This was kept by a witch who was here in Salem during the trials. It's old—I mean, so old that even *I* can feel the power coming off the pages. This witch could work some serious magic."

Her words worked like a shot glass of optimism at a positivity party. "Good to hear. So what's the bad news?"

She swallowed. "I haven't found anything about possession—nothing at all. Maybe . . . what happened with Owen . . . it was just an accident and it's never happened before in the history of mankind."

My optimistic shot glass shattered.

"Possession can occur either by spirit or demon. It's been documented throughout history." Thierry's voice didn't reveal a fraction of the strain I felt right now after hearing about Heather's uninspiring findings.

"Yes, but . . . I did some research last night. A possessing spirit never literally pushes out the original soul. *That's* the part that doesn't happen. Grandma's never heard of anything like this, either. Normally, in a regular possession, the spirit takes hold of the body long enough to get across its message, but then the original spirit pushes it back out. That should be the end of it. But here . . ."

"That's not the case," Thierry finished.

"Which means this *has* to be caused by magic." She turned back to the grimoire. "But there's *nothing* in here to help me fix this. If this is my fault from the séance the other night, I'm so sorry. I don't know what to do to make this right again."

The sad look she gave me then reminded me of Princess, the puppy I'd had once that soiled the carpet every single day. My father had wanted to smack his butt (yes, I named a male dog Princess—I was only a kid!) with a rolled-up newspaper, but that wouldn't have helped him learn. Instead, I insisted on patience and time. As my reward, I got to be the one to do the cleanup until he finally learned.

I'd clean up this mess, too.

I looked at Thierry, my stomach churning. "Suggestions for that alternate plan would be awesome right about now."

He crossed his arms over his chest, his expression thoughtful. "We could contact the necromancer I mentioned the other day."

"The one in California."

He nodded. "She's very powerful. It's possible she could help."

I leaned against the edge of the couch, glancing at the still-sleeping Owen. His eyelids fluttered as if he was having a vivid dream. "I currently will cling to possible with both hands. How do we get in touch with her?"

"I have a contact who might be able to locate her. The only problem is time."

Right. We didn't have much of it left. "Then tell me what to do."

He did, letting me know who in his address book to call. I dug out the BlackBerry from the pocket of his jacket—now draped over a chair by Heather's wooden desk in the corner of the room. Without delay, I called and spoke to the deep-voiced and suspicious-sounding man on the other end who seemed to reply in one-word answers only. I told him what we needed—although not specifically *why* we needed it, only that it was a favor for Thierry de Bennicoeur—and ended the call after he promised to get back to us soon.

Heather watched the proceedings tensely. I noticed that her fingers were literally crossed. I could use all the good luck I could get, frankly.

The call had not filled me with endless optimism. I scrolled through Thierry's address book, seeing dozens, hundreds, of names and phone numbers I didn't recognize. Then I found one I did.

"Don't, Sarah," Thierry said softly from over my shoulder. I'd paused on Markus Reed's name.

His stubbornness about this was seriously going to drive me batty. "He helped us before."

In Las Vegas, Markus had saved us from a serial killer who'd wanted to add both of us to his growing list of victims. Even though Markus had been after Thierry at the time, believing him to be a killer himself, he'd still stepped in without hesitation when we needed him.

Call me crazy, but that earned him some big brownie points in my book.

"That was then, Sarah. It doesn't change anything. I want nothing to do with Markus while he's acting on behalf of the Ring."

"Fine." I hissed out a breath. "Let me look at that grimoire. Maybe I can find something."

Heather handed the book to me and I sat in the chair next to the sofa, trying not to be distracted by Owen's magically unconscious presence only a couple of feet away from me. I flipped through the pages one by one. They were dry and brittle, and I had to be gentle for fear of tearing or cracking them.

Heather was right—the magic in this book was palpable. It made my skin literally tingle while in contact with it. Most of the pages were written in Latin, but there were some English words and phrases as well. The witch had been a decent artist. Adorning the pages of writing were portraits of faces, landscapes, and specific herbs, plants, and animals needed for some of the spells.

"What's this?" Halfway through the book I came to a thicker page. After inspecting it for a moment, I realized that it wasn't one page, but two pages stuck together.

Heather's eyes widened. "I didn't notice that."

I slid my fingernail between and gently worked on pulling them apart. It took a couple of minutes, but finally they separated and fell apart.

On these pages the handwriting was so small, if I hadn't had vampire vision I'd need a magnifying glass to read it—if I *could* read it at all.

"Does that say 'vampyr' there?" I asked, pointing. "With a *Y* and no *E*?"

"It does," Thierry confirmed.

This had to mean something. I mean, we *were* vampyrs. Or—vampires. Same difference, I figured. "Vampyr magic. That sounds seriously old-school."

Thierry's expression had become unreadable and

guarded. "You must put that book away, Sarah. You're now treading onto dangerous territory."

My heart skipped a beat. "Well, that sounds much more promising than the nothing we had to work with before. Talk, Thierry. You're our expert here in all things historic."

He turned away and crossed the room to the sofa, where he glanced down for a silent moment at his body lying there unconscious. Then he flicked a glance back at me and Heather.

"Some witches throughout history have used vampire blood to strengthen their magic. It can be a potent and highly dangerous ingredient."

"Vampire blood magic." I'd never heard of this before. A chill shot down my spine.

Heather gasped. "Wait a minute. If Raina has this book, and if this original witch was an ancestor of hers, she'd know about this. Raina could be responsible for those vampires you said have gone missing. And—and even for Owen's murder."

His expression became more grim. "It's possible."

I frowned, running my index finger along the parchment. "But these pages were stuck together. It looks like they've been that way for ages. Maybe she has no idea what's in this book—that's why she shoved it up in her attic and forgot about it."

"This is also possible," Thierry conceded.

When the phone rang, I nearly jumped out of my skin. Heather rushed toward the table where it sat next to the archway leading to the front hallway and looked down at the call display. She gave me a squeamish look. "Guess who."

Three guesses which witch was calling, and the first two didn't count. "Don't answer it."

Her face had paled to a ghostly shade. "Wasn't planning on it."

I caught Thierry's curious look.

"Is your recent criminal past coming back to haunt you?" he asked.

"Great, now he's making ghost puns. I'm so proud," I mumbled to myself. Then I shifted my attention to the redhead. "Okay, Heather, let's talk vampire blood magic. Can it help us?"

She scurried back to the open grimoire and studied the pages. "One spell draws energy from a vampire and uses it to help strengthen a witch's magic—just like Thierry said."

Thierry nodded. "I'm familiar with that spell. It usually requires the blood of not just any vampire, but a master."

Heather shivered, her finger tracing the words as she read. "He's right. It says right here that makes it more powerful."

I turned my attention back to him. "I'm afraid to ask, but how do you know that?"

"I've encountered many witches in my life. A few have been interested in this particular sect of magic. Their daggers were sometimes unexpected, but always sharp."

My own vampire blood ran cold. "Thierry . . ."

"It's past. Nothing to concern yourself with now."

I hated to think he'd been at the mercy of some bloodletting witch, but he was right. I forced myself to put it out of my mind and focus on the task at hand. "Are there any other spells there, Heather?"

"Yes." Her finger skimmed across the Latin words. "Oh, this is very interesting, but it won't help with a possession."

My stomach sank like a stone. "What is it anyway?"

"This spell uses a vampire's blood to trace his or her history."

History, quite honestly, was never one of my favorite subjects. "What does that mean?"

"It seems to be like . . ." She frowned as if struggling to describe what she was reading. "I want to say time travel, but is that even possible, even with magic?"

"Time travel?" I repeated, stunned. "Thierry, have you ever heard of anything like this before?"

He gave me a pensive look. "There have always been rumored methods of walking through time—either physically or metaphysically—but I've never seen a shred of proof that it's actually possible."

I stared down at the page. "But wouldn't it be interesting if it was?"

"Wouldn't what be interesting?" Rose entered the room carrying a vase of freshly cut roses in water. Her gardening gloves were tucked under her right arm, and there was a smudge of dirt on her nose.

Heather looked up from the grimoire. "I think we found a time travel spell in here."

"How exciting!" Rose smiled brightly. "We never did interesting spells like that in *my* secret coven back in the day. Although, I must admit, we conjured a couple nice potions that worked just as well as alcohol but didn't have the calories."

I glanced at Thierry, who'd gone very quiet. "What are you thinking?"

He met my gaze directly. "That this is a very dangerous grimoire. Also, unfortunately, of no use to us."

He was right about one thing—it was dangerous. And it didn't have the answers I'd originally been seeking in it.

All we could do now was hope Thierry's contact got back to us quickly with information about the necromancer.

I began wracking my brain for a Plan C.

The doorbell rang. I froze and glanced at Heather's stricken expression.

"Well, this *is* a bed-and-breakfast, girls," Rose said after a moment, clearing her throat. "And potential customers *do* ring the doorbell. It's not necessarily someone unfriendly."

"Of course," I agreed tightly. "It's probably another honeymooning couple. Don't let them be intimidated by the unconscious vampire on the couch."

Heather wrung her hands and slowly crossed the room toward the foyer. "I'll ask whoever it is to come back later."

I joined her at the door as she slowly opened it up, but there was no one on the porch.

"I'm over here," someone called out.

Raina Wilkins currently stood on the sidewalk in front of the Booberry Inn. She waved at us.

I waved back, my stomach busy tying itself into gruesome origami shapes. "Hello."

She hitched her shoulder bag higher. "Just thought I'd drop by in person since you're not answering your phone."

"What do you want?" Heather asked, her voice crisp. A trickle of perspiration slid down her forehead. I was impressed the timid girl hadn't already turned around and run upstairs with her tail between her legs.

"I was wondering if you returned to my house earlier when I wasn't home."

Heather glanced fearfully at me. "What should I say?"

I had a feeling that lying wasn't going to help us very

much. It was clear that Raina already knew the answer to that question without needing any confirmation from us. And the fact that she stood twenty feet from the front door spoke volumes.

"Hey, Raina," I called to her. "Why are you standing on the sidewalk? We can barely hear you from there."

"It's the darnedest thing. I can't seem to come any closer." Her cold smile held. "So why don't you come outside and we can speak more easily?"

That wasn't going to happen. In fact, I'd decided to make the Booberry Inn my permanent home. Still, I couldn't blame her for coming here to confront us. She might be pissed off enough to have "dark intentions" toward us, but we were the ones who'd broken into her house and stolen her property. I wasn't saying I was the innocent one here.

Still, she was the more dangerous one. The magic I now felt crackling down my arms proved it.

"I'll fix this, Raina," I called out to her. "Just give me some time, okay?"

Even from a distance, I could see her blue eyes turn witch red. "I want my property back. Now."

"Whatever do you mean?" Heather squeaked.

I eyed her. She was an even worse liar than I was.

"You know what I'm talking about. A book? From my attic? It's missing. And my front door is broken."

I wanted to take over for Heather, since the bleak, scared expression on her face automatically made me want to protect her. Miranda was wrong about her. She might have stolen a boyfriend in the distant past, but the girl was harmless.

"I asked for your help, Raina," I said firmly. "But you said no. Then you worked some mojo on me to get me out of your hair."

"Return the book."

"I fully plan to. But I can't—not yet. I'm not done with it. I assure you, as soon as I am, it'll be returned to you undamaged. My word is good—I promise. And I'll also pay for the door. It was my fault. Heather had nothing to do with that. So hate me, not her."

I closed the door to block out her vicious glare. I'd just made an enemy of a witch of uncertain power. That never turned out very well.

The doorbell rang again.

I looked at the door, feeling queasy now. Then I shot a glance at Thierry, standing a few feet away, who'd witnessed the entire exchange. "How does she ring the doorbell if she can't approach the house?"

His expression darkened. "Magic."

"That's not very reassuring."

"You're right. It's not."

I pushed the door open a crack and glanced outside again. Raina still stood at a safe distance, but her cold smile had returned.

"I've taken out a little insurance that I get my book back." She pulled something out of her handbag. "I believe this is important to Heather. Am I right?"

I peered closer. "What is that? A rock?"

"Hoppy!" Heather exclaimed. "She has Hoppy!"

"Oh no!" Rose gasped from the living room, her hand over her heart. "I left him in the backyard when he discovered a tasty flower. Hoppy hopped away!"

"Most want a cat as a familiar"—Raina looked down at the animal—"but you have a frog."

"Toad," I corrected uneasily. She was combatting our thievery with kidnapping. Heather loved that little creature, so this was low, even for a witch.

"Whatever it is, I'll be holding on to it for now. I do have a perfect recipe if I hear nothing from you very soon. A vegetarian lasagna, but I'll make an exception this time for one of the layers." Her smile widened. "Have a nice day."

I had my hand on Heather's arm, and the girl had started to tremble.

"Hey, Raina," I called after her, "did you know a witch hunter's ghost is haunting your house? Well, he is. Sweet dreams."

Her shoulders tensed, but she didn't turn back around.

It was petty, but I couldn't help it.

By the time I closed the door, Heather had grabbed the grimoire from the living room table and had returned to try to push the door open again.

"What are you doing?" I asked, alarmed.

"I need to give her this. It's no use to us, and I can't let Hoppy become an Italian casserole. She'll do it, you know! I don't doubt it!"

I grabbed her arm. "She won't do that. Toad lasagna would be really gross. It was just a random threat because she's mad. And yeah, we're evil, devious creatures of darkness for taking that spell book from her, but we need it."

Thierry caught my eye. He'd remained silent while we had our witchy standoff. "Sarah, there's nothing in there to help us. What difference does it make now?"

I shook my head. "Wrong. It *does* have something that can help us."

He frowned. "What?"

"The time travel spell."

"I'm not sure I understand."

I'd been thinking about this ever since Heather told me what it was. Thierry was right—there was nothing in that grimoire that could help us with his possession problem. However, that wasn't our only trouble. I wanted to deal with our mounting issues with the Ring and get it over with. Then we could focus better on the problems here in Salem.

"This is an opportunity," I said firmly. "One I can't just ignore."

"What are you talking about, Sarah?"

I took a deep breath. "I want to go back to the night you disappeared and find out what really happened."

Chapter 10

Sometimes it was hard for me to remember that I'd had serious trouble reading Thierry's shifting moods when I first met him—ever since that November night when I'd first been bitten by a vampiric blind date. That jerk was long gone (actually, he was dead, courtesy of vampire hunters). But the *other* vampire I'd met that night—the one that tolerated my endless questions and my tendency to get myself neck deep in trouble; the one who tried to push me away until he realized it was a losing battle and that I wasn't going anywhere—was giving me a look that could only be described as *incredulous*.

I recognized that look. I got it from him a lot.

Thierry shook his head. "Sarah, this is *not* a good idea. Actually 'not a good idea' is a vast understatement."

"Hear me out." I moved over to where Heather clutched the grimoire to her chest. "This spell book can help us figure out what happened to you. The Ring wants to know and Markus gives me the distinct impression they're not going to take "leave us alone" as an answer."

"You believe they mean to seal me away somewhere and torture me into revealing what I don't remember?"

He said it half jokingly, like I was overreacting, but I didn't think it was very funny at all.

"I wouldn't put anything past them, actually." When he opened his mouth to interject, I held up a hand. "And before you try to argue with me, I do realize they'd have a hard time locking up a spirit, but I am going with the optimistic presumption that we *will* find a way to successfully fix this and you'll be back in your body very soon. Therefore, you and your body will be fair game for the elders to pick at like a science project."

He was so close to me that I could reach out and touch him if this was a normal situation. I had to fist my hands at my sides so I wouldn't attempt it. Touching cold air and seeing him turn to smoke was too disturbing.

"You're trying to protect me from them," he said, his gaze steady on mine.

"Of course I am. And you'd do the same for me." I didn't wait for his reply, since I already knew the answer. He already *had* protected me from them by taking this job in the first place, even if he refused to admit it in so many words. "Heather, do you think you can do it? This time travel spell?"

She exchanged a look with her grandmother. "I don't know."

"What do you mean, honey?" Rose said. "Of course you can do it. I just want you to be very careful not to hurt yourself. The nosebleeds, you know."

Heather chewed her bottom lip. "Well, it *is* grimoire magic. I've had some luck with that in the past. But it's also blood magic, so you're going to need a blood sample from the vampire whose lifeline you want to travel along."

"Sarah . . . ," Thierry said.

I spun to face him again. "Save your breath, Thierry. Or . . . or whatever you have in that ghost form. I need to try. If it can help you—"

"If I ask you not to do this, will you respect my wishes?"

I didn't understand why he wanted to fight me on this when it was something that could get the Ring off his back. But then I realized his misgivings had very little to do with the Ring at all. "I know you don't want to share your past with me in all of its unedited glory. But what exactly are you afraid I might see?"

He gave me a look like I'd just slapped him. "I'm not afraid."

"Then let me do this for you. Please. You told me before that you trusted me. Trust me enough to let me try."

He opened his mouth as if ready to continue to argue with me, but then closed it. "If this doesn't work, you must promise to walk away and let me deal with the Ring."

"Thank you." The tight feeling in my chest eased by a fraction. I studied his strained expression. "But if it *does* work I'll be able to figure out where to find this amulet they want. We can get them off your back, once and—"

But then Thierry disappeared right before my eyes as if someone had flicked a switch.

I turned around in a circle. "Thierry? Are you still here?"

"I think he's gone again, honey," Rose said. "He was getting all uppity and upset. That'll do it."

Every time he disappeared I was afraid it would be the last time I'd ever see him.

Just as I was about to run upstairs to check if Thierry had reappeared in our room, I heard a groan. It came from the couch.

It came from Owen.

Uh-oh.

But then I had a thought—a wonderful thought, since

Thierry had just disappeared a moment ago . . . "You don't think Thierry was able to get back into his original—"

"Sexy mama," came a half-garbled outburst from the still-slumbering vampire. "She's so sexy—look at that body. Oh yeah. Daddy thirsty now. Gimme a taste."

"Nope," I said, my stomach souring. "Still Owen."

"Oh dear," Rose said. "I think the Baxter spell's wearing off. He's waking up. I really wanted him to stay asleep and out of trouble until later."

Me too. The timing on his awakening was horrible. I needed him unconscious if I was going to get a blood sample. "Heather, can you renew it and keep him unconscious?"

She gave me a squeamish look. "Afraid it only works once."

I stared at her. "It only works once? What kind of a stupid spell is that?"

"Sorry. But, I mean, it was originally meant for a dog."

"If it's any consolation," Rose said, "the original location spell should be intact for quite some time. He'll still be unable to leave the inn."

I watched the vampire with growing dread. "He's going to tear this place apart."

Owen was the key to the time travel spell for one very important reason—he was currently residing in Thierry's body. For this vampire blood magic spell to have a chance to work, I needed a sample of Thierry's blood.

But to have Owen awake and cranky about being magically trapped and sedated . . .

This was not going to be fun.

"Can you two give us a little privacy?" I asked.

"What are you going to do?" Heather watched me warily.

I gave her a look. "Whatever I have to."

She grimaced. "Grandma, let's go into the kitchen for a few minutes."

Rose didn't argue. Heather left the room with the grimoire clutched to her chest, her grandmother right behind her.

Rose glanced over her shoulder at me. "Try not to break anything, dear."

"I'll try my best."

They disappeared.

It wasn't more than a few seconds later when Owen slowly opened his eyes, then blinked rapidly. "Wha—what happened?" He squinted at me as if I was slowly coming into focus for him. "Oh, it's *you*."

I forced a smile. From his unfriendly tone, I didn't think he'd give me another opportunity to run away on a romantic adventure with him. Fine by me. "Good afternoon, sunshine."

My good cheer—however forced—was met with only a scowl. My worst fear right now was Owen going postal, destroying the house, and possibly hurting Rose and Heather in the process. After his rigorous escape attempt last night, I didn't put anything past him.

"I'm out of here." He shakily got up from the couch, flicked the afghan to the floor, walked in a semistraight line toward the front door, and exited the house. I waited tensely, ready to run after him, but he got as far as he had last time before he hit the invisible barrier.

"Problems?" I asked from the open doorway.

He gave me a withering look over his shoulder. "You totally suck, you know that?"

"Feeling's mutual, body snatcher."

Owen brushed past me as he came back into the house; then he stomped up the stairs to the second floor. I followed right on his heels.

"What are you looking for?"

"Thierry's cell phone," he said. "I'm sure there's somebody in his speed dial who can come and help him out when he's being held prisoner by his crazed wife from hell."

He wasn't going to be winning any Nobel Prizes for brainpower—or congeniality. Besides, the phone was downstairs by his jacket, where I'd left it after calling Thierry's contact. "That's your master plan to get out of here? To call for backup and pretend to be Thierry? Good luck with that."

"Why do you have to be so mean to me?" he asked, his expression pinched.

"Just because I don't want you stealing Thierry's body and gallivanting all over the world with it while he takes a one-way trip to the spirit world? Yeah, so mean." I blew out a breath and tried to stay calm. "Listen, Owen, I need a favor from you."

This made him pause before he started to laugh. "You need a favor from *me*."

"Pretty much."

"You're just as crazy as you look. What is it?"

I didn't think I looked *that* crazy. I cast a glance toward the special mirror. Nope, totally sane, if a bit stressed, in my humble opinion. "I need some of your—well, *Thierry's*—blood. And I need it right now."

He cocked his head. "Thirsty, Sarah?"

"What? No, that's not why. I need it for a spell. However, I can take it by force if you keep giving me a hard time."

This only made him laugh harder. "You think you can take my blood by force."

"I can try. But I'd really prefer if you cooperate."

I was trying for that optimism thing again. It would have to do until I thought of something better.

"A spell using master vampire blood, huh?" He looked intrigued by this. "Sounds dangerous. That's pretty hot."

It was something. "Glad you approve."

Owen crossed his arms over his stolen chest. "Here's the deal. I give you some blood and you let me leave."

I glared at him. "Forget it. I'll find another way."

I turned toward the door, but Owen was next to me in a heartbeat. He grabbed my wrist tight and spun me back around to face him.

His expression was fierce. "You're going to help me get out of here, Sarah. The witches like you. They'll break this doggy spell if you ask nicely."

I gave him an icy look. "I strongly suggest you let go of me."

His gaze moved over my face and down my throat. "How about another deal? I'm willing to negotiate. One kiss of your own free will for a little blood."

I made a face. "Is that all you ever think about?"

"I said *kiss*, not anything horizontal." He grinned now. "Come on, these are Thierry's lips, after all. It's not like it would be cheating. Kiss me, Sarah, and don't hold back."

"Owen, I'm seriously going to knee you in Thierry's groin if you don't let go of me in three seconds."

He laughed softly and moved closer so he could whisper in my ear. "You know what? You're kind of—"

But then he froze.

"Owen?" He hadn't let go of my wrist and he was still

positioned to whisper to me, but he said nothing at all. "What happened? What's wrong?"

"So strange," he said, his words now muffled. "It—it's like nothing I've ever felt before. You smell so good."

I rolled my eyes. "If this is some kind of a cheesy pickup line, it's not going to—"

And then he sank his fangs into my throat.

I shrieked and tried to get away from him, but he held me firmly in place. This was *not* the way this scene was supposed to play out. *I* was the one who was supposed to get the blood sample, not him!

He pulled away from me, his lips red with my blood. His eyes were black and glazed and filled with endless hunger—and also, confusion. "What's happening to me? It's horrible . . . this thirst. I can't stop this."

All I could do was stare at him in shock before he dove back for a second helping.

It never occurred to me that Owen would have to deal with Thierry's drinking problem. Thierry didn't drink blood at all, since even the smallest taste of it would push him over the edge of his control—similar to an alcoholic dealing with the aftermath of a shot of vodka, only way more deadly. Thierry had tried to fight this constant urge for centuries, and it was much worse than the regular thirst other vampires dealt with. His was true bloodlust.

He'd fought it hard and well—and almost always abstained from drinking blood. At his age, he could go a long time without it. Like, a *very* long time.

But Owen was brand-new to this body. And if he was now experiencing the same bloodlust Thierry did . . .

Then I was in serious trouble. As far as I knew, being drained of every drop of blood could kill a vampire as surely as a wooden stake through the heart. And Owen seemed ready to satisfy his endless thirst right here and right now. With me.

Before I could figure out how to stop this, something shattered and Owen jolted against me. He spun around angrily to see Rose standing behind him holding the remnants of a broken jar.

"Ouch!" Owen touched the back of his head. He pulled his fingers away bloody and he frowned. "Wait a minute. Did that bottle contain . . . pickled garlic?"

She nodded. "Yes, it most certainly did."

"Well, damn." Owen fell to his knees, then collapsed all the way to the ground.

Contrary to popular myth, garlic doesn't *repel* vampires. Once in the bloodstream, it actually knocks us out cold.

I held my hand to my throat and stared down at the unconscious vampire before turning my grateful gaze to Rose.

"Thank you. I was doing my impression of a damsel in distress really well."

"Don't mention it." She pulled a pair of handcuffs out of her pocket and flashed me a grin. "Brought these up, too. They're silver. Should hold him nicely, don't you think?"

"You're brilliant."

Silver worked on a vampire like a magical metal. It burned our skin if we pressed against it. It was good for restraints. Not so good for jewelry. Trust me on that.

It took me a minute to transport Owen onto the bed, and Rose restrained him with the cuffs so I wouldn't have to touch them. Then I went to the kitchen to fetch a glass and a sharp knife, which I brought back up to the room.

With only a moment's hesitation, I held the glass under

his arm and made a shallow cut in his skin. His blood flowed red into the glass.

Master vampire blood. More valuable by the ounce than gold. For a fledgling to feed on a master made the fledgling stronger, more powerful. Masters were very careful about whom they shared blood with.

In seconds, the wound healed before my eyes. Master vampires had many special skills. Rapid healing—much faster than that of a mere fledgling like me—was one of them.

"Good luck with the spell, dear." Rose pulled a wooden chair from the desk up next to the bed. "I'll stay here and watch over our resident troublemaker. I have more garlic in my pocket if he causes any more problems."

"Thanks, Rose." I gazed down at Thierry's face for a moment and stroked the hair off his forehead. I exhaled shakily. "He doesn't want me to see his past. That's why he got so upset that he disappeared earlier."

"He's ashamed?"

"I don't know. I guess. But he doesn't have to be. When I chose to be with him, I wanted the whole package. I've told him this before, but I don't think he listens."

"You really love him."

"More than anything."

She nodded, smiling wistfully. "I loved someone like that once. He was my past, present, and future. Hold on to that love with both hands, Sarah. There's nothing more valuable." Her gaze shifted away from me. "Is there, Thierry?"

I glanced over my shoulder, and my heart leapt to see the ghostly Thierry standing at the doorway watching us.

"Nothing more valuable," he confirmed.

"You're back," I said, breathless with relief.

"I couldn't let you do this time travel spell without

me." He glanced at the glass of blood I held. "I see you haven't changed your mind."

"No, I haven't."

Thierry's gaze brushed my throat and his eyes narrowed with anger. "He did this to you."

I touched the fang marks, flinching. "He has your thirst."

"I was afraid of that. It must be horrible for him, but if he tries to hurt you again, I will kill him—even if he's still in my body."

I tried very hard to put that out of my mind as we left Rose and Owen in the Batberry Suite and went back downstairs. Quickly I snatched up Thierry's phone and checked it for messages from his contact, but there was nothing.

A thud of disappointment went through me.

Heather waited for us at the table where she'd performed the séance. She took the blood from me with trembling hands. The grimoire was spread out before her to the page she needed to read from.

"I've read this over several times," she said; then her eyes went large. "Is that a bite mark on your neck?"

I touched it and grimaced. "Maybe."

"Owen bit you?"

"Well, it wasn't your grandmother. Forget it. It doesn't matter. What did you learn? Can you do the spell?"

"Yes. I mean, I think so." She twisted her necklace, as if summoning strength from her mother, the more powerful witch. "It's spirit travel, not physical. So that's . . . I mean, I think that's better."

I nodded as if I knew what she meant, then stopped. "Um, what?"

"The spell, it . . . Well, I'm not really sure how to explain it." She glanced down at the Latin.

"Allow me," Thierry said. His expression was grim.

"This spell, with the help of my blood, will rip the spirit out of your body, Sarah, and cast it back through time, hoping that you'll be returned to your body here in the present once all is said and done."

I blinked. "Gee, don't try to sugarcoat it or anything."

"I wasn't."

"I was being sarcastic."

"It is a risky spell," he said firmly. "And I wish you'd reconsider."

Heather was now standing, staring down at the book, as if trying to absorb the knowledge through her eyeballs. "I'll be very careful."

Thierry sent a glare in her direction. "If it feels wrong, then you must stop. Nothing is worth Sarah's safety. Do you hear me? Nothing." There was a dangerous edge to his voice now.

Heather's gaze showed a glimmer of fear as she looked at me.

"It'll be fine," I assured her. It was a spell. It would work. I had to hold on to that thought and be positive enough for the three of us combined. Heather might not trust her own skills, but I'd seen enough to make me feel she had the right stuff to do this.

"This blood," Heather said, her voice stronger now, "I can feel how powerful it is. Exactly how old are you, Thierry?"

He flicked a glance at her. "Old enough."

"The blood is the key to everything. Blood like yours . . . to help with powerful magic like this . . ." She frowned, as if disturbed by her own thoughts. "Many witches would kill for it."

He studied her for a moment. "Yes, they would."

How many witches had he come across over the years

who were interested in him for his powerful blood? He didn't like even a minor witch like Heather having a sample of it. His blood really was like gold.

"Are you going to try to talk me out of doing this again?" I asked him.

There was a challenge sent to me through his gray eyes, which faded only a little at the edges. "No. But please don't make me regret this."

"I'll be fine."

"You better be."

I sat down next to Heather. Then she dipped her finger into the blood and traced a symbol on my palm before dragging the makeshift ink over my wrist and all the way up to the crook of my arm. I was glad I'd worn a T-shirt today.

"Let's begin," she said solemnly.

I nodded, pushing away any doubts that poked their heads up like an invisible game of Whac-A-Mole. I was driven by my search for the truth. If I could catch a glimpse of what might have happened to him to erase his memory all those years ago . . . and, better yet, if I could figure out where the amulet the Ring was after might be—or at least, where it was back then—then that might be enough ammo to keep them away from us.

"Here it goes," Heather announced nervously, just before she began to speak the spell out loud, Latin words I didn't understand. Thierry stood to my right, his arms crossed tightly across his chest, his expression tense.

"When exactly are we aiming for?" she asked.

After hesitating, Thierry spoke, "The twenty-third of September, 1692. Dusk."

Heather nodded and began to write that date on my other arm with Thierry's blood. Then she went back to reciting the spell. And I tried to ignore the blood on my arms, which had made my heart start to race.

Vampires and blood—two things eternally entwined. Blood was life. It fed us, sustained us. Without it we would get a little less civilized, a little more monstrous. Blood to vampires was the beginning and the end of our existence.

I felt the magic—a swirling sensation of energy, that prickly electricity that raised the hair on my arms—as the room became charged with it. It made my breath catch.

When Heather finished reciting the spell, she watched me carefully. "Well?"

I raised my eyebrows. "Well what?"

"Did it work?"

I blinked. "Is this 1692?"

"No."

"Then it didn't work."

The swirling energy had stopped. The room felt normal again.

She frowned and looked down at the grimoire. "I did everything it said to do. I don't know what happened. Is a page missing? I think a page is missing!"

Or maybe Heather wasn't the right witch for the job. Disappointment crashed over me. Another failure. I wasn't sure how much more I could take.

A buzzing began to come from Thierry's phone. My attention snapped to it; then I got up from the table and moved toward it to see the call display.

"Thierry, it's your contact!"

Just as I was about to jab the answer button, the room suddenly began to swirl in front of my eyes as if I'd climbed aboard an amusement park ride.

I grabbed hold of the back of the sofa. "Whoa."

"What's wrong?" Thierry asked, while his phone continued to buzz.

"The spell—" The phone slipped from my grasp and hit the floor. "I think it's—"

But before I could say anything else, the room before me disappeared completely.

Chapter 11

For a second, I thought I'd passed out right on Heather's floor. After all, I'd spent a disturbing amount of time since first becoming a vampire being knocked unconscious, so I was kind of used to it.

I didn't think I was unconscious.

Instead, I was doing an uncanny imitation of Dorothy when her house was picked up by a tornado. Only—there was no house. Only me, in the midst of that tornado, the world spinning and spinning all around me, blurs of color and light.

But then it stopped.

I braced myself with my hands on my thighs, then pushed my hair back from my face to glance around, stunned.

Heather's living room was gone. Instead, I was outside. It was dusk, the air clear and the moon already visible in the darkening sky. The scent of burning wood wafted past my nose.

I heard the clip-clop of horses' hooves and I jumped out of the way as a wooden cart rolled past on the muddy road.

"Did it work?" I whispered. "Did the spell really work?"

There was a cluster of houses nearby, and they certainly didn't look modern. This definitely wasn't the Salem I'd left. This was like something out of a movie. One with no electricity or cars. And definitely no Starbucks.

I was here. *Literally* here.

"Excuse me," I said to a couple passing me, dressed like something out of *The Scarlet Letter*—the version with Demi Moore (which was the only one I'd seen). The man had long hair and a thick beard. He wore a black hat with what looked like a buckle on it. The woman wore a cloth kerchief to cover her hair and a dull, austere, long dress. Total Pilgrim chic—just like everyone else I could see.

They ignored me.

I ran out to block their path. "Hey, can you help me?"

The next moment they walked right through me.

Right. Through. Me.

I gasped for breath, as if I'd just been punched in the stomach, and looked down at myself. My body swirled like formless gray smoke before it slowly took on a more recognizable form.

"Holy crap, I'm a ghost." Thierry had said that this would be spirit time travel—and this was the proof. My body was still in the present, but my spirit had been magically transported more than three hundred years into the past.

I looked down at my arm, then poked it with my fingers.

Solid, at least to me. If this was how real ghosts felt, then I totally understood why finding out they were actually dead could come as a shock.

The spell worked.

I turned slowly in a circle to take in the incredible scene around me. "It worked! Heather, you are amazing!"

Not wanting to waste any time overthinking this, I began to hurry down the dirt road, which was busy with foot traffic. No makeup. No high heels. No designer labels. No bling to speak of as far as the eye could see.

I would not have liked living in 1692. I was very fond of all those things.

"—took her to the jailhouse," one woman whispered to another as I passed them. Her expression was filled with anguish. "Goody Connolly accused her of being a witch."

At the word "witch" I froze in place and spun around to face them. Of course, they didn't see me, although they did glance around as if fearful that someone more corporeal might overhear.

The woman's companion paled. "You must have nothing to do with her. Do not visit her. Do not even speak her name. Do you hear me?"

"I hear you. But . . . but I don't understand. Why can't she free herself? Her magic is powerful."

"Shh." The second woman cast a furtive glance at the common area. "They could hear you."

"The witch hunters."

She nodded gravely. "They have ways of keeping those gifted with magic detained and helpless."

"Do the hunters also work with magic?"

"They would never call it that. But yes. They have enlisted witches to help them imprison others of their kind."

I listened with a sick, sinking feeling in my gut. I did know enough about Salem and the outlying towns that had the trials, mostly thanks to my tour of the town and its historical sites with Thierry yesterday, to understand what they were talking about. Two dozen people had died here in less than a year, either put to death or dying in captivity. The colonies were incredibly religious and afraid of anything they thought might be the devil's work—and witches definitely fit the bill.

I hated to think what they might do to a vampire.

As sickening as it was to be here at the time of such a horrible injustice as the witch trials, I couldn't let myself get distracted by the sights and sounds. I didn't know how long this spell would last and I needed to find Thierry. If this was the date he'd told Heather—and *if* the spell worked as it should have—then he was here. Somewhere.

And so were the answers I needed to find to help him unravel the mystery of his disappearance—the one that happened on this very day.

It was like a really scary Easter egg hunt.

I started jogging through the town, past the small brick houses with thatched roofs, past the people out with their children. Past the church. The edge of the ocean was nearby, with ships with tall white sails docked there. The early evening air felt cool on my incorporeal face.

Finally, I saw someone out of the corner of my eye. A very familiar, handsome man dressed in black—black hat and a long black coat. His dark hair was longer than it was now, and he had a short, well-groomed beard. His sharp gray eyes scanned the town and the people he passed as he swiftly moved down the road.

My breath caught. "Thierry."

I started to follow him, catching up enough to be right next to him. I couldn't stop staring.

"It's amazing," I managed. "I'm here. Can you see me?"

He didn't reply or give any indication he felt anything but the evening breeze.

"Okay, fine, you can't see me or hear me, but I'm here. I found you." Giddy excitement swept through me. "You look really good in those clothes. I see black is not a recent fashion choice for you. No Hugo Boss suits in the seventeenth century, are there?"

Thierry still had that intimidating air about him, that cold and cutting gaze that looked right through anyone he passed as if they, too, were ghosts. Those on the road parted like the Red Sea to let him pass, eyeing him with uneasiness as if they guessed there was something threatening about this new guy in town.

He was intent on something, some goal, and his steps did not slow until he reached a tavern that was close to the meeting hall where others gathered out front. He entered the tavern without hesitation, his gaze traveling over the men there. Candlelight and lanterns lit the establishment. After a moment, he approached a wooden table in the far corner. A man watched him, a ready smirk on his face. The man was blond, his eyes green and sparkling.

He stood up and clasped Thierry's hand before he sat down across the table from the man. "You've arrived."

"I have."

My heart leapt at hearing his familiar deep voice.

"Was it a pleasant journey?"

There was no friendliness on Thierry's face. "Three months in a stinking, overpacked ship to bring me here. To say it was pleasant would be a lie."

"That is too bad."

Thierry's lips thinned. "Indeed."

He scanned the tavern again, his gaze watchful,

shrewd, appraising. That was my Thierry—this attractive, untouchable man who let go of his tight hold on control only on rare occasions. He currently seemed as if he expected a team of deadly ninjas to burst into the tavern at any moment. Still, I looked on through this window into my husband's past with barely restrained glee.

And really, he was rocking that beard. So hot.

The man gestured for someone to bring over a beverage for Thierry. A moment later a glass was delivered filled with an amber-colored liquid.

Thierry passed the glass under his nose. "Ale?"

"The water here is questionable at best. Ale is therefore readily available, although public drunkenness is frowned upon."

"I can imagine."

The man grinned. "Don't worry, Thierry. It's not poisoned."

"Wouldn't matter if it was." Thierry set it to the side anyway. "It's not my beverage of choice."

"No, I don't suppose it is." The man cocked his head. "I've heard some recent rumors about you, Thierry. That you have difficulties with your thirst, more so than any other vampire your age."

"Rumors are usually started by those who wish ill upon their subjects."

"You deny the truth of it?"

"That I drink blood to sustain myself? I can't deny that. I am a vampire."

"No, that you are a danger to any human—or even any vampire—that you come across since you are always at the very edge of your control."

Thierry's expression darkened. "Does that concern you?"

"Not particularly. I just like to be as knowledgeable as possible about those I choose to do business with."

"My thirsts were sated on the ship. Several who began the journey in England did not make it to this shore. A desire for blood is not my concern at this moment."

A chill went down my spine to hear him basically admit that he'd left some victims in his wake, Bram Stoker–style. I couldn't say it came as a huge shock, but hearing it stated so bluntly made my stomach churn. I wondered if satisfying his thirsts, as opposed to abstaining as he did in the future, helped his blood addiction or made it worse.

Thierry slid his index finger around the rim of the glass, though he didn't take his gaze from the man's. "I've traveled a great distance to meet with you, David. Let's get on with it, so I can begin my lengthy journey back."

"For one blessed with immortality and the gift of time, you're always in such a rush." David shook his head. "Can't you at least pretend to enjoy yourself?"

"No," Thierry said, his gaze tracking through the room for a third time. "I can't."

"Where is your beautiful wife, Veronique?"

That drew Thierry's attention back to David. "Not here."

"Stunning woman. How can you ever bear to let her out of your sight?"

"It's not nearly as much of a hardship as you might imagine."

"Yes, but to leave such a woman on her own—"

"Trust me, Veronique is rarely alone. But I did not come here to discuss my wife, David. I came here for one reason and one alone. Where is it?"

My ears perked up at that like matching exclamation points. Was he talking about the mysterious amulet?

David took a sip of his drink. "If I said I couldn't get it, would you be disappointed in me?"

"My disappointment would be the least of your worries." Thierry's tone turned glacial. His distaste for this man was palpable. I couldn't really blame him. There was something about David that rubbed me the wrong way. Something in his gaze, something slick and serpentine.

"You are quite the renowned collector." David leaned back in his chair and took a swig of his own glass of ale. "You must have amassed a fascinating collection after all these years."

"I have."

"Obtaining this particular object would be quite an accomplishment. Do you know how many also look for it?"

"I'm certain there are many. Which is why I required your particular skills to locate it and was willing to go to great extremes to cross an ocean at your request for this exchange. So let me see it."

"I couldn't get a message to you on the ship, but . . . well . . ." The man giggled. *Giggled.* "There's a problem, I'm afraid."

I realized now what it was about him that was slightly off, other than a creepiness that seemed to permeate his very skin. The man was inebriated. So much for public drunkenness in a highly religious village. Naughty Pilgrim.

Thierry did not giggle in response, of course. His eyes glittered dangerously. "If you're as smart as I thought you were, you won't waste my time with these foolish games."

David glanced around as if to check if they were being watched. But no one was close enough to see or hear their exchange.

Well, except for me—the ghostly eavesdropper from the future. I waited with bated breath. It took a great deal of effort to keep my gaze on David and not on Thierry. I could barely look away from him.

At first glance out on the road, I'd assumed Thierry would be exactly the same as he is in the future—only with a bit of a fashion makeover. But there was something about this Thierry that felt darker to me. Colder. *This* Thierry was a man who looked at everyone as a potential enemy or saboteur. A man who was married to a beautiful woman but didn't give a damn if she remained faithful to him in his absence. A man who fed his dark addictions whenever the urge struck, one who didn't feel any remorse.

He hadn't wanted me to see his past. I'd thought it was due to some moment, some specific act that he now regretted. But perhaps he simply hadn't wanted me to see who he was as a whole.

Perhaps he felt no remorse for the lives he'd taken due to his overwhelming bloodlust, but still—there was the edge of *something* in his familiar gray eyes, something lost and pained, that told me that the real Thierry was in there, too.

"I wish I was really here," I said, even though I knew he couldn't hear me. "I'd tell you everything would be better one day."

David finally pulled something from the leather satchel by his feet. It was wrapped in cloth. He unwrapped it, holding it out to Thierry. I drew closer to see that it was a timepiece, a gold pocket watch. However, it didn't have hands to tell the time, only numbers.

"This is not the amulet," Thierry said, unimpressed.

"No, it isn't."

"Where is the amulet?"

David's expression finally shadowed, the drunken pleasantness disappearing and an edge of fear entering his gaze. "I'm told it was destroyed five years ago."

Anger sparked in Thierry's gaze, and he stood up, his chair scraping against the floor like fingernails on a chalkboard. "Then meeting you here is a waste of my time. I won't pay you for something I don't want, if that's what you're thinking."

"Sit, Thierry," David hissed, glancing nervously around. "Just sit down and let me explain. Do not draw attention to yourself. Not here, not now."

I was certain he was going to storm out of the tavern, but instead Thierry sat back down and faced David. "Then explain."

"I know you want the amulet."

"The amulet has been destroyed. You're not the first to tell me this, but I haven't wanted to believe it's true. Perhaps it is."

"But that's why I have this for you." He held out the gold watch again.

A little of the impatience faded from Thierry's eyes, replaced by a fraction of curiosity. "What is it?"

"A timewalker."

Thierry's eyebrows shot up. "I thought they were only legend."

"Not true. While exceedingly rare, they do exist."

"How do I know this is real?"

David's lips stretched into a smile. "Because I know if I try to fool you, my life may be significantly shortened. Remember, your reputation does precede you, Thierry. This is legitimate. I guarantee it. You can use this to go back to when this precious amulet still existed and snatch it away from any other interested party. Not simple, but certainly effective, yes?"

Thierry was silent, studying the timepiece with more interest now. "How does it work?"

"Be careful, since it is very delicate. You wind it up like this, setting the numbers to the date you wish to travel. This way to go forward. This way to go back." He demonstrated with the winding stem. The wheels and cogs in the watch moved and shimmered in a way that made it clear that this was no normal watch. "It can also be triggered remotely by magic."

"What difficulties are associated with using such a device?"

David nodded, as if expecting the question. "For a human, it would kill them. The use of a timewalker is out of the question for their delicate bodies. For a vampire . . ." He gave Thierry a guarded look. "Well, I won't lie to you. There is still great risk involved. I would advise you to write yourself a detailed letter and put it somewhere upon your person. Your mind will be affected; there's no way around it. Timewalking can cause problems if one does not take precautions."

Thierry's gaze snapped to the man's face. "How will my mind be affected?"

"Memory gaps, mostly. For the hours leading up to the usage as well as several hours after you arrive at your destination."

I'd watched their conversation with my mouth hanging open, not believing my own ears.

A timewalker. Thierry was about to purchase a *timewalker* from this strange man, in order to retrieve the amulet that might have been destroyed five years prior.

And *I'd* traveled into the past to learn this.

Did that qualify for irony?

"Carefully consider your options before using this," David said, before hesitating. "Your collection doesn't need this amulet in it. No one's does."

Thierry's jaw tightened. "Let me be the judge of that."

"Your obsession with dangerous pieces of power will be your undoing, de Bennicoeur. Be very careful."

"I appreciate your concern." Thierry reached into the inner pocket of his black coat, then tossed David a small silk drawstring bag. "Even though this isn't what we agreed upon, neither is this what you promised me. This is the payment I will offer you for the timewalker. And your silence."

David undid the ties and glanced inside the bag, nodding. "It's acceptable."

"Is our business complete here?"

"It is." David handed the timepiece to Thierry, who then tucked it inside his jacket. "It's an interesting time to be here, Thierry. You should stay for a while and observe. Such fear these humans have, so wrapped up in their religion, with their God, that they think any shadow, any problem, any illness, can be blamed on the devil. Wouldn't it all be so much easier if that were the truth?"

"I've heard what's been happening here with the trials. It's distasteful."

"A little blood and death shouldn't bother you. In fact, I'm surprised you're not as fascinated by it all as I am. You've witnessed many atrocities before. Sometimes you've even stepped in to lend a hand—although the side you fight for seems to change with the seasons. Are you a friend or a foe this month to those who are weak and needy?" He said it with a sneer, half insult, half observation.

Thierry didn't seem to care. He sent a gaze toward the front door when a few men entered and gathered around a table near the fire. "If I help anyone, it would be my own kind. Witches wouldn't be my concern even if I was feeling particularly generous."

David nodded. "Understandable. Didn't that one witch hold you for some time, bleeding you for her own power? Nearly killed you, I'd heard."

"She sought to increase her magic through the blood of a master vampire. Some witches do."

"But she didn't achieve it. You killed her, didn't you? But you killed her husband first, while she watched, as punishment."

My gaze shot to Thierry's face to find it had turned to stone. Totally unreadable, even to me.

Thierry's lips thinned. "Another rumor?"

"Perhaps. Is it true?"

"She made her choice. It was the wrong one."

"Yes, don't worry. I know not to upset you. I prefer to blend in and appear as harmless as possible."

"And yet, you're far from it. You're one of the most powerful wizards in any of the American colonies."

"And then some." There was a sinister note to David's smile.

"Then I don't understand. Why would you allow your kind to be tortured and murdered by those who fear their abilities? Not to mention those humans only accused of witchcraft who hold no magic at all."

David spread his hands. "It's none of my business."

Thierry studied him. "I would almost say that you're enjoying this. As if it's entertaining to you."

"Entertaining seeing witches and innocent humans murdered?" David looked appalled for a moment before humor lit his eyes again. "Perhaps a little. But you do know that witches' blood is almost as potent as vampire blood when it comes to black magic. Without a steady supply, I might not be able to find trinkets to please my wealthier clients such as yourself."

Thierry's expression soured further. "You're helping them, aren't you? The witch hunters."

David laughed at this and then drained the rest of his drink. "These witches, these humans, they're weak, Thierry. The weak must be destroyed so the strong can flourish."

"And you've made some sort of deal in which you have access to these accused witches, either before or after their deaths, so you can take their blood."

Something unpleasant flickered through David's eyes. "Don't you dare judge me, de Bennicoeur. Not you of all people. You've profited from the pain and misery of others for centuries. I don't care if you deny it; your insatiable thirst has become legendary."

Finally, a dark smile touched Thierry's lips, one that chilled me. "I assure you, I have total control over my thirst. But blood is essential to the existence of any vampire."

"Of course you're right." David's words were now guarded, as if he'd suddenly realized he'd been doing business with a supernatural creature with sharp fangs and malevolent intentions. "I know you don't wish to delay your journey back to England. Our business is done here. Farewell, Thierry."

He put on his hat and strode out of the tavern without another word.

Thierry sat there for another moment in silence, his eyes straight forward, his shoulders rigid, his brows drawn together in a deep frown.

Then he pushed up from the table and began to follow David.

He moved so fast that I had to jog to keep up to him. "Don't do anything crazy, scary Thierry from the past. It's not worth it."

His gaze was razor sharp as he scanned the street searching for the man who'd just left his company. David strolled down the road in no hurry, nodding and smiling at those he passed.

Thierry stayed twenty feet back but continued to trail after him.

"He's a jerk," I said. "A complete and utter bastard. But don't do anything you're going to regret. You said yourself that guy's a wizard. You don't want to mess with that."

Thierry swiftly stalked after David until the man turned a corner near a river that looked like a shimmering ribbon of darkness under the evening sky.

"David," he said.

David's shoulders froze and he turned. His eyes had shifted to that familiar witchy red and I felt the crackle of energy charge the air.

Uh-oh.

"You mean to bite me, de Bennicoeur? To drain my blood?"

"No, of course not. I'd never bite you," Thierry said, offering a smile. "I regret how we left things in the tavern and I wanted to tell you that before we part ways."

David's tension eased a fraction. "Well, that is good to hear. I know many might hold my recent decisions against me, but I've always known we were two of a kind—survivors in this harsh, unforgiving world."

"Two of a kind indeed." Thierry drew closer. "I have been pondering the deal you've made with the local hunters to acquire the blood of dead witches . . ."

"Oh? What about it?"

Thierry reached forward, his movement nearly too fast to see. He grabbed David's head between his hands and twisted sharply. I heard a crack and David crumpled to the ground.

Thierry looked down at the wizard's dead body. "I don't approve."

Chapter 12

I clamped my hand over my mouth to hold back my scream.

Thierry turned his face away from the body with a hiss. His eyes had turned black with hunger. David had hit his head on a sharp rock when he fell to the ground. Blood now trickled down his temple.

"Don't even think about it, Thierry." My shock at witnessing the murder had swiftly turned to fear.

Dead blood, even *freshly* dead blood, was like poison to a vampire. It was like some sort of magical trap for a vampire, since the blood of a dead person was still red, still fresh, still tempting.

But potentially deadly.

He turned away, his hands clenched into fists at his sides. He began to move away from David's body with long, determined strides.

I kept pace. "Good. I approve. Well, not of the cold-blooded murder, but still. Good for you for walking away from temptation."

His lips drew back from his straight white teeth until I saw the sharp tips of his fangs. He scanned the road near the tavern, near the meeting hall. Finally his predatory, black-eyed gaze fell upon a woman in an indigo blue dress. She was walking unchaperoned after leaving the company of her friends.

Thierry began to trail after her.

I picked up speed. "Oh, no, you don't. Don't even think about it!"

Of course, he couldn't hear me.

He was in the middle of a sudden and overwhelming wave of bloodlust—the same kind of bloodlust Owen now had to deal with and that present-day ghost Thierry was free from. This wasn't present-day Thierry. This was scary-vampire Thierry and he needed to feed. And this unlucky young woman, whoever she was, was going to be playing the part of victim number two in this evening's program.

I grabbed for Thierry's arm, but my hands slipped right through him and turned to smoke for a horrifying moment. I swore under my breath. I didn't care if I was no better than a ghost at the moment; I couldn't let this happen.

It was one thing to hear about the horrible things Thierry had been responsible for, the murders aboard the ship that brought him here. But for me to witness him kill a helpless girl with my own eyes . . .

I honestly didn't think I'd be able to look at him the same way again.

He hadn't wanted me to see any of this. I now realized he did that to protect me—to protect how I cared about him. And yes, admittedly, perhaps I had put him on a bit of a golden pedestal in my mind—which he was currently attempting to knock himself off of.

But I was here; there was no turning back. And there *had* to be a way for me to stop this from happening.

I scanned the street looking for inspiration until my

gaze fell on another woman. Dark hair, dark eyes. She read a Bible while seated on a lantern-lit bench in front of the church.

Without thinking, I moved directly toward her.

I might not be dead, but I *was* currently doing an excellent impression of a wandering spirit. That gave me only one option I could think of to use.

"Here goes nothing," I said under my breath. As the woman got up, tucked her Bible under her arm, and moved forward, I remained standing right in her path, bracing myself with my hands on my thighs like a sumo wrestler. Instead of her walking through me, I walked into her. Headfirst.

She shivered as we met, as if she'd just strolled into a freezer.

And then, suddenly, I was looking out of her eyes.

"Awesome," I said now in the voice of someone else. I could already feel a pressure building. Sort of like in an airplane when it's descending. If my ears popped, so would everything else. I'd pop right out of this body like a half-cooked Eggo.

I worked the borrowed legs, the skirt flapping and threatening to tangle me up. I never wore long skirts except for the odd time I was in somebody's wedding and didn't have a choice of bridesmaid outfit.

I'd never dressed like a Puritan before. Actually, scratch that. In college I'd dressed up like a Pilgrim for Halloween. A sexy one with a high slit in my black skirt, a red garter, a plunging neckline, sky-high buckled patent leather heels—and a plush turkey for good measure.

This was a bit different.

I was literally running by the time I spotted Thierry again. He followed the girl down a dark road lit by the full moon. She appeared utterly unaware of who was ominously trailing after her.

As she left the road, he followed. And I followed, my steps quickening to a full-out sprint when I heard a shriek.

He now had her by an oak tree, pressed up against its thick trunk with his hand to her throat.

I didn't hesitate to yell: "Hey!"

I threw the Bible directly at his head, and it successfully knocked his hat right off. A tad sacrilegious to use it as a weapon, I'll admit, but surprisingly effective.

He turned with a snarl to send a chillingly dark look at me.

I chose to ignore the immediate fear that raced through me, since it really wasn't helpful right now.

"Don't do it!" I forced as much conviction into my voice as I could manage. "Don't you dare even think about it!"

"Leave me in peace, woman," he snarled.

"Help me," the girl gasped. "He's a demon. He's a monster from Hell who will destroy all of us."

My borrowed heart hammered against my borrowed rib cage. "Well . . . no, he's not. But he *is* acting like an ass right now."

He glanced over his shoulder at me and raised an eyebrow. "An ass."

"A huge one," I confirmed.

"His eyes . . . ," the girl managed. "They're black as pitch. He's been sent by Satan to devour our souls."

I blinked. "Actually, he just wants your blood. But the soul thing does sound a bit more impressive, doesn't it?"

Thierry's darkly curious gaze didn't leave mine—it pinned me. Even three hundred years in the past I could still be effortlessly held in place by those eyes of his. "Who are you, woman?"

Dangerous question. "Consider me your guardian angel."

"My guardian angel?" His lips curved into an unpleasant smile. "It seems to me that you're attempting to be *hers*."

A moment later, he released the girl.

"Run," he suggested.

She didn't hesitate. She sped off into the night without a backward glance.

Thierry was in front of me a split second later. He took hold of the front of my borrowed dress and pulled me back toward the oak tree as if I weighed nothing more than a Puritan Chihuahua.

That fear I'd been trying to ignore came back in spades.

"So kind of you to take the place of your friend," he growled.

"Not my friend. Never even met her before."

"Then perhaps the word I should use is 'foolish.' "

That would certainly be one word to describe my recent decisions.

Still, I stared up into his face, half-freaked-out, half-fascinated. I reached up to touch the line of his jaw.

He watched me warily, frowning now, but he didn't swat my hand away. "I think you must be a bit mad to be so bold."

"I am mad. Furious, actually."

"You don't fear me."

"I fear you. Oh, absolutely, Thierry. I fear the hell out of you right now."

His dark brows knitted closer together. "How do you know my name? Tell me who you are." His eyes hadn't shifted to any color but black. I'd put this woman's body in danger by approaching him in order to save another girl. I hated to think I might endanger this one in exchange. I'd never forgive myself for that.

Now I was faced with the problem presented in time travel movies. How was I supposed to tell him anything that might help? Didn't that mess with the whole past/future time paradox, or whatever it was called?

However, since Thierry was the one who said I couldn't lie to him, and time was of the essence here, I quickly opted for the truth.

"I'm from the future," I said evenly. "I needed to stop you from hurting that girl. You can't hurt anyone else, Thierry."

He cocked his head, perplexed. "The future."

"Yes. I know you in the future. More than three hundred years from now. You're not a killer. You're wonderful, actually. At least, *I* think so."

A long, silent moment went by before he began to laugh. The sound coursed pleasantly through me—another reminder that this guy might be half his age and seriously troubled, but he was still *my* Thierry. And I could still make him laugh.

Even though at the moment I wasn't exactly *trying* to.

"Amusing," he said. "*Wonderful*, am I? And I live for three more centuries; is this so?"

"You do."

His smile fell. "You expect me to believe such nonsense? There's only one thing right now that I do believe."

"What?"

"Your blood is something I need." He came closer, sweeping the pieces of dark hair that had escaped this woman's kerchief away from her throat. I felt his breath, hot on my skin as he pressed me against the tree.

"You've amused me," he whispered in my ear. "I won't take your life, only a taste of it."

"You're sure you'll be able to stop in time?" I drew in a ragged breath as his lips brushed against my throat—the sexy preshow before the scary movie began. "I know you hate that you can't control this . . ."

He pulled back from me, his expression quizzical. "It's like you *do* know me."

"I do."

Uncertainty slid across his face. "It's impossible."

I started talking. Quickly. "You were sired by Veronique during the plague. You married her shortly after, but you were never happy with her. You might have been somehow dependent on her in the beginning, maybe you even thought you loved her—I mean, she does look like a Victoria's Secret model"—not that I needed that particular reminder right now—"but there's nothing between you deeper than a shared history. She's vain, selfish, thoughtless. She cheats on you all the time. She doesn't care what you do or who you do it with."

He stared at me as if my words shocked him before he tempered his reaction with skepticism. "Many know of Veronique's reputation."

"Even some random human girl in Salem?"

His gaze moved over my face, my throat, before returning to my eyes. "Perhaps you're a powerful witch—one who can see into my mind to pick out words to use against me."

"Look at me, Thierry. I know you don't know me right now. I know I'm in the wrong body. I know this is the wrong year, wrong century. But you have to see that there's something in my eyes. Something you recognize. Something that time can't steal from us."

The blackness in his eyes began to fade back to his regular stormy gray.

He shook his head. "I don't know you."

"Yes, you do," I insisted. "You know me. And you know I love you more than anyone else in the whole wide world."

"Love?" He whispered the word, his brow furrowing.

I knew I had to keep talking. The original owner of this body was fighting hard to launch me out of it. The pressure built like a teakettle about to start whistling. If this was what real possession was like, then it was proof that something truly unnatural had happened with Owen. "That man you met with—the one you killed. I don't know how, but he's somehow involved with your disappearance. It happens tonight. You vanish for fifty years."

Yeah, I was breaking the time travel rules big time now, but I couldn't stop myself from warning him. I'd deal with the ramifications later.

"Despite the madness of your words, I can't deny that there's something about you . . ." He studied my face, as if trying to memorize it. "Perhaps *I'm* the one going mad tonight."

I was getting through to him. I knew I could do this! "You told me that I wouldn't like what I saw if I witnessed your past. But see? I can handle it. What I see is a man who's lost his way, who chases after treasures to fill his empty days. One who's lived long enough that there's nobody he trusts anymore. But you can trust me. And I trust that you can control this thirst, even when it feels like it's going to overwhelm you."

"Your words are so sweet, every bit as sweet as you are." He studied my face, brushing his fingertips across my cheek. "But you're wrong."

I froze. "What?"

"There will never be any control for me."

His eyes shifted back to black, and then he pressed my

head to the side. I felt the bite of his sharp fangs as they sank into my borrowed flesh—total déjà-vu to what had happened with Owen. And it stung just as much as it would in my own body. I grabbed his arms, but there was no chance for me to fight him. He was way too strong.

I barely had a chance to panic when he let go of me with a gasp and staggered back a few feet.

My hand flew to my neck to press against the wound. "Okay, so maybe I was wrong. You don't have any control. Like, zero. *So* not impressed right now!"

Seriously, I should have saved my breath. He'd just shown me definitively that I was like a wounded goat trying to bargain with a hungry lion. I'd go with the good old-fashioned knee to groin if he came near me again—as any wounded goat should. Even lions—or master vampires—were affected by that handy self-defense move.

I watched him cautiously when he didn't come any closer. "Not that I'm complaining, but why did you stop?"

There was a strange glow coming from his chest. He reached into his inner jacket pocket and pulled out the timewalker, but it was barely recognizable anymore. It now resembled a piece of bright light.

He swore under his breath. "David said it could be triggered remotely with magic. He must have done this before I—"

"Before you snapped his neck like a Thanksgiving turkey," I finished for him.

His gaze shot to mine. "What does this mean?"

My heart was pounding right out of my chest. This is what happened! It had to be. "It means that you're going on a little trip. And you're not going to remember anything about it."

"A trip where?"

"Fifty years into the future."

He looked at me, stunned.

I gave him a frustrated glare in return. "I mean, you just bought a timewalker from an evil wizard. What do you think it's going to do? Give you a bikini wax?"

"This can't happen. I won't let it."

"Right. Well, good luck with that." I crossed my arms. My borrowed neck hurt from his fangs and I felt absolutely horrible that I'd put this woman's body in harm's way. "I guess you should look at the bright side."

"What?"

I shrugged. "You're actually fifty years younger than we thought you were."

A moment later, a tornado of bright white light swirled around him, obliterating his body from view. And then he vanished into thin air.

I stared at the spot where he'd vanished for a full minute in utter silence. "Note to self: three-hundred-year-old Thierry? Less awesome than expected."

And here I thought we were going to have a romantic, star-crossed, soul mates moment. Nope. He was just a vampire who wanted to suck my blood.

As if to punctuate that thought, my incorporeal body was launched right out of the one I'd borrowed. I landed ten feet away on my back and looked up at the star-studded sky before I propped myself up on my elbows to see the dark-haired girl.

"What in the heavens?" She glanced around. "What happened?" When she touched her throat, her fingers came away tipped with blood. "Goodness! Have I been bitten by an insect?"

"Yeah, a six-foot-tall mosquito," I said dryly. Still,

other than the neck wound, I was extremely relieved she seemed otherwise unharmed and untraumatized.

I watched as she picked up her Bible and scurried away from the oak tree and back to the moonlit dirt road.

"So, Thierry," I said out loud. "I figured out the mystery of your disappearance and why you can't remember a single thing about it. Mission accomplished."

It was because there was nothing to remember—those years never happened for him.

David said that the hours leading up to and after a timewalker journey would obliterate the traveler's memories. Since Thierry hadn't originally asked David to get the timewalker, he wouldn't remember having it on his person. And David had triggered the timewalker earlier, probably when his eyes had turned red, just before his death.

It was a delayed reaction, but it had worked like a charm.

Right now, Thierry would be standing in this very spot in fifty years, looking around and wondering how the heck he got there.

As for me, I hadn't gone anywhere.

"Okay, I'm ready to come back to the present." I turned around in a full circle. "Anytime now, Heather."

I was met only by silence. Actually, scratch that. Crickets literally chirped.

I'd defied Thierry's wishes and his better judgment to do this spell—one that came with no money-back guarantee.

One that could keep my spirit trapped in the past forever if I was very, very unlucky. But I wasn't going to panic. Not yet. This delay didn't mean something was wrong. I just had to be patient and wait it out.

I walked back to the village and scanned the streets. Maybe while I was still here I could investigate a bit more about these witch hunters and who they were using as their hired witches. The thought disgusted me. Who would ever agree to such a horrible thing?

Two hours later, I was still there, with no further answers.

"Okay, maybe I was wrong." A nervous gnawing was growing in my incorporeal gut. "Maybe getting back isn't going to be *quite* as easy as I hoped."

Yeah, maybe you're going to be stuck in 1692 as a ghost forever, my unhelpful inner voice informed me.

Well, that was actually impossible. It would only be 1692 until December thirty-first. Then it would be 1693. And so on. And so on.

So not good.

Already, I was working on my backup plan, which mostly consisted of me possessing another body and getting a witch to help my sorry butt with another time travel spell.

I stood in the middle of the road, thinking hard, before I finally turned, ready to take another walk through the town. Then—*bam*—somebody walked right through me. I gasped at the jarring sensation. It felt as if I'd hit a wall—or rather, as if a wall had hit *me.* My entire body turned to smoke for a moment before it re-formed. I stood there stunned while I tried to gather myself together again. Literally.

The man who'd walked through me paused as if he'd felt something. For him it likely felt as if he'd walked through a cold spot. He glanced over his shoulder in the direction he'd come from.

I stared at him, shocked.

It was Jonathan Malik, the witch hunter.

"How strange," he said under his breath before continuing on.

Holy crap.

I followed, my feet quickly developing a mind of their own. I couldn't deny that finding out more about Malik interested me, and not because he was the sexy, deadly, alpha type some women really went for, hoping that their true, pure love might help soften his hard edges and redeem his evil ways.

No, I was just curious what motivated a monster like this, and what he might do in his spare time—when he wasn't torturing witches for fun. It might give me a better understanding of the darkness I faced more often than I'd like to.

He moved easily through town, his gaze sharp, but his stride wasn't as swift as Thierry's had been earlier. It was leisurely.

For some reason, this infuriated me more than anything else.

"You think you're so tough," I said to him. "Well, you're just a man. I'm not surprised you're stuck haunting Salem now. Must be boring for you. Too bad."

Not surprisingly, he ignored me completely, as if I weren't even there.

Suddenly, I realized where he was headed. There was a dark-haired woman up ahead, and his gaze fixed on her as he followed her through this mazelike village.

She didn't seem aware of him.

Just like with Thierry earlier, a predator had fixed his sights upon unsuspecting prey. My hackles went up, my immediate need to protect something smaller and weaker from something dark and malicious. I scanned the area to see how I might be able to raise the alarm, but no one was nearby.

He caught up to her and grabbed her wrist, halting her steps. She turned to face him with surprise.

But then a smile stretched across her face.

"Malik," she whispered. Her gaze then became guarded. "You said it was unsafe for us to see each other."

"I tried, but I can't stay away from you." He raised a dark eyebrow. "It seems you've managed to bewitch me."

"Not with any spell." Her smile returned as he gathered her into his arms and kissed her passionately, pressing her up against the side of a stone mill.

I stared at them with shock. Not because they were a couple living in Puritan times who were obviously romantically involved, but because I now recognized the woman.

It was Raina Wilkins.

I stared at her, stunned. How was this possible?

Maybe I was wrong. Maybe this wasn't Raina, but instead an ancestor of hers that looked identical.

"Raina, your beauty brings me back to you every time," Malik breathed. "I need you."

It could be an identical ancestor with the same name.

Even I had to admit that was stretching things. Something bizarrely supernatural was going on here, and all I could do was stare.

"I need you, too." Her voice broke. "I hate this, Malik. I hate it all so much. Why can't we run away? No one has to know."

"You know why. I must stay and finish my work here. The jail is full of the accused."

Her expression shadowed. "Leave your work behind. You said you loved me."

"I do love you."

Moonlight lit her beautiful face but also showed the pain in her blue eyes. "Then it's not right."

"You're absolutely right. It's not."

Her expression tensed as if his words were like a slap. "Don't say that."

His lips curved. "You are a woman who doesn't know what she wants. Either it's me or it's freedom from this colony of fools."

"There are many here I consider friends, family."

"So you stay. So we can be together. You've been endlessly valuable to me."

Her eyes brimmed with tears. "Don't remind me of what I've done to help you."

I literally gasped out loud at this. Raina was one of the helpers, the horrible witches assisting the evil witch hunters.

Malik's gaze burned into hers. "When it's all over, when the darkness is purged from this place, only then can I move on. With you. I promise we'll be together."

She stared at the ground as tears dripped down her pale cheeks.

"You still want that, don't you, Raina?"

Her gaze lifted to meet his. "Of course. I want that more than anything. I want *you* more than anything."

He touched her chin and lifted it so she'd meet his eyes. "Then there's nothing more to say, is there?"

She shook her head. "Nothing more."

"That's my Raina. Today, tomorrow, forever."

"Forever," she murmured as he kissed her again.

Then another wall hit me head on, stealing my breath completely.

My vision went nearly black as the storm landed right

on top of me and obliterated my view—the tornado of the world swirling before my eyes. For a terrifying moment it was as if the floor fell away from beneath my feet and I dropped like a penny thrown into a wishing well.

And then my vision lightened, cleared, and suddenly I was staring into Heather's face.

She was slapping me. Hard.

"Sarah, snap out of it. Sarah!"

I grabbed her wrist before she struck again. "Stop."

"She's back!" Her expression lit up, shifting from fearful to joyful. "Thank God you're back! Your husband was ready to tear this entire town apart if you didn't open up your eyes again."

"My husband . . ." My gaze shifted to Thierry, standing next to Heather, his face grave and pale, his gaze intense. I shifted a little on the hard sofa. Someone—probably Heather—had tucked a pillow behind my head.

"Are you all right?" he demanded.

I licked my dry lips. Seeing him now, after dealing with him in the past . . . it was more jarring than I would have guessed. "I—I think I'm fine. How long was I gone?"

"You weren't gone. You were unconscious. For half an hour."

Right. My body had been here the whole time. "Half an hour? Is that all?"

"All? It was a small eternity." There was a tenseness to his words, like he was barely able to control his tone. "How long was it for you?"

"A few hours." I shook my head. My limbs tingled; every one of them felt as if they'd fallen asleep and now the blood was rushing back. When I was able, I shakily got up from the sofa.

"It worked?" Heather asked.

"Perfectly." I nodded, then glanced at Thierry. "I was there. I saw you."

This did nothing to remove his strained expression. "And what did you see?"

It was almost funny now. "I tried to give you a message by possessing a body."

"A message?" His brows drew tightly together. "What did I say to you? What did I do?"

I laughed at that, slightly hysterical. "You bit me."

Then my head spun like I was still stuck in the time travel theme park from hell, and I sank to the ground. This time when everything went black, I knew it was a good old-fashioned bout of unconsciousness.

I could totally work with that.

Chapter 13

This time when I opened my eyes, someone wasn't slapping me across the face. That was progress.

"You're awake." It was Thierry.

I blinked a few times until he came into focus. He stood next to the bed where I currently lay, his arms crossed, his expression strained but relieved.

"How long was I out?"

"Not long. Heather and Rose managed to bring you up here since, unfortunately, I couldn't help. How do you feel?"

Good question. I pushed myself up on my elbows and took a quick assessment. "I feel okay. I think."

He nodded, his eyes twin storm clouds. "Before you fainted, you said I bit you. Was that a joke? I can't always tell when you're trying to be funny."

I held back a quip about me *always* being delightfully hilarious. "I wasn't joking this time."

His face was stone and he nodded once, then crossed to the window to look outside. "Tell me what happened, Sarah. All of it."

I did. I told him everything from the moment I realized where I was, to seeing him, listening in on his meeting with David, and the discussion of the amulet.

"What does the amulet do?" I asked, not for the first time.

He sent a short glance over his shoulder. "You say he didn't have it."

"You're evading my question."

"Did he do something to corrupt my memory, since I don't remember this meeting at all?"

He *was* evading my question. I could take a hint. I continued to tell him about the timewalker and then David's murder.

He turned fully around to face me. "You can't be serious."

"About the timewalker or you treating David's neck like a Pez dispenser? I'm serious about both. That's why you disappeared. That's where you went. No fifty years of nasty behavior covered up by amnesia. They simply didn't happen, but you just don't remember that you time traveled."

I could tell he wanted to argue with me, to deny that this could be the truth, but then he nodded once. "If you say this happened, then it happened. But I thought timewalkers were only a myth."

I shrugged. "I thought the same about vampires once."

"If this is true, it must have been destroyed or stolen while I was still coming out of this magic-induced daze. What happened when you say I spoke with you? What led to me"—his expression shadowed—"biting you?"

I told him, his face and posture growing more tense with every word I spoke. I didn't leave anything out. Me possessing the girl, him about to attack the other girl, me stopping him—including my handy use of the Bible as weapon. I watched his expression carefully, since every word I spoke chipped away at his carefully constructed stone exterior.

"I could have killed you," he said softly.

"But you didn't. However, it's more proof that your thirst for blood . . ." I swallowed hard, and what I'd been considering since earlier bubbled up inside of me like a supernatural soufflé. "You don't have it anymore, do you? Your thirst? It's gone now that you're having this out-of-body experience, right?"

Thierry nodded, holding my gaze. "It's completely gone."

I swung my legs around and out of the bed to sit on the edge, expecting a wave of dizziness, but there was nothing. "What does it feel like?"

He didn't speak for a moment. "Being free from a dark compulsion I've fought against for as long as I can remember? It's as if a horrible curse has finally been lifted."

Of course he felt free. To deal with a blood addiction for all this time and then have it taken away . . . it had to be a wonderful feeling.

Unfortunately, I couldn't exactly be happy for him, since this was only temporary. If we succeeded in finding the answer to shift his spirit back into his body, he'd have to deal with that constant thirst once again.

"So you were successful. You learned one of my dark truths. You faced me at one of the bleakest times of my existence, when my self-involved obsession with magical trinkets sent me on quests to the far reaches of the earth."

He didn't like that I'd seen him that way, but it didn't change anything. In fact, it changed nothing at all with this situation and with those who were also interested in Thierry's past. "And it doesn't even matter, does it? The Ring isn't going to take my word for anything. Only if we hand this amulet over to them tied in a pretty ribbon would they leave you alone, if that's what they're really after."

He gave me a wry look. "You're learning."

I stood up. While I'd felt rather accomplished at surviving my trip to the past—for many reasons—we had to keep moving forward on our lengthy to-do list. No time to lick our wounds and feel sorry for ourselves that things weren't perfect. Fact of life: Things were *never* perfect. "Tell me what happened with the necromancer. Your contact was calling when I took a time travel nosedive. What did he say?"

Thierry's lips thinned. "I had Heather call him back."

"And?"

"There is good news and bad news."

His face was frustratingly unreadable again. "Good news, please?" I prompted.

"The necromancer could have done the job. It was within her abilities. And she would have been able to get here in time."

My heart lifted. "So what's the bad news?"

"She was murdered last week by a zombie she'd raised from the dead." He raised his hand. "And before you ask, yes, brains were involved."

I sat down on the side of the bed again, heavily enough that the springs creaked, disappointment crashing over me. "Damn."

"We'll figure something else out."

My gaze snapped to his. "I already have: Markus Reed. He can help us."

Thierry's expression tightened. "No, he can't."

A frustrated sound escaped from the back of my throat and I leapt back up to my feet. "So what happens in two days when we can't figure this out on our own and you're stuck without a body forever?" Then something occurred to me, an idea I normally would have dismissed without a second thought. "Wait a minute. Is that what you want? Now that you're free from your bloodlust, do you *want* to stay this way?"

Before he could answer me, a roar filled the air. It came from down the hall.

"Oh, my God. That's Owen!" I ran out of the room.

In our original room, where I'd handcuffed the vampire possessing Thierry's body, things were not looking good. Owen turned his furious gaze on me—his eyes were black and filled with hunger and outrage.

"Let me out of here!" he snarled. "I'm dying of thirst!"

I shot a worried look at Rose. "Run out of garlic?"

The old woman wrung her hands, standing a few feet away from the bed. "I have more. I didn't want to keep giving it to him since I was afraid too much might damage him. I thought I could reason with him."

"Yeah, reason with a thirsty vampire. Good luck with that." I went directly to the minifridge and pulled out a glass container, unscrewed the top, and brought it over to Owen.

"That won't help him for long," Thierry cautioned by the doorway.

"It'll buy a little time." I held the container to Owen's lips. "Drink. This should hit the spot."

He drank. Greedily. Relief filled his black eyes and he literally whimpered.

So much for my ready supply of blood. It wouldn't be long before random necks started to look appealing to me, too. Another of many bridges I'd cross when I had to, even if the trolls beneath them were starting to get bigger and uglier.

"Better?" I asked once he'd drained the container. I winced in sympathy to see that his wrists were chafed from yanking at the silver handcuffs. Even though Thierry's skin healed rapidly, it would still be painful.

"You have to release me," he said pleadingly. "Come on, Sarah. Be a pal."

"Let me think." I tapped my chin, pretending to consider his request. "*No.* You're not going anywhere. In fact, *you're* the one who's going to be a pal and get out of Thierry's body right now."

His brows drew together. "I can't. I tried. Really, I did."

"Yeah, sure you did."

"I did! I can't live like this. I thought I could, but . . ." He cocked his head to the side. "Although, I am feeling *way* better now. That blood really helped. Maybe I'm okay again."

Thierry crossed his arms over his chest. "The hunger will return. If you're not strong enough, it will overwhelm you. And before long you will find a way out of those handcuffs and out of this house and you will cause harm to innocents. Hunger is an incredible motivator."

Owen glared at him. "You are a serious buzz kill—you know that, de Bennicoeur?"

"Does the truth sting, Owen? I know you tend to avoid any pain, seeking only pleasure in life. This must be a severely unpleasant experience for you."

Owen mumbled something then that could not be repeated in polite company.

I had to cringe at the reminder that this was what Thierry dealt with all the time. I looked at him over my shoulder. "How have you handled it, then, if it's so torturous?"

"You've seen for yourself more than once, past and

present, that I, too, weaken when it overwhelms me. I can only imagine how it is for him, one lacking in any discernable personal restraint."

"Sure, keep insulting me, you pompous windbag," Owen grumbled. "Whatever. I'm used to it."

I ignored their squabbling and studied Owen's stolen face. He did not look well at all. This possession wasn't turning out to be the dream come true he'd originally believed it was—a handsome new body he could wear for the rest of eternity. No, Thierry's body came with a warning label: Use at your own risk.

So Owen wasn't staying in the body of his own free will. We had no necromancer to pitch in and help. Thierry would have an incorporeal aneurism if I went against his wishes and contacted Markus or the Ring.

So now what?

"There has to be another way to fix this," I said.

"There is," Rose replied.

I shot a look at her. She'd stood there patiently at Owen's side watching the three of us discuss matters. "What is it? Please, I am *so* open to suggestions at this point, you have no idea."

"Well, I know you wanted to find a necromancer, but that's basically a powerful witch, isn't it? One who specializes in both life and death magic? Therefore, you need to find yourself an alpha witch—one who can do all kinds of magic. Unfortunately, there are none in Salem."

"An excellent suggestion," Thierry said, nodding, "but there are no alpha witches in all of North America. They were destroyed by witch hunters decades ago."

"Wrong, both of you," I whispered. "There is one here."

Owen strained against his handcuffs. "Who?"

I could barely breathe. "Raina Wilkins."

"What?" Rose exclaimed. "But Raina isn't an alpha witch. She's—well, she's a witch, certainly, but not a very powerful one."

"She is. I saw it myself." I quickly explained what I'd seen in the past—of Raina and Malik's illicit romance, and Raina's assistance to the witch hunters, making her an enemy and a traitor to her own kind.

The woman who looked no more than thirty had been alive for well over three hundred years. To me, that screamed alpha witch.

"Impossible," Rose breathed. "Witches are human. They age just as anyone else does."

"Not always," Thierry said. He glanced at me. "I told you that regular vampire blood is potent to some witches' spells, and you saw for yourself the truth of that in the grimoire. Master vampire blood can be used in even more powerful spells, including one for immortality, which has been known to a rare few."

The pieces clicked for me. "David said that a witch imprisoned you, bled you. Was it to do a spell like this?"

His expression shadowed. Another of his closely guarded secrets had been laid bare for me to see. "Yes, among other plans for my blood, she wanted to live forever. However, she didn't succeed."

A shiver went down my spine. David said that Thierry had killed her—*and* her husband.

I studied the face of *my* dangerous husband, equally disturbed by his dark acts as I was by the thought of somebody using his blood for their own gain. How much pain and suffering had he been subjected to in all of his years of life? I wished I could take even a fraction of it away, erase it like those fifty missing years.

"So Raina's found an eternal fountain of youth," I said. "But it's a spell that needs to be maintained, I'm guessing. Not just a one-stop beauty shop."

He nodded. "Correct."

"She could be the reason for the disappearances of those vampires. They were all masters. All to maintain her youth, like walking, talking, fanged Botox."

"It's possible."

"Unbelievable," Rose said, disgusted. "If this is all true, that woman gives a bad name to every witch who's ever existed."

"You're right. Raina Wilkins has basically sold her soul in order to stay young and beautiful forever after helping her witch hunter boyfriend kill others of her kind. She's evil." My breath caught and my gaze flicked to his. "But that evil witch is the only one who can fix you."

Silence fell in the room before Owen began to laugh.

I shot him a look. "What is so funny?"

"Me and Raina had a thing recently."

"A thing?"

"Never knew I was sleeping with an older woman. She sure hid it well. Huh. *That's* what's so funny."

I failed to see the humor in Owen's cougar revelations. I glanced at Thierry, not surprised that he was now glaring at me. "Problem?"

"You're staying away from that woman." He enunciated each word precisely, so there would be no mistaking his meaning.

"So give me another option."

"We'll contact Markus like you suggested."

This time *I* was the one to laugh. "This is the straw that broke the vampire's back, is it? Me seeking out an alpha-witch-slash-murder-suspect is enough for you to agree that Markus is not the worst evil in this equation."

He scrubbed a hand over his forehead, giving me a frustrated look. "I'm trying to find a middle ground here and prevent you from getting yourself killed."

I rolled my eyes. "Honestly, do you really think I'm going to march up to Raina, tell her I know what she really is, and demand that she help us? Hardly. I'm not naive enough to think I'd have a frozen margarita's chance in hell. However . . ." I flicked a look at Rose. "Please keep an eye on Owen."

She nodded. "I'll do my best."

"Sarah!" Owen roared after me as I left the room without a backward glance. "Let me out of these cuffs! Oh, come on! This isn't fair!"

"What are you doing, Sarah?" Thierry was right on my heels.

"Stuff," I replied.

"That's not an answer."

"What does the amulet do?" I asked pointedly.

His jaw tensed. "Stuff."

"Exactly."

Down in the living room, Heather was poring over the grimoire. When she looked up at me, there was relief in her eyes.

"You're better!"

"I'm getting there." The grandfather clock chimed to announce it was six o'clock. I could barely believe it had been only six hours since we'd crashed Raina's book club meeting.

"There's nothing in here," she said, returning her focus to the weathered pages. "I keep reading it, flipping through it, but there is literally nothing else. I can't believe she only has a couple pages of vampire blood magic spells. If there were more—"

"Forget that right now." I sat down next to her on the couch. "I need to find Miranda. I need her address. And do you have any idea where she might be right now other than that karaoke bar?"

She made a face. "Miranda? Why?"

"I have questions for her about her pal Raina. Miranda's part of the coven, but she seemed pretty genuine when I talked to her at Mulligan's last night. I think she might be able to help me."

For a moment, I thought Heather's distaste for the blond witch might keep her from being open to this idea. But instead she closed the grimoire, stood up from the couch, and moved toward the table in the adjoining room where we'd done the séances. I followed, ignoring the glaring master vampire's spirit behind me.

"Sarah, stop this right now."

I didn't even look at him. "No, don't think I will."

Heather grabbed the local newspaper. "This is where pretty much everyone will be this evening."

I glanced down at the headline to see there was a street festival going on. "She'll be here?"

She nodded. "Miranda sells handmade jewelry. She's normally at these events hawking her wares to anyone who likes her glass beads and fake breasts." Her expression soured. "She'll definitely be there."

I scanned the article, noting where it took place—not all that far away from the inn. "What about Raina? Has she been by again?"

"No. It's been really quiet."

"You stole the grimoire of an alpha witch," Thierry said stiffly. "It's hers, not some ancestor's."

I finally glanced at him, bracing myself for a multitude of arguments. "I'm sure you have a point."

"She'll do whatever it takes to get that spell book back."

"I have no doubt she will. Therefore, I need to work fast and get the info I need."

"By questioning Miranda about her coven leader."

"Exactly." I looked up at his face, my chest tense. "So now what? Are you going to try to stop me? Or is this the point when you tell me that you're super-happy being a ghost and you want to stay like this forever?"

He cocked his head. "Do you really think that's a possibility?"

I ignored the lump in my throat. "Well, gee, let me think. You've fought this horrible thirst for six centuries. Now it's gone, you're free, and everything's peachy again. I think there must be a part of you that is relieved right now."

"I won't deny it; there is." Finally, the smallest edge of a smile played at his lips as he studied my face, noting my distress. "But that doesn't mean I've given up this fight. I don't want to stay this way if I can help it. Not being alive, not being able to touch you, to be with you, Sarah . . . it's far worse than any thirst I must deal with."

The tightness finally eased, both in my throat and in my heart. It was a rather huge understatement that his words had given me relief. "Then you're okay with me going to the festival to talk to Miranda alone?"

"Absolutely not." He began to move toward the front door, glancing over his shoulder when I didn't automatically follow. "I'm going with you."

I was at his side a moment later, looking up with surprise into his face—which glowed just a little with ghostly luminescence in the darkening hallway. "You are?"

"Argument?"

"None at all." I grinned. "An excellent idea, I think. You'll be my ghostly sidekick. The Nearly Headless Nick to my Hermione Granger."

He raised an eyebrow. "Are you aware that you reference *Harry Potter* nearly every day?"

I shrugged. "I can't help it. Those books rock."

And I had renewed optimism about our team effort in getting to the truth about Raina and figuring out how to enlist her help—with Miranda's assistance. I was totally open to blackmail if necessary, but I knew I had to play these cards just right. After all, in this town, they weren't playing cards; they were tarot.

"We'll be back as soon as we can," I called over my shoulder to Heather.

"Okay! I'll stay here with Grandma and Owen. Good luck!"

I pushed open the front door and slipped out with Thierry at my side. I made it to the bottom of the porch steps and started toward the sidewalk. "It's only a few blocks away. Ten minutes tops if we hurry."

"Sarah . . ." Thierry's tone made me stop, turn around, and look at him with alarm.

"What's wrong?"

He stood just at the bottom of the steps, holding his hands out in front of him. "A problem, I'm afraid."

It took me a second to realize who he reminded me of, but it was Owen—in *his* body—last night. "Oh, crap. Heather's doggy spell."

He nodded. "It seems that it also affects me. Owen

possesses my body, but the spell believes we are the same person, whether my spirit is separate or not."

Disappointment was like a sucker punch to the gut. "Well, that blows. Can she remove the spell? I mean, Owen's tucked away safely upstairs, and she's got to . . ." I frowned. "Why are you looking at me like that?"

His expression had suddenly grown stricken. "Sarah—"

"Hi, Sarah," Raina said.

I froze and then swiveled slowly on my wedge heels to see the raven-haired witch standing only a couple of yards away. My stomach dropped.

"Raina . . . hey there. How are you doing?"

"Fine, thanks." She gave me a cold smile.

"Gee, I really do appreciate the offer," I began, "but I'm not interested in joining your book club. I'm only passing through Salem, so I can't commit."

"That's too bad." Her eyes flashed red. "We could have had some deep discussions about theme and metaphor."

"Sarah, come back to the house," Thierry growled. "Now."

I couldn't stop looking in the witch's eyes. "I would if I could, Thierry. But—I can't move."

"Make no mistake, witch." Thierry's words were as sharp as blades. "If you do anything to harm her, I will kill you."

She didn't look away from me, or else she'd risk breaking this mojo holding me frozen to the spot. "He sounds like he means it, but in his current state I'd really like to see him try."

I knew this was one of Thierry's worst fears—not that he was afraid of much after his long life of trials and struggle. But he wanted me to be safe, to be happy, and he'd put his own life on the line in order to ensure my continued well-being.

And now he couldn't do anything to save me. He couldn't do anything but watch as the witch reached out to touch my face. The smile on her red lips was the only friendly thing about her. Her gaze held only malice. Only evil.

She patted my cheek. "Sleep now."

I couldn't fight it. I did exactly what she told me to do. I slept, afraid I'd never wake up again.

Chapter 14

Luckily, I did wake up. And when I did, I noticed two very different things.

The first was a headache from hell, reminding me that I'd been magically knocked out by a revenge-seeking witch and now, judging by the dark, dank place where I'd gained consciousness, I seemed to be in serious trouble. Understatement.

The second thing I noticed was a toad. It was staring at me.

I raised my head enough to meet its direct gaze.

"Hey there, Hoppy," I managed in not much more than a hoarse whisper. "Glad to see you're still alive."

Hoppy croaked.

"For now," another voice said.

I swiveled my head in the opposite direction to see Raina standing a half dozen feet away with her arms crossed over her designer blouse. Next to her, looking even less amused, was her second in command from the coven book club, the perky blonde Casey.

So my plan to talk to Miranda, the comparatively "nice" one, who could help ease me into a meeting with the alpha witch and, essentially, make a deal with the devil for a spell to fix Thierry, seemed to have hit a snag. A big one. A big, ugly, warty one.

But I didn't have the luxury of time to panic. I needed to deal with this situation as best I could. Although the "not panicking" thing would take some effort.

"I want my grimoire back," Raina said bluntly.

Stay calm, Sarah.

I exhaled shakily. "So you, what? Kidnapped me and dragged me to your dark, nasty dungeon?" I glanced around uneasily. This place actually *did* look like a dungeon. That really wasn't a good sign.

The witch's eyes sparked with anger. "That book has been around for a very long time."

So had she. But I didn't dare say that out loud. A big part of me wished I'd never seen her cozying up to Malik. I had to fight to keep my disgust off my face.

Instead, I forced a disarming smile. "So why don't we talk about it? I'm finished with it, so let's go ahead and arrange a trade with Heather. No hard feelings. Nothing's been damaged. Release me and Hoppy, and you get your book back. No problem."

Her expression soured, turning her beautiful face momentarily ugly. "Do you even know what kind of magic is contained between those covers?"

Even her voice made me shudder—and not just with fear. This witch had no soul, she'd helped murder her own kind, and she still lived in a big house, with a nice car and a fabulous wardrobe. Karma sure hadn't worked properly for her. Not yet, anyway. "Magic, huh? And here I thought you were all part of a book club and that grimoire was just another book."

"Let's not play games, Sarah," Raina hissed.

"Yeah, no games," Casey agreed.

I flicked a look at Raina's eager sidekick. "Can't really play any games with my hands tied behind my back, can I? Are you admitting you can do magic, Raina?"

Raina's lips thinned. "Perhaps."

Maybe I *did* want to play games after all, but I was going to play very quietly and stealthily to try to eke out some information.

Bottom line, despite this unfortunate situation, I still saw Raina as the only chance I had to get Thierry's spirit back into his body and to end Owen's possession of it. I wasn't happy that I'd run out of choices, but I knew I was rapidly running out of time.

"So what does that mean?" I said, as if completely ignorant and confused by all of this. "You're a . . . witch?"

Her eyes narrowed. "And *you're* a vampire."

Looked like I wasn't nearly as stealthy as I would have liked.

I tried to recover from that surprise blow. Three vampires had disappeared in Salem without a trace. Owen had been murdered remotely by a witch's death spell. The dark-haired witch standing before me was my prime suspect as the resident vampire killer.

And now she knew what I was, too.

"I don't know what you're talking about." Thierry had it wrong. I *could* lie when I had to—when it really mattered. And right now, it *really* did.

"Oh, give me a break!" Casey yanked my hair away from my neck to bare my wound from Owen's bout of bloodlust. "Typical. Vamps love to suck each other's blood. It's so weird." Then she grabbed my lip and pulled it up so she could poke at my teeth. "You have fangs. Don't try to deny you're a bloodsucker. We know exactly what you are. What do you have to say now?"

Say? Nothing.

I bit her. Hard. After all, her finger was in my mouth. She was asking for it.

She yanked her hand back, shocked. "You bitch!"

"Casey," Raina growled. "Leave us. You're not helping matters."

"I'm bleeding!"

"Go get a Band-Aid. It's only a flesh wound."

I glared at Casey. "Is that O-negative? You're lucky that's not my favorite blood type."

"Yeah, more like *you're* the lucky one."

I rolled my eyes. "Good comeback."

She finally left, holding her barely injured hand close to her chest for protection. I glanced at Hoppy, who continued to watch us, as pensively as a toad could, and tried to concentrate on something other than the fleeting taste of blood, which had triggered my thirst. It was nothing like what Thierry had to deal with, but it was enough to distract me.

The door clicked shut behind me. While Casey had been annoying beyond belief, she seemed relatively harmless. At least, next to Raina. Now I was alone with an evil alpha witch who kept herself young and beautiful eternally, thanks to a constant rinse and repeat of vampire blood magic.

There had to be a way for me to turn this around. Either I needed her to help me—which, let's face it, wasn't looking good—or I needed to get out of there so I could call Markus and put my backup plan into action.

"Are you thirsty?" Raina asked. "Has it been a long time since you last fed?"

"I'm okay." I leveled my gaze with hers. "But if you

want to offer yourself up, I prefer a wrist. I mean, I barely know you and I am a bit of a germaphobe."

"Don't worry, it takes a long time for a vampire to starve themselves into a corpse-like state."

I repressed a shudder. So that was what happened if a vampire didn't drink blood? *A corpse-like state?* "You know this from personal experience?"

She absently brushed a bit of lint off her tailored jacket. "Yes. Actually, I do."

Oh boy. Never trust a witch with a medieval dungeon at the ready. Lesson of the millennium.

Her jaw tensed. "What did you want with my grimoire, vampire?"

I shrugged. "I was searching for a spell. Duh."

"What spell?"

"One to help me fix a problem."

She gave me an unpleasant smirk. "A problem with your husband?"

My chest tightened. "I have lots of problems."

Raina walked a slow circle around my chair. I swear the woman was wearing Eau d'Intimidation as a cologne. "Here's what I know about you, Sarah. You're newly married to a master vampire named Thierry de Bennicoeur. He's old. Ancient, in fact. You're clearly not. He's currently cast out of his body, which is why I saw his spirit back at the bed-and-breakfast—and he seems to be trapped there. I don't know much more beyond that. I honestly don't care what happened to him. What I want to know is why you came to Salem in the first place. It's not a popular vacation spot for vampires."

"I'm a huge fan of *Bewitched*." I ignored my racing heart. "Had to come here for my honeymoon. Always been a big dream of mine."

"You're lying." She grabbed my chin and forced me to meet her gaze directly as her eyes shifted to red. "Now tell me the truth."

Just like before, I couldn't seem to look away. A tingling, electric sensation slid down my throat; then my words spilled out before I had a chance to stop them. "Thierry works for the Ring as a consultant, which is another way of saying he's an investigator for them. He was sent here to check out the recent disappearances of three master vampires."

Her eyebrows rose just a little at this, starting with my mention of the Ring. "And what have you discovered?"

"Mostly that I'm pretty sure *you're* the one to blame."

My stomach sank as I listened to the words fly out of my mouth like a swarm of gossipy butterflies.

She cocked her head. "What else are you pretty sure about, vampire?"

I tried to force the words back, but they had minds of their own. "You killed Owen Harper in Heather's driveway, whacking him remotely like a vampire-shaped piñata."

This received no reaction at all, other than a slight tightening of her cheeks. "Sounds like I've been very busy."

She'd put some sort of truth-telling spell on me, but now I struggled with every ounce of my strength against it. It was like trying to move through sticky taffy.

"What else?" Her words were sharp.

"You were Jonathan Malik's lover during the Salem witch trials." Nothing but duct tape over my mouth would have had a chance of stopping this outpouring of the truth. "You helped him hunt the other witches he tortured and killed, you heinous red-eyed bitch."

The moment the words were out, her expression froze

and she staggered back a step, finally breaking eye contact with me.

She wanted the truth—she'd magically forced me to spill all of it against my will.

I'd always known my mouth was going to be the death of me someday. Looked like it was going to be today.

At this point, I pretty much had nothing to lose.

"That's right." I raised my chin and glared at her. Only I wasn't glaring directly into her eyes anymore. That was a danger zone if I wanted to keep from getting bespelled again. I stared at the point between her angry slashes of eyebrows. "You're an alpha witch. And you've kept your collagen levels high for over three hundred years thanks to an immortality spell that uses master vampire blood. I know it. And I'm not the only one who does. If you kill me it won't matter. Your secret doesn't die here."

I waited, holding my breath for her reaction, hoping it wouldn't be: "Well, okay then, smarty-pants. I guess I'll kill you."

"Anyone ever tell you that you talk too much?" she said through clenched teeth.

"Frequently." But I wasn't dead yet. I was taking that as an encouraging sign. "But I just don't get it. Why are you still here? Vampires leave a place before people start to guess they're getting a little long in the fang. Pick up, leave town, start again somewhere new where nobody knows you. But you're still here. Does Casey know? Miranda? They're your covenous trio, right? Does anyone know the truth about who you really are and all the nasty things you're responsible for that didn't quite make it into the history books?"

The fine hair on my arms stood up from her magic. It felt big enough to reach out and grab me by the throat without her making a move toward me. A remote death spell, just like what killed Owen. No need to get her hands dirty.

But Raina didn't unleash her magic. She did the opposite and caged it.

Slowly, the charge subsided. I was able to notice how fast my heart beat and feel the cool slither of perspiration down my back.

"Wait a minute," I said, thinking it through. "It's Malik, isn't it? That's why you stay here in Salem? So you can be close to your old lover's trapped spirit."

Her gaze snapped to mine again. "You know nothing, vampire."

I think I'd found her Achilles' heel—it had a witch hunter–shaped blister on it. "You shouldn't feel too loyal to that guy. After all, he's the one who told me where to find your grimoire."

The crackle of violence, the sheer alpha witch magnitude of her power, slid over my skin. I couldn't help but shudder in fear.

Then she swore under her breath, clenched her fists at her sides, and stormed out of the dungeon, slamming the door behind her.

Finally, I let go of the breath I'd been holding and slumped down in the chair. I didn't know how long I had before she returned, but I had to use that time to figure out how to escape.

I pulled at the ropes and felt the burn of the silver. I forced myself to breathe, to somehow find the strength to ignore the pain long enough to break through the ropes. After all, they weren't handcuffs. Ropes were just ropes, and I did have some extra vampire strength at the ready. It would be five, maybe ten seconds tops of sheer agony, and then . . .

Then I'd pick up my severed hands from the floor and walk out of here with my head held high.

Okay, bad plan.

A few minutes passed and all I heard was the sound of my rapid breathing. If I wasn't careful, I was going to hyperventilate.

"Calm down," I told myself. "All is well. You can figure this out."

"I have no doubt that you can."

A fresh, icy shiver coursed through me at hearing Malik's voice.

The ghost studied me from the far corner of the cavernous but very underdecorated dungeon. His arms were crossed over his chest and his black eyes glittered in the shadows.

I shook off any dread and distaste at seeing him again. "What do you want?"

"That's not very polite, is it?"

"I'm sorry. How are you today, Malik? You're looking rather . . . dead."

His lips stretched. "Have you ever heard the saying about honey and vinegar? Why take such a vinegar-like tone with me? What have I done to deserve this?"

"Do you want a list?"

His smile held. "Do you want my help while the witches have left to run an errand?"

I blinked, surprised he'd even suggest it. "How are you going to help me? Ghosts have no power in the mortal world, even chatty ones like you."

This comment made his smile fade just a little. "Tsk-tsk, Sarah. You aren't doing such a good job with the honey."

"They left? How do you know that?"

"I saw them leave through the front door."

"This is Raina's house?"

"It is."

I took a deep breath and let it out slowly. Malik *had* shown me where to find the grimoire. My disgust over what he'd done in the past clouded my opinion now—I'll admit it. And if Raina and Casey had left the building, I needed to use this opportunity any way I could. "Okay, fine. If you're serious—if you really can help me—then please do. I could use all the help I can get."

He eyed my ropes. "Raina brought you here."

"Your girlfriend is a problem."

His expression darkened. "You know about us."

I glanced back at the locked door, fearful that it was going to open at any second. "I know what you did, Malik. I know you hurt a lot of people—with Raina's help. That's why you're trapped here now, right? One of those witches you murdered managed to trap your spirit here to punish you."

He didn't speak for a moment. "You're right. This is a punishment. One I entirely deserve. I am responsible for everything you believe I am. And I regret it to my very soul."

Okay. *This* I didn't expect. "You regret what you did? Seriously?"

"I can't change what has happened. I am trapped here, forever reliving my dark decisions, but I believed what I did was right. I see now that witches come in many different forms—both evil and good. Just as vampires do. I truly believed I was helping humanity. But I wasn't. I was ignorantly harming innocent people I assumed were demons. I harmed them with Raina's help. Unfortunately, there's nothing I can do now to make amends."

It couldn't be possible. Was he being serious? He existed with regret, having enough time as a ghost to see the wrong in what he'd done.

He was just like Thierry. Thierry had also been responsible for his share of darkness, but now I knew that time had made him into a different man entirely from the one I'd met in the past.

Three hundred years was a very long time. Maybe it was enough to change someone from evil to good.

I shook my head. "I don't know what to say."

"I don't expect you to say anything. I'm not asking for forgiveness. I know I'll never get it from anyone." He glanced toward the door. "I don't have much time. She doesn't want me in her house—I can't stay here for more than a few minutes before I'm cast back into the spirit world. I remind her of what she's done. And who she was. She's evil—one of the witches who should have been executed. Instead, she directed me toward the others, the good ones who didn't deserve death. She used me to gain more power through the blood of fallen witches." His voice broke. "I loved her and she betrayed me. She was not the woman I believed her to be. She must be stopped."

A shudder of fear and revulsion went through me. "How do I stop her?"

He looked down at his hands to see he'd started to fade. "Damn it." His gaze shot to mine. "You must free yourself and disable Raina tonight, any way you can. Tonight is very important for me, and she can't try to stop me. There's no other—"

And then he was gone. Vanished. As if he was never there to begin with.

I stared at the spot where he'd been standing, my mind reeling from what he'd told me.

Or, rather, what he'd all but confirmed for me.

Raina Wilkins was an evil witch. One I was 99.9 percent certain was responsible for at least four vampires recently going the way of the dodo here in Salem.

And I was currently at her mercy.

Chapter 15

Malik had left me with an encyclopedia full of information to consider. But I didn't have time to contemplate his regret over his past actions, compare his path to Thierry's, or consider where Raina and Casey had gone and what torture device they were going to bring back. Bottom line, redemptive ghost or not, I was still tied up in the dungeon of despair, and at this rate I wasn't going anywhere unless I went back to the "severed hands" plan.

I sent a bleak look toward Hoppy. "I'm going to die here, you know. And so are you."

Hoppy croaked mournfully.

"Yeah," I said under my breath. "Exactly what I was thinking. But how about a little less croaking and a little more help?"

It wasn't bright down here, so I figured my eyes were playing tricks on me when, a moment later, Hoppy suddenly seemed bigger. Just a little.

Then a little more.

The next croak he let out was deeper, louder.

"What are you doing?" I asked uneasily. "Are you going to explode? Please don't be an exploding toad."

He didn't explode. But he was still . . . changing.

Or, really, I guess a better word would be "shifting."

Shape-shifting.

My eyes widened. "Oh, you have got to be kidding me."

Hoppy grew larger and larger, his form turning less toad, more something else. Something taller and broader. His brownish green mottled skin became less mottled and much less green. And there was a lot of it.

Shoulders, arms, a torso, legs, and feet.

Human form. Hoppy had *human form* now. Six feet tall, well built, broad shouldered, dark haired—very attractive for someone who'd been a palm-sized amphibian two minutes ago. Tall, dark, and handsome for sure. Less toad and way more . . . Toad Prince.

Did I happen to mention he was totally naked?

Hoppy gave me a sheepish look while strategically shielding part of his body with his hands. "Right. So . . . you probably have some questions for me, huh?"

My mouth was open so wide by now that my fangs had dried out. "You're . . . you're a—a *weretoad*?"

"I'm not a weretoad," he said, as if insulted by the suggestion. "I'm a shape-shifter. We can change into lots of different animals."

I blinked. "And you chose a toad?"

"Yeah. This time." He gave me a distraught look. "I only changed so I could help save you, so please spare me the judgment."

I could barely form words. I literally shook my head to try to clear it. "Save me. Yes, excellent plan, um, naked toad shifter man. Ropes?"

"I'm on it." He scrambled to untie the tight knots holding my hands behind me. Finally, the painful silver-infused ropes fell away.

"Thank you . . . Hoppy." I averted my gaze so I

wouldn't get too much of the floor show when he moved into my view again.

"The name's actually Todd."

"Todd," I repeated.

"That's right."

Todd the toad. *Okay.*

I swallowed hard. "Does Heather know?"

He didn't reply to this.

"Does she?" I said it louder as I shakily got up from the chair I'd been stuck in for far too long. I needed to get the H-E-double-hockey-stakes out of here.

"No, and I'd really, really prefer that she doesn't find out." His hands currently were doing a great and much appreciated impression of a fig leaf. He cringed at my sharp look. "It's not as creepy as you might think. Heather—she needs my protection. That vampire she had the hots for was big trouble."

"You mean the dead one."

"Yeah, him. He's still trouble."

I couldn't argue with him there. "If you wanted to protect Heather, then you could have shifted into a Rottweiler. Or a grizzly bear. Or a sharp-horned unicorn."

He shrugged. "She found me when I was a toad. I didn't have much of a choice. It happened. And"—he swore under his breath—"now it's over."

"And you sacrificed this . . . this—whatever it is you think you have with Heather—all to save me."

"Yeah, well, if those witches come back, I'll be sacrificing a lot more. So let's get out of here."

An excellent suggestion.

I swiftly moved to the door and tried the handle, but it was locked. Not a huge surprise.

"Stand back," I said, giving him a sidelong glance.

"Don't want any splinters to, um . . . well, just stand back. You're vulnerable right now."

He did as I asked without comment.

I focused myself, tapping into more of my vampire strength, and kicked the door as hard as I could. It splintered and flew open on the very first try.

It was the second door of Raina's I'd broken today. I might have to start running a tab. However, since she'd kidnapped me and tied me up in her dungeon, I currently considered us even.

The dungeon was in the basement of Raina's house. I raced up the flight of stairs, found another door, which happily wasn't locked, and we were suddenly in the kitchen. Todd grabbed a dish towel from its holder next to the stove to semicover his nakedness. The next room was the living room, where the coven's book club meeting had been held.

Todd followed me, his bare feet squeaking on the hardwood floors.

I quickly got to the front door, peeking outside before I let myself out. It was definitely unlocked, hanging on its hinges from earlier. I eyed Todd as he also emerged onto the porch. "You need clothes."

He looked around nervously. "I know you think I'm some sort of weirdo, hiding out in Heather's home, Sarah, but you don't understand why I do this for Heather."

"So tell me." I glanced over my shoulder with surprise as I left the porch and hit the sidewalk. The evening air was cool, the skies darkening. Streetlamps flickered on all along the street. Freedom felt fan-frigging-tastic.

His breath hitched. "I love her."

"You love her?"

He nodded. "We were involved—I thought we had something really special. But then two months ago she broke things off. She couldn't let herself be with me since she was too busy imagining herself in love with that loser."

Aha, so *this* was Heather's ex she'd mentioned in passing, the one who'd left Salem without saying anything. "But little does she know, you never went anywhere."

"No, I didn't." He cringed as he kept pace with me. "And it's not just that vampire. I need to watch over her because of her magic. You've seen what it does to her—those nosebleeds. That's not normal, Sarah. Something is wrong with her."

Concern spiked inside me. "What's wrong? Do you know?"

He shook his head. "That's what I've been trying to figure out."

A passing car beeped at the sight of a half-naked man walking along the sidewalk. To Todd's credit, he didn't move his tiny dish towel and give anyone the full monty. "Damn it. I need clothes. I'll catch up with you in a minute."

The next moment, he ducked through a fence into a backyard.

I didn't wait. I had to get back to the inn and get my hands on a phone so I could call Markus. I had to get Thierry back in his regular body. And then the two of us had to escape from this dangerous, witch-filled town as soon as vampirically possible.

Still having trouble believing I'd managed to escape Raina's dungeon without too much opposition, I got two blocks from the witch's house before I saw a huge crowd ahead. It took me only a second to realize it was the street festival—my original destination, but now the last thing I needed. However, unless I took a time-consuming detour, the best way would be to go straight through it on my way back to the Booberry Inn.

The festival had closed off an entire tree-lined street, and there were at least a hundred booths offering everything from palm readings to used books to portraits and caricatures done on the spot to homemade perfumes. There were also costumes to buy for the thousand-plus attendees, everything from cloaks to capes to pointy witches' hats. The scent of hot dogs and other street food wafted through the air.

For a moment, I paused at a booth that sold reproductions of old portraits of former Salem residents. One was of Jonathan Malik himself—no doubt about it. I stared into his dark eyes for a moment, transfixed, comparing what he'd told me about his past to what I knew about Thierry's. Were they really similar?

I wished I knew what to believe. He'd asked me to disable Raina any way I could. Disable her? Did she plan on stopping him from doing something? Contacting someone? Ending her quiet but steady reign of terror here, right under the noses of the general public, which had no idea there was an alpha witch in town?

It didn't make any sense. And knowing that alpha witch had it in for me kept me from lingering very long.

"Thirty dollars and I'll throw in the frame," the man in the booth said. "Handsome guy, isn't he? They say his ghost haunts this town to this very day. It's my most popular print. The ladies think he has that mysterious quality—a dangerous edge."

"He definitely has that." I grimaced, turning away from the booth. "But no, thanks. I have to go."

But then, as I started to swiftly walk away, I saw her. And she saw me.

"Sarah!" Miranda waved at me and my footsteps slowed. The blonde wore a low-cut, tight red dress, which, just as Heather had suggested earlier, did show off both her beaded necklace and her breast implants to their full advantage. Standing next to her was Hoppy. Or, rather, Todd. He'd made it here fast. Or maybe I'd been staring at that portrait of Malik for longer than I realized.

Todd had managed to find something to wear very quickly, although it wasn't what I would have expected.

"Nice kilt," I told him.

The shifter was wearing a Scottish tartan kilt that came a few inches above his knees. And, well, nothing else.

Oddly enough, with the other costumed people milling about the crowded festival, he didn't look entirely out of place.

"You two know each other?" I asked.

"Oh, yeah," Miranda said, putting a hand on Todd's muscular biceps. "We go way back." She cocked her head, studying me. "Everything okay with you?"

I considered my words before they left my mouth. My original plan had been to come here and find Miranda, to gauge if she might be willing to give me more information about Raina that could somehow secure the powerful witch's help. Well, here I was—and maybe *I* was now the one with the useful information. If I revealed the truth about Raina, Miranda might be able to help stop the witch from hurting anyone else. But I knew I had to be careful.

I flicked a glance at Todd, who seemed relaxed and totally at ease. He grinned at me. Not sure this was a grinning situation, but I'd take it as a good sign.

"I need your help," I said to her.

Miranda's brows went up. "My help? With what?"

I wrung my hands. "I'm in trouble. It's Raina."

"What has she done now?"

I hesitated only a moment. "She wants to kill me."

Her eyes widened. "Kill you? But why?"

"I stole her grimoire. And I . . . well, I've found out some disturbing things about her."

She didn't speak for a moment. "Like . . . what kinds of things?"

Todd didn't give me any indication that I should hold my tongue, so I didn't. "Do you know how old she is?"

Miranda's brows drew together. "She's forty, isn't she? She says she's thirty, but I just *know* she's had work done."

This chick was as clueless about the real Raina as I thought. "Try more like three hundred and forty and you might be in the right ballpark."

She stared at me. "What?"

"She's an alpha witch. She uses vampire blood to stay young, stay immortal. I think she's behind the recent disappearances of three master vampires here in Salem."

Todd let out a low croak.

"Frog caught in your throat?" I asked him. "Or is it a toad?"

He just kept smiling at me. But there was something in his eyes . . .

They *weren't* smiling.

"Tell me more about Raina," Miranda insisted. "And these vampires. Are you seriously saying that vampire blood has some sort of magical power?"

What was that old saying? Out of the basement dungeon and into the boiling cauldron?

Damn it. I knew that escape had been far too easy.

Miranda was no ignorant coven member. Her green eyes glittered with knowledge, with pointed curiosity. But they weren't filled with innocence and shock.

Crystal balls that revealed the hidden truth, eyes were. Had to remember my own metaphor. It would help a lot.

I swallowed hard. "Oh, I don't know. It's just a theory—a silly theory. I'm sure Raina isn't killing vampires and draining their blood. Wacky, right?"

"Killing them? That's does sound extremely wacky."

I shrugged a shoulder. "Come to think of it, I'm probably completely wrong. Witches aren't immortal. And that hocus-pocus stuff that could help someone become immortal—I know it's not real."

Miranda's expression became grave. "I think I might be able to help you. You were right to come to me. Hang on a sec."

She turned away toward her jewelry stall.

I looked at Todd and tried to communicate with him, searching his frozen face. *What's wrong with you? Are you okay?*

His brows moved closer together, his eyes strained, a direct opposite of that happy perma-smile his mouth was in. *No,* he seemed to be trying to convey. *I'm not okay in the slightest.*

"Here it is," Miranda said.

I turned to face her uneasily. "Here what is?"

"The best way to deal with a vampire."

In her right hand she clutched a carved wooden stake with a razor-sharp point.

I only had enough time to register what it was. Before I could say anything, turn away, or run, she arched it toward my chest—

And sank it straight into my heart.

Chapter 16

So this was how it would end for me. Staked in the middle of a street festival by a crazy bimbo witch in a red dress.

Not too many of the wide variety of vampire myths were true, but three definitely were: (1) We needed to drink blood to survive, (2) we didn't have a reflection in a regular mirror, and (3) getting a wooden stake plunged into our hearts meant certain death.

She hadn't missed.

White-hot pain blinded me. I staggered back from her and looked down at the weapon sticking out of my chest. With a cry, I curled my hand around the base of the stake and tried to pull it out but failed.

I fell to my knees.

No one seemed to notice. The crowd of people milling around the festival walked past Miranda's beaded jewelry stall as if we weren't even there, which told me she'd cloaked it with magic. Only Todd stared at me with horror, while that eerie, bespelled smile remained frozen on his lips. It was the clarity of that expression—that sheer shock and panic in his eyes—that finally won me over to his side. He wasn't just a creepy shape-shifter who'd been secretly stalking his ex-girlfriend as an innocent-looking toad. He was a good guy down deep. He cared whether I lived or died.

That made two of us.

"Should have minded your own business, vampire," Miranda said, wiping her hands on the front of her dress. She moved toward me, pushed my hands out of the way, and yanked the stake back out, letting it clatter to the ground. I screamed and pressed my hands against the wound. The world around me began to grow dim and fuzzy at the edges as the remaining moments of my existence literally bled away.

My life flashed before my eyes—preschool, high school, a year of university, my failed attempt at becoming an actress, my working years, roommates from hell, dates from hell, waking up in a shallow grave with blood on my throat, being chased by vampire hunters, finding Thierry, falling headfirst in love and never looking back . . .

All of it gone like sand through my fingers.

I gasped. "Why?"

"Why?" Miranda glared at me. "Because you know too much. I saw what Raina did with other vampires. With Owen. She drains their blood and she recites a secret spell. I worked that spell for myself. I'll be young and beautiful forever."

A coldness swept over me. I thought it was coming from the inside, my body dying. But no. It came from the *outside.* My breath formed frozen clouds as if this were the dead of winter, not the middle of June.

An arctic wind swept through the street festival, but nobody else seemed to notice. It took me only a moment to see where it came from.

Raina was swiftly walking toward us, her eyes red. Her long dark hair swept back from her face and the black cloak she now wore swirled around her calves from this strange, unnatural wind. Magic crackled through the air and skittered up my arms.

She thrust her hand out toward me, and that icy sensation wrapped itself tighter around my chest in a viselike grip. I couldn't breathe.

She was helping Miranda kill me so no one would learn their dark secrets.

And yet, I wasn't dead yet. And with a deep stake wound through my heart, I knew I should have been.

My heart had stopped beating completely, but I was still conscious. Raina had frozen me in this state, in the exact moment before death would have snatched me away. But why?

"Raina." Miranda cleared her throat nervously. "What are you doing here?"

"Why don't I ask you the same question?" Raina's words were cool and crisp. "What are you doing, Miranda?"

"Taking care of a problem."

"In public?"

"No one can see."

"I thought we discussed this before. We don't perform magic out in the open. Period."

"Yeah, well." Miranda gulped. "It's fine. Everything's fine."

"No, I don't think it is." Raina captured Miranda's gaze in hers. "Tell me the truth—why have you killed this vampire?"

Killed. Not "tried to kill." *Killed.* Past tense.

Raina might have pressed the pause button, but it was all over for me.

"She knows." Miranda's voice sounded strangled, as if she was fighting the truth-telling spell with every ounce of strength she had. "About the vampires you bled. That *I* bled."

"You've been bleeding vampires, Miranda? Why?"

"I saw you do the spell. Every six months you find a vampire, you take their blood, you work your spell. You even did it with Owen—and you slept with him, too."

This took Raina by surprise; I could see it on her face. "Jealous, Miranda? I know you thought he was yours for a brief time. Owen wasn't anyone's."

"I don't want Owen anymore. He's nothing to me. But I want so much more. I want what you have. Your power."

Raina laughed at this coldly. "So you watched me do my spell. And you tried to emulate it."

"I did better than try. It worked. I'm immortal, just like you."

Raina swept her gaze over the woman. "You fool with power much stronger than you can handle."

"I can handle it fine."

"What about the vampires you bled? What did you do with them when you were done?"

Miranda pressed her lips together, her body visibly shaking with the effort she expended trying to fight the truth-telling spell.

My eyes widened. "You killed them, didn't you?" My words came out quiet and raspy but audible. "You bled them and then you killed them when you were done."

Miranda flicked a glance at me. "I dated a vampire hunter once. He explained to me why a vampire's life is worthless. I needed a lot of blood. It took me forever to get the wording right from the notes I made. But the trial and error was all worth it."

Raina's face was strained. "You would kill to remain young?"

The other witch gave her a withering look. "You bleed vampires to stay alive, stay young. Why can't I be as vain as you are?"

Raina's eyes flashed. "What I do has nothing to do with vanity, you pathetic fool. And to think, I believed you were a friend."

"We were never friends. You only want obedient minions, like Casey, who hang on your every word and follow after you like trained puppies. She's weak and pathetic, can't do any magic at all. I had to get everything I have the hard way. Nobody's ever helped me!"

Then Miranda wrenched her gaze away from the other witch, gasping in pain as if it caused her agony to break the spell. Raina came toward her and gripped her throat. Her lips curled back from her clenched teeth.

"You would sacrifice your soul for beauty and the love of worthless men who will still throw you away like garbage, you ignorant, vain child."

Miranda couldn't break away from Raina's grip on her. The crackle of magic only increased. Her eyes also shifted to red, and she grabbed hold of Raina's cloak.

"I only do what I have to do. And I only kill who I have to kill. It'll be better when you're gone, Raina. Not everyone should get the chance to live forever."

She reached a hand toward the bloody wooden stake she'd used on me, and it flew from the ground into her grip. Without hesitation, she stabbed it upward into Raina's stomach.

There was a boom of thunder in an otherwise cloudless evening sky. Dozens of festival attendees in my peripheral vision jolted in surprise at the sound and looked up as if expecting to see a storm had suddenly gathered.

My attention returned to the witches as Miranda slowly collapsed to the ground, her head lolling to the side, her eyes opened and glazed.

Raina's eyes weren't red anymore; they were *black*. Her hands were clenched into fists at her sides; her breath came in short, frantic gasps. She wasn't dead. Wasn't stabbed.

I thought Miranda had her. But it was the other way around.

She'd killed Miranda with magic—black magic. *Death* magic.

It had turned Raina's eyes as black as a hungry vampire's. Slowly, they shifted back to red.

More eyeball truth to prove my theory.

Todd drew in a ragged breath as the spell that had held him in place finally broke. He was at my side an instant later. His hands trembled as he touched my arms. "Sarah! I'm sorry. I saw her and she saw me. It's like she just knew. I couldn't warn you to stay away."

Still, no one paid any attention to us, their gazes moving over the witch's stall as if they saw nothing out of the ordinary here. If the spells Miranda cast had disappeared when she died, then Raina must now be keeping us hidden from the crowd with her own magic.

I held my hand tight against the mortal wound in my chest. The coldness drew back and then numbness began to creep over me. I'd rather feel pain, since I knew what the numbness meant. My heart remained silent, unbeating.

My mouth was dry. "Please, Todd . . . tell Thierry that I'm sorry." Thierry was going to be so mad at me that I'd let this happen, that I'd leave him after I'd only just promised to be with him forever. "Tell him I'm sorry I couldn't stay out of trouble and . . . and that I love him so much, more than anything else in the whole world. That I'll *always* love him."

He nodded, his eyes glossy. "I'll tell him. I promise."

Raina sighed. "How sweet. Her last words are that of love for her darling husband."

I had just enough life left in me to shoot her a dirty look. "Go to hell, you evil witch."

"Not today, vampire." She sank down to her knees so she faced me and pushed Todd out of the way. "I don't do much magic these days—beyond the immortality spell—because it makes me want to do more. It's like a drug addiction, the worst kind you could possibly imagine. And yet, here we are."

Raina bled vampires, killed vampires, all so she could stay young. Miranda had learned everything from her. Just because she'd eliminated the competition didn't mean anything had changed.

She swept her gaze over me. "Hold still, vampire."

"Don't touch me."

But she didn't listen. Raina pressed her palms against my chest and began to whisper words under her breath, words I didn't understand, in some language that felt more ancient than Latin. What was she doing? Punishing me for escaping from her dungeon? Prolonging my death so she could toy with me, taunt me, tell me how amazingly I'd failed?

The crackle of energy charged the air again, this time entering me. It tingled as it slid up my limbs, joining together in the core of my chest—my heart.

Slowly, very slowly, the pain faded. The scary, creeping numbness withdrew like movie vampires seeking shadowy safety as the morning sun rose.

The evil alpha witch wasn't trying to hurt me. She was *healing* me.

Finally, it was done. She pulled her hands away. Todd had been trying to wrench the witch away from me but wasn't having very much luck, even though he outweighed her by at least sixty pounds.

Raina sent a glare in his direction. "I wasn't harming her."

He looked confused. "Sarah?"

I touched my chest, then looked under the edge of my now bloody T-shirt, which had a stake sized hole in it. My skin had healed. It was as if I'd never been staked.

I'd been milliseconds away from death. I'd been staked through the heart, but I was still alive. And other than the destroyed shirt, there was no evidence that anything bad had happened to me.

But Raina was an evil witch who killed vampires, had helped Malik kill her own kind in the past. Why would she do this?

I stared at her with wide eyes. "You saved my life."

She shrugged.

"I didn't know witches could heal."

"It drains our own life energy and can potentially kill the witch herself. Luckily for both of us, I have plenty of life to go around."

"So the vampires you've killed in the past to do your immortality spell have contributed to my continued breathing." The words felt bitter leaving my mouth.

She sighed. "You believe that, don't you? That I killed vampires, just as Miranda has done."

"Do you really care what I believe?" I looked away, toward the happy crowd of ice-cream-eating, hotdog-munching, oblivious humans who didn't see the dead body and the literally bloody vampire only a few yards away from the festivities.

"Not particularly. However, you should know that I am a much more accomplished witch than Miranda ever could have dreamed of being. Yes, I bleed master vampires to use their blood in my magic; I won't deny it. But then I usually make them forget it ever happened. Miranda couldn't do that, so she had to kill them."

My gaze snapped to hers for a split second before I shifted my eyes away. I didn't trust her enough to let her have the chance to enchant me again. "How can I possibly know if that's the truth?"

"You can't. But it is. These vampires you've been searching for here in Salem—they're gone. Miranda killed them. Master vampires don't leave evidence behind that can't be mopped up. So there's no proof either way, only my word. I know you won't believe it, but remember, I just saved your life. I didn't have to do that, did I?"

Todd nodded. "She does have a point."

He offered me a hand and helped me up from the ground. I rubbed my chest. I'd been literally a moment from death, and I couldn't just snap back from that like it was nothing and start making amusing, sarcastic comments.

But I was alive. And I had an alpha witch to thank for it.

My legs were as shaky as my thoughts. It all didn't click for me, not yet. But I desperately wanted it to.

"I saw you with Malik. I know you loved him. Enough that you helped him hunt and kill witches during the trials."

Her brows drew together. "You saw—" Then clarity and an edge of anger entered her gaze. "My grimoire. You did a spell from it to see into the past. Do you know how dangerous that was? You could have been trapped there forever."

"But I wasn't." She could kill both me and Todd with one of those well-placed thunderbolts. I had to be very careful if I still wanted us to leave this festival intact.

"Trapped where?" Todd frowned. "What are you talking about?"

"A spell, one passed down to me through generations." She hissed out a breath. "I hid that grimoire to keep its dangers out of the hands of those too foolish to understand its power. Nobody knew where it was. Nobody except Malik." Her words cut off and her jaw tensed. "And he showed you where to find it."

"He feels bad about what happened, what he did. It's been three hundred years, him trapped here in Salem, and now he knows that what he did was wrong. That not all witches are evil. He wanted to help me."

She stared for a moment longer before she laughed. "Oh, Sarah. You are not the first to be taken in by the words that come out of that bastard's mouth. Is it because he reminds you a little of your husband? A man who has changed with time, who's become better, not worse, as the years have passed?"

I flinched at the possibility I'd been manipulated. I hadn't totally believed Malik, but I was open to the concept. I liked the idea of redemption. Then again, my Achilles' heel *was* the fact that I trusted too easily, especially handsome men with dark pasts.

"The ghost *sounded* sincere," Todd cut through the silence between us. "I mean, *I* believed him, too."

Raina groaned. "So let's get this straight. You think I'm one of the bad guys because I'm a witch, and he's the potential hero because he says he's sorry for a few mistakes he's made. Fabulous. I hate this town."

I exchanged a look with Todd while I tried very hard to ignore Miranda's body. It was not curling up on itself and disappearing like the wicked witch in *The Wizard of Oz*.

Raina caught my glance. "I'll take care of the body in a minute."

"You do both murder and cleanup. Handy." I exhaled shakily. "Look, I'm not going to debate this any longer. You saved my life. Thank you for that, seriously. I owe you one. But I need to go now. I need to get back to Thierry so he doesn't fret. The man is a major fretter."

I turned away, but she grabbed my arm. I spun back around, alarmed that her grip was even stronger than I expected.

Her eyes were red again. My newly healed heart leapt into my throat.

"What are you doing to her now?" Todd demanded.

She shot him a dark look. "Stay where you are or you'll regret it, toad."

There was suddenly a dagger in her other hand. For a moment, I thought she'd stab me, but instead she sliced it across her forearm. Blood welled up.

"Get away from me!" I tried to pull away from her, but I couldn't quite manage it.

Using the blood, she began to write on my arm.

"You won't believe my words," she said, "so you must see for yourself."

Finally she released me. I wiped her blood off my arm, both disgusted by what she'd done and disgusted with myself for letting it trigger my thirst like she'd just waved a can of salmon under a kitten's nose.

"You need to stay away from—" I didn't get any

further before a dark whirlwind swirled all around me, and the next moment the street festival, Raina, and Todd vanished before my eyes.

I blinked a few times before I realized what she'd done.

I'd been sent back in time. *Again.*

Chapter 17

It had been a hell of a day. Breaking and entering, spell casting, time traveling, kidnapping, getting killed, and now back to time traveling.

I seriously needed a nap.

But here I was, back in Pilgrim times. The town looked just as it had before. It was night. There was a small crowd of people milling about near the church. Another gathering clustered around the town hall.

I couldn't tell if it was the same day I'd been here last time, or a month, a year, a decade later. Now there was a chill in the air and the sky was dark, but the stars and moon were bright enough to light the area enough to see well enough with my vampire eyes.

When Heather had done the spell, it hadn't been perfectly precise. She was an amateur, one who didn't have very much magic inside her. I knew I was lucky to have found Thierry at all when I searched the town.

Raina was different—and this was *her* spell. An alpha witch had alpha control. She knew where she'd wanted to send me and had delivered me to that exact spot and that exact moment.

I knew this because only seconds after my arrival I saw her.

Raina zipped past me, seemingly in a major hurry to get somewhere. Or to *escape* from someone.

Then I saw him. Malik trailed closely behind her.

I followed both of them swiftly. Nobody could see me. Nobody could hear me. But I could see and hear just fine.

Raina knew I wouldn't believe anything she said—I needed proof. So here was history in the making, right in front of me. Fair enough. I would be an observant observer. All I lacked was some popcorn for the show. Still, part of me was afraid of what might happen next. What I might see.

"Stop," Malik growled after her.

She ignored him and kept walking, nearly running, until she'd left the main part of town and was near the forest, wild and dark. It was somewhere that didn't look safe for a woman on her own, even one able to wield powerful magic.

He finally grabbed hold of her and wrenched her to a stop. "Why are you leaving me?"

Her eyes flashed. "It's over, Malik. I can't be with you anymore."

"I won't let you leave me."

Tears streaked down her cheeks. "You killed them. Without a moment of kindness, without listening to them beg you to spare their lives. Even those not officially on trial . . . now gone, and no one will ever know where they disappeared."

"You were on my side."

"I came to my senses. I was blinded—"

"Because you love me."

A sob caught in her throat. "How can I love someone who enjoys causing such pain to those who don't deserve it? Please, let me go. I want to forget."

He didn't let go of her. Instead, he shook her. "No, you're too powerful. I still need you."

"Why?"

"You must teach me your magic and help me become what you are. So I can be immortal—so we can be together forever."

She gaped at him, her lovely but strained face lit only by the moonlight. "You would destroy the lives of witches only to try to become one yourself?"

"It's different."

"I can't teach you witchcraft. Such magic is born within us."

"Don't lie to me. You can do a spell to give me power—I know you can."

She turned her face away, her expression anguished. "I won't."

He grabbed her wrist. "Don't you want to be with me?"

"Once I did. No longer. It's over between us, Malik. Forever."

"It will never be over between us. Do you think that a passion such as we have shared can be forgotten, even in death? I won't let it and I won't let you leave me. You said you'd be mine forever, and that's exactly what you'll be."

She shook her head. "Let me go. Please."

"Never." His eyes were filled with anger, with fury, but also with pain, as if the thought that she'd run from him was something he'd never considered before. "Do you really think me a monster, my love?"

"Yes." She said it quietly.

His handsome face hardened. "So be it. Then be a monster with me. We could be so powerful together if we face our true natures. If you truly give in to your magic, we could be omnipotent."

"I thought you said you loved me."

"I do."

"If you loved me as I love you, you would not wish to use me in this way."

His brows drew together as if he didn't understand.

I watched all of this, barely breathing. Raina wanted to show me that she'd chosen to turn away from the evil she'd done because she regretted it bitterly. But Malik didn't see that it *was* evil. Either that, or he didn't care.

"I'm leaving and you can't stop me," she said evenly.

"Wrong. I can. And I will." He grabbed hold of her throat and shoved her up against a tree. Any emotion left his dark eyes, making them cold and hard. I imagined it was the same chilling look he got when he killed an accused witch. "If you insist on turning your back on me, I'll find another. There will always be a beautiful young witch who'll do as I ask. But I wanted it to be you. Remember that, Raina."

He squeezed tight enough that her eyes began to bulge.

I wanted to do something, say something, scream something to stop this, but it was impossible and there was no one nearby for me to possess even if I had half a chance to stop him.

She gasped as her face began to turn purple, and then grasped hold of his wrists. Her gaze sought his and held—then turned red. The next moment electricity charged the air and he flew back from her, losing his footing and falling hard to the muddy ground.

He looked at his hands, which had nearly killed a woman he claimed to love. "Change your mind, Raina. There's still time. It doesn't have to end like this."

"Wrong." The word was nothing more than a soft gasp. "It does."

"So be it." Malik leapt to his feet and charged her again, his expression fierce and determined.

And then I heard a sound I remembered all too clearly: an echoing boom that could be mistaken for thunder or a cannon.

It was neither.

Malik's eyes grew wide. Then he fell to his knees before collapsing completely to the ground.

Raina let out a wail and dropped at his side. She touched his face.

"I'm sorry, my love," she said over and over again. "I'm so sorry. I should have done this months ago to stop you, but I couldn't bring myself to lose you. I won't lose you. No matter what, I'll honor our promise. We'll still be together forever."

She pressed her hands against his chest and began to speak in that strange, ancient language, the one she'd used to heal me. For a moment I thought she was healing him, too, and bringing him back to life like a necromancer could.

But that wasn't her goal.

Malik's spirit now stood nearby, watching her with confusion. "What have you done, Raina?"

She finally tore her gaze away from the man on the ground to look at the ghost before her.

"I've bound your spirit to this town. To me." Her eyes were black—just as they'd been when she'd killed Miranda. Slowly they shifted back to red.

Malik didn't look horrified by this; he looked awed. "You're even more powerful than I thought you were. Resurrect me. There's still time."

She turned away from him and began to dig into the ground with her bare hands.

He watched her with growing horror. "Raina! Do as I say!"

"I'll bury you here," she whispered. "You're dead, Malik. You'll never hurt anyone else. I won't let you."

He stood there in impotent fury, his hands clenched into fists at his sides. "So you curse me to haunt this town. For how long?"

"Forever."

"Why?" he demanded. "Why would you do this to me?"

She looked up, her hands coated in mud and dirt from the shallow grave. Tears streaked down her cheeks. "Because I love you."

At that moment, the dark whirlwind swirled around me, obliterating my view, and spun me back to the present.

I found that I was now seated on the ground, with Todd crouched in front of me.

"Hey," he said, relieved. "You finally snapped out of your daze."

"Snapped out of my daze, traveled through time. Same diff." I didn't pause too long to nurse my spinning head. I immediately jumped back up to my feet, then checked myself. I felt okay. Last time at Heather's house I'd passed out, but I didn't think that was going to happen again. Different witch, different results.

I slowly looked toward Raina, where she stood with her arms crossed over her chest. Miranda's body was gone without a trace.

"Did you see?" the witch asked, her expression solemn.

I nodded. "You're the one who trapped his spirit here in Salem for all these years. I don't understand why, though."

"If I'd let his spirit free, he would have gone to Hell for his deeds. I—saved him from that because . . . despite everything, I did love him. Part of me still does." Her expression tensed. "It's punishment enough for both of us. I can't leave. My magic is what sustains his curse."

"For three centuries."

"Yes."

I regarded this woman now with more wariness than when I thought she was totally evil. Evil was way simpler than what she'd done. "You're incredibly powerful."

"I am. My magic was strong from the very beginning. It's what makes me, as you say, *alpha*. Only an alpha witch has the ability to do that time travel spell."

I blinked. "Heather could do it."

"Then Heather is also an alpha witch," Raina said.

Todd stared at her in disbelief. Behind him walked an oblivious family of four, carrying helium balloons imprinted with black cats and friendly-looking ghosts. "She's not. She can't be. I mean, she's always had *some* magic, but it's not very much."

Raina spread her hands. "All I know is that the spell to send someone's spirit through time, no matter if it's witch blood or vampire blood helping to power it, must be done by an alpha witch. End of story."

My mind raced. "Thierry thought an alpha was responsible for Owen's murder—death magic. And if it wasn't you—"

"It wasn't," Raina said firmly. "I meant that vampire no ill will. He was . . . fun. He made me laugh. I'm sorry he's dead."

I turned to Todd, but he shook his head. "Don't even suggest it, Sarah. There's no way Heather had anything to do with Owen. I wasn't thrilled about it, but she was crazy for the guy. And she'd never hurt a fly. I mean, she fed me cat food for the last two months. Not that I would have been thrilled with flies, but"—he made a face—"either way, it was really gross."

Miranda had wanted me to have the impression that Heather was deceptive, that she wasn't as innocent as she let on. Had Heather been keeping this secret from everyone?

Raina gasped. "Oh, it can't be."

"What?" I asked, alarmed.

"Malik . . . he could have gotten to her. Maybe he knew she was more powerful than she let on. Maybe she found the spell . . ."

"What spell?"

Her face paled. "A spirit transference spell. He's tried to convince me to attempt it to find him a new body to possess and give him the chance to live again. I found the spell a year ago, after many decades of research. I couldn't go through with it. I didn't want to destroy another life. He was furious and he hasn't spoken to me since. But maybe . . . maybe he's been speaking to someone else."

A spirit transference spell? "Thierry's body was possessed by Owen's spirit—and it was strange; Owen claimed he had nothing to do with it. He can't get out of the body even though he wants to. Is that the same thing?"

"If it isn't, it's quite a coincidence, isn't it?" She was breathless. "Malik is up to something."

My throat tightened. "He wanted me to disable you. He's planning something—tonight. He could be planning to possess a body with that spell . . . and another witch's help."

"Whoa, whoa, wait a minute." Todd held his hands up. "Calm down, both of you. Heather has nothing to do with this. It's got to be a coincidence. There have to be lots of ghosts in Salem capable of possessing bodies, right? And lots of witches to help them? People die all the time!"

"It's different here in Salem." Raina's gaze drifted across the happy people and families moving through the street festival. "A spirit has attachments to the mortal world for three days after their death. In those three days they are very vulnerable. After that time has elapsed, they can move on to their final destination. But a spirit like Malik, eternally bound to the mortal world rather than free to move on to the spirit world, he becomes . . . very hungry."

My mouth went dry. "Hungry how?"

"Just as a vampire is driven by its hunger for blood"—her face paled—"a trapped spirit like Malik hungers for the energy of other spirits."

My mind raced. "If he finds Thierry . . ."

Raina's gaze was as haunted as her doomed romance with the witch hunter. "Pray that he doesn't, vampire. For he will destroy your husband without hesitation."

Chapter 18

Malik hungered for other ghosts like a vampire hungered for blood. He'd lied to me, trying to use how I felt about Thierry's dark past to gain my sympathy toward his own. I was ashamed to say it had worked—until now.

He wasn't a redemptive man who regretted anything. He was a cursed spirit who manipulated others whenever he could. He was no better than he'd been three hundred years ago. He might not be a danger to me, or anyone else currently breathing, but he was a direct threat to Thierry.

That was all I needed to know.

I turned and started running in the direction of the Booberry Inn without saying another word. I arrived only a few minutes later and burst through the front door.

Heather looked up at me, her expression strained. She sat on the living room sofa with Raina's grimoire spread open before her.

"Sarah!" She jumped to her feet. "Are you all right? I haven't known what to do! I was about to go to Raina's house myself. I . . . I was scared, but I was coming!"

I found myself momentarily speechless, faced with the girl I'd considered to be a new friend. If Raina was right, then Heather had lied to me from the beginning about her magical ability. Lied to everyone. This timid, shy girl who had secret crushes on vampires and ran a quaint bed-and-breakfast was an alpha witch, every bit as powerful as Raina herself. But I couldn't let on that I knew the truth. It was too dangerous.

Her gaze swept over me as if fully seeing me for the first time. She gasped. "Oh, my God! You're covered in blood! What did she do to you?"

I glanced down at my destroyed shirt and my arms, which still bore dried-up evidence of Raina's time travel tracings. Heather was right; I looked like the walking dead. "Forget about it. I'm fine. Well, now I am. Where's Thierry?"

I craned my neck and searched the general area, hoping he was lurking in a dark corner, but there was no sign of him.

She pressed her lips together and looked down at the floor.

I was in front of her in an instant, grabbing hold of her shirt, and tried to ignore the danger presented by pushing her too far. "Where is he?"

She was an excellent actress, because an edge of fear crossed her gaze. An alpha witch wouldn't be afraid of some panicky fledgling vampire she could squash like a bug.

"I tried to break the doggy spell so he could follow you when Raina . . ." She swallowed hard. "Thierry demanded that I do it, even if it meant that Owen might be able to escape. I tried, but I couldn't do it. He wasn't able to leave. He got so upset that he lost his hold on the mortal world. I haven't seen him since. But—um, I'm sure he's fine. Try to calm down."

Seeing me knocked out and kidnapped while he could

do nothing to save me must have exploded a few of his brain cells. The anger mixed with helplessness worked to flick the switch that sent him away.

"I can't calm down, Heather. Malik devours the energy of other ghosts. And if he learns that Thierry's trapped here, all delicious and devourable . . ." I couldn't finish my sentence.

Her eyes bugged. "I—I don't know why I couldn't break the spell. I cast it, so I should have been able to break it. It would have been my fault if Raina had killed you. Oh, Sarah, I'm sorry. I can't tell you how much."

"My goodness, you look like you were trampled by a herd of elephants!" Rose gave me an alarmed look as she entered the room. She held a cup of tea, which she brought to Heather.

"Just one, but she's not a problem any more. I'm okay now." Other than the fact that I was dealing with Rose's granddaughter's lies about her level of witchcraftitude to her and everyone else. But what was Heather's goal? What was her scheme? Was she connected to Malik? To Owen's murder? How did it all fit together?

"Besides, if this Malik fellow is as dangerous as you say, Sarah," Rose continued, "then Thierry is better off not here."

She was right. While I desperately wanted to see him, to know he was okay, I'd rather he be somewhere safe right now. I sent a look toward the staircase. "How's Owen doing? Still using Thierry's body as a Holiday Inn?"

Rose's expression darkened. "He's not doing so well, I'm afraid."

"What do you mean?"

"He's weakening. Poor thing. I hope he recovers."

Before I could ask any more questions, Todd burst

through the front door, kilt swishing around his legs. Heather and Rose regarded him with surprise.

"Todd?" Heather gasped. "What on earth are *you* doing here?"

"Hi, Heather," Todd said, crossing his arms over his bare chest as if he'd just remembered he wore only a kilt and literally nothing else. "How's it going?"

"How's it going?" Heather put down the grimoire. "I don't see you for two months, I figure you've left town completely without saying a word to me and worry the hell out of me, and you're suddenly here asking how's it going?"

"You broke up with me," he reminded her.

"Yeah, I did, but . . ."

"You were worried about me?" He looked pleased about this. "Really?"

"I—um . . ." She seemed to grapple for her words as a blush colored her cheeks. "Where have you been?"

"Good question. And not one that's easy to answer." Todd swallowed hard and glanced at me. "Um, Sarah? Some help?"

I knew this was a delicate situation. Todd had stayed in toad form for two months all to keep watch over the girl he loved. It was sweet . . . in a seriously twisted way. This needed to be handled extremely delicately.

Too bad I wasn't feeling delicate. "Good news: Todd is madly in love with you and wants desperately for you to be safe and protected always. Bad news: He's a shape-shifter who's been playing the part of Hoppy the toad for two months."

"What?" Heather's mouth fell open as she stared at the half-naked kilted man standing in her front foyer.

"Oh crap," Todd breathed.

"Work this out between you two, okay? I have to go rip Owen's spirit out of my husband's body." I started for the stairs, past the mirror that didn't show my reflection.

Rose glanced out the front window. "There seems to be not one but two angry witches now standing on our front lawn."

I froze and glanced out the front door's side window. Raina stood at the edge of the magical warding. Next to her was her loyal sidekick, Casey.

I'd deal with them in a minute.

I took the stairs two at a time and hurried into Owen's room. My breath caught as I saw Thierry's body, still handcuffed to the bed. Rose was right; he didn't look so well. His handsome face was pale, his dark hair slicked back from his face.

I sat down next to him, concern gnawing at my gut. "Owen, are you still in there?"

He blinked a few times, and then he opened his eyes. My heart wrenched to see the familiar stormy gray eyes I loved so much, even though the personality behind them wasn't the same. Not nearly the same.

"Hey, Sarah," he said weakly. "Heard Raina got hold of you. Glad to see you're . . . well, you're incredibly bloody right now. Oh God, the thirst. The thirst is back! This sucks so bad!"

I got up from the bed and put some distance between us. "Sorry."

He groaned. "Finished your blood—Rose gave the rest to me to keep my strength up. You're going to have to restock."

"Did it help?"

"Not really." He met my gaze. "I don't know how Thierry deals with this. He's a lot stronger than me; that's for sure."

"Is that why you look so sick right now? The thirst is draining your energy?"

He swallowed hard. "I don't know. I guess. It was way worse an hour ago, but it's getting better, I think. I'm recovering."

I remembered what Raina had said about the spirit transference spell and hissed out a breath. "I think I know what happened to put you in that body in the first place. I need to get you out of here. Something crazy's going on, and I don't think we've seen the end of it yet."

Rose was at the doorway. "Do you think that's a good idea? Moving him? I think he should stay right where he is."

"I don't think we have a choice anymore." Not if my guess that Heather might be involved with Malik in some way and that this spirit transference spell was meant for him, not Owen, was right.

Malik wanted Raina out of his way tonight. Something was going to happen and he didn't want a powerful witch like her close by.

Owen looked fondly at the old woman. "Rose . . . you've been so good to me, better than I deserve, staying by my side all this time. I think Heather hates me. Two out of three. It ain't bad."

I turned to Rose. "What do you think's wrong with him?"

Her expression was tense. "I think he's not strong enough to keep his hold on the body, but something's trapped him there."

Something. Or some*one*.

I moved past Rose into the hallway, to look over the railing to the first floor. Heather stood by the bay window, the grimoire clutched to her chest, staring out at Raina and Casey on the front lawn.

Waiting. Watching.

I turned to face Rose and lowered my voice to a whisper. "Did you know that Heather's an alpha witch?"

Rose gasped softly. "You can't be serious."

"I know it's hard to believe, but I think she has something to do with what's happened to Thierry. To Owen."

"Impossible," Owen said, shaking his head. "She can barely do any magic at all. What about the nosebleeds? You saw that yourself."

I did. And I didn't have an explanation for it. Not yet, anyway.

Rose looked at me, her eyes wide. "Why do you say this about Heather?"

"Raina told me."

"And you believed her?"

I blew out a breath. "I'm having trouble figuring out who to believe, to tell you the truth. I don't trust anyone at this point."

"Smart vampire," said a low voice by the door.

My gaze shot to the open doorway, where Malik now stood watching us, leaning against the doorframe casually, as if he didn't have a care in the world.

Rose inhaled sharply at the sight of him.

I put a hand on her arm so she wouldn't be afraid. "It's okay. He's harmless. To the living, anyway. What do you want, Malik? To lie to me some more?"

I hated being manipulated, and he'd done a bang-up job. Now, with my newfound clarity when it came to Jonathan Malik, witch hunter, I saw that nothing about him had changed in three hundred-plus years. Not even his fashion choices. He wore the exact same clothes as a ghost that he'd died in.

Malik simply regarded me coolly. "I'm so very glad that you're here tonight to be a part of this."

"A part of what?"

His smile before he turned away from us sent new shivers coursing through me. I ran after him into the hallway. Malik now stood by the railing, overlooking the main floor. Heather had left her station at the window to stare up at him in shock.

"What's going on?" she managed. "Who are you?"

As if she didn't know.

I approached him cautiously. "Talk to me, Malik. What's your plan? Did you have anything to do with this? With Owen? Have you hurt Thierry?"

He glanced at me. "Those are several questions. Which would you like answered first?"

"Thierry. Where is he?"

"Your husband." He cocked his head. "Yes, he's like me right now, isn't he?"

"He's nothing like you. He's capable of change, of redemption. You're not."

He rolled his eyes. "Let me guess. You've been talking to Raina again, have you? Don't trust that woman, Sarah. She'd kill you as soon as look at you."

"Maybe I don't trust either of you. What are you doing, Malik? What's the game plan?"

"Can't you figure it out?"

I already had. Partially, anyway. I spoke in no more than a whisper: "The spirit transference spell."

"Yes." The word was a hiss.

My throat was tight, almost too tight to form words.

"Thierry's body. It was supposed to be for you, not Owen. A witch is helping you and you think it's going to happen tonight."

"More than *think*, vampire. I *know*."

He drew closer so that sinister smile was way too close for comfort. I swatted at him, meeting only cold air in the process. He looked down at himself as his misty body swirled and re-formed.

"Nice try. Now it's my turn."

He backhanded me. My head whipped to the side, my face stinging from the hit. I clasped my hand to my cheek and stared at him with shock.

"How did you do that?" I gasped.

"Magic."

He came toward me and grabbed hold of my shirt, shoving me against the wall so hard that I shrieked. A framed embroidery sampler was knocked off the wall and crashed to the ground.

I tried to fight back, but it didn't work. For some reason, he could grab hold of me, hurt me, but I couldn't do the same.

"Not fair," I gritted out.

"Life's not fair. But I'll tell you what life *can* be: very painful."

Suddenly, an arm came around his throat and the ghost was wrenched back from me. He spun around to face Thierry—Thierry!—who'd appeared in the hallway.

Thierry grabbed hold of Malik's shirt and launched him to the side, where he hit the wall—and disappeared. Thierry searched for a sign of him, even looking in the empty room, but the ghost was gone.

Thierry's furious gaze snapped to mine and shifted

immediately to one of relief. "You're all right. I was so—" His attention fell to my torn, bloody shirt. "Sarah, what happened to you?"

I couldn't talk. I was too happy to see him. I reached out toward him, going so far as to touch his face. Or try to, anyway. My hand didn't make contact.

"Sarah," he growled. "Tell me why you're covered in blood or I'm going to freak out."

I couldn't help but laugh. "Freak out? *You're* going to freak out? That's something I'd say."

"Maybe so. But trust me, I've never been closer to it in my life."

I looked down at my train wreck of an outfit, wishing I had enough time to have a shower and change clothes. I couldn't tell him exactly what had happened with Miranda, with Raina, not now. It would only be a distraction. "I . . . got hurt. But I'm better now. Don't worry."

My words didn't do much to ease the torment in his eyes.

"When that witch took you and I couldn't stop her . . ." His brows drew tightly together. "I thought I'd go insane. I thought I'd lost you."

My heart twisted into tight, painful knots. "I'm back. I'm okay. And we can still fix this." I had to explain what I could quickly. "There's so much I need to tell you. The witch hunter . . ." My breath cut short. "Thierry, watch out! He's right behind you!"

The ghost in question grabbed hold of Thierry and yanked him away from me. Thierry staggered down the hall before he regained his balance.

"Stay away from him!" I yelled. "Thierry—he can devour the energy of other spirits. It makes him stronger. Be careful!"

Malik launched himself at Thierry, and they fell through the railing. When they hit the ground floor, both bodies turned into gray smoke, which swirled and then disappeared completely from view.

Rose stood by the doorway to Owen's room, her face etched with worry. "This is bad, isn't it?"

I shot her a look. "Well, you guys did name this place the Booberry Inn. Looks like it's finally living up to its potential." I searched my mind, hoping that a fantastic plan to fix everything would form effortlessly. Sadly, it didn't. "Can *you* do anything to stop this, Rose? A spell? Anything that could help us?"

Her forehead wrinkled deeper. "No, I can't. I'm sorry, dear. And Heather, oh my Heather . . ." She pressed her hand to her mouth. "If she has power like you say, then it's been hidden from the world all this time."

"So you can't help."

She shook her head and cast her gaze back toward Owen. "I wish I knew who could."

"Luckily, I do," I said.

Her eyes widened. "Who?"

"Raina Wilkins." I turned and raced downstairs, scanning the floor for any sign of Thierry or Malik, but there was nothing.

I moved directly toward Heather, not pausing to consider how best to approach a powerful witch who tried to hide her powers. "Break the spell keeping Raina outside. I need her in here."

She shook her head, her face going very pale. "We stole her grimoire. She hates me."

"Do it anyway. Please." I was certain she'd refuse to even try. That would be the last piece of proof I needed to convince me she was a deceptive, lying witch and had been all this time. But if she did help get Raina in here . . . Well, I didn't know what that would mean. But it would be a good start.

Todd sat on the couch quietly, his hands clasped together. "Heather will help you. I know she will."

Heather groaned. "I thought I told you to leave."

"I'm not letting you face all of this without protection."

She hissed out a breath. "That's what this was to you? You were protecting me as a stupid toad? Now you want me to forgive you after you lied to me for two months?"

He got to his feet and took a step toward her while she watched him warily. "I don't expect you to forgive me. As long as you're okay, I'm happy. I didn't trust Owen, Heather. I didn't trust him from the moment you met him, and—yeah, I made a dumb choice because I was stupid and jealous and my feelings were hurt when you dumped me. But I don't regret a single day we spent together before or after."

She let out a harsh, annoyed cry from the back of her throat and shot him a look so withering I was certain he'd turn into a toad again. Permanently.

"She'll help," Todd said to me, although his gaze didn't leave Heather. "She'll break the spell because she knows it's the right thing to do."

She really shouldn't kick Todd out. He was currently the only unwavering member of her fan club. I just hoped he wasn't setting himself up for disappointment . . . or worse.

Finally, after another anxious moment, Heather closed the grimoire and placed it on the coffee table.

She sent an unfriendly glare in my direction. "Fine. But if that witch kills everybody, it's *your* fault."

I nodded. "Noted."

Heather grabbed her grandmother's grimoire from a side table and moved to the front door, opening it. Raina and Casey stood at the boundary of the protection ward.

"Well?" Raina said impatiently.

"Sarah wants me to let you in my house. For me to break this spell."

"And are you going to?"

There was a pause. "I don't know yet."

"He's here, Raina," I said tensely.

The witch's expression tightened. She knew exactly who I meant. "Let me in, Heather. I can help. I have unfinished business with that ghost."

Heather let out a shaky breath. "Fine. This is a mess, and all of it seems to be my fault. If somebody—anybody—can help fix it, even you, then I can't just turn my back on it." She flipped forward through the pages. "I renew the warding every week as magic practice. This should do it."

She spoke the words of the spell under her breath. After a moment, she grimaced when her nose started to bleed. She wiped it away as if she was used to that side effect. I looked at her with concern. Owen was absolutely right; that was not a normal reaction for an alpha witch.

Raina approached cautiously, eyeing the empty air before her as if she expected it to slap her in the face. It didn't. I watched her tensely as she drew closer and closer, hoping I hadn't just made a horrible mistake. I wasn't in Vegas anymore, but every choice I made lately seemed to be yet another roll of the dice.

Finally, she stepped fully into the inn and glanced around. "How quaint."

Casey was right behind her. I glanced down at her finger. "Nice Band-Aid."

The blonde glared at me. "Bite me again and it'll be the last thing you ever do."

"Ooh, I'm so scared." Why was she even here? Two witches I didn't trust were more than enough to juggle, let alone Raina's Mini-Me minion joining the group. I swallowed hard and looked at Raina. "Are you really going to help?"

She hesitated. "Yes. I suppose I am."

I let out the breath I'd been holding. "Thank you."

"Do yourself a favor and don't thank me until this is all over."

"Maybe that's a good idea."

"Where is Thierry's body?"

"Upstairs."

"Bring him down here so I can do the transference spell and put your husband's spirit back into his rightful body. Malik doesn't get the chance to live again on my watch."

My mouth was dry. "I hate to ask, but why are you doing this, Raina? Why are you helping us? What's in it for you?"

Her eyes turned red, and magic crackled through the air. A sinister smile curled up the corner of her mouth. "Closure."

Chapter 19

Ten minutes later, we all gathered around the table where Heather had done her previous séances. There were seven of us this time: me, Owen, Raina, Heather, Todd, Casey, and Rose. It was a tight fit around the small round table.

"The vampire looks like he's about to croak," Todd said uneasily. "And I don't use that word lightly."

"I'm conscious now, you know," Owen growled. "I can hear you."

Todd shrugged. "Sorry, but it's true."

Owen hadn't fussed at all or tried to make a break for it when Todd and I went up to his room, unlocked his handcuffs, and helped him downstairs. He was pale, his energy low, and it worried me deeply.

"We'll have to do a spirit summoning first," Raina said. "We'll need your husband's spirit here, Sarah."

I nodded. "Okay, let's do it."

Rose cast a wary glance at the rest of us, ending with Raina. "You're not planning to double-cross us and resurrect Malik yourself, are you?"

She was giving voice to my worst fear, that I'd allowed myself to be manipulated by the alpha witch and that what she'd shown me of the past was all smoke and mirrors.

Raina's lips thinned. "No double-crossing, but feel free to leave if you're not comfortable with me here. Everyone who's staying must now join hands."

Rose stayed without further commentary. I took hold of Raina's and Owen's hands.

Raina cast her gaze straight forward. "I call forth the nearby spirits into the mortal world. Appear to us now and be bound to this realm until I say otherwise."

I searched for any sign of Thierry. When a chill entered the otherwise warm room, I literally held my breath in anticipation.

But it was Lorenzo's face that popped into view before me. "Oh, hello, everyone! I seem to be back once again!"

Raina hissed out a sigh. "Not you. Go away."

Lorenzo disappeared with a frown.

A moment later, Thierry's form shimmered into sight near the doorway. I almost leapt to my feet and ran toward him, but I forced myself to remain exactly where I was.

Concern twisted through me to see that he looked tense and tired. "Are you okay?"

He met my gaze. "I've been better."

If he'd said he was fine I would have called him a liar. He wasn't fine. Malik had stolen some of his energy just as Raina had warned he could. The proof was that Thierry's ghostly form didn't appear solid this time; it was translucent.

"Hurry," I urged Raina, my voice shaking. "Let's get this over with."

She nodded, squeezing my hand. "I'll set this right. I'll undo the damage that's been done and return your husband to his rightful body right now."

From across the table, Casey rose to her feet. "Like hell you will."

A crackle of magic filled the room, and Raina flew back from her chair and hit the wall, pinned there for a moment with sparkling bands of magical energy binding her wrists, ankles, and throat. She stared at Casey with absolute shock.

"What are you doing?" she demanded.

Casey's eyes were bloodred, and a sinister smile twisted on her face. "Do you know how sick I am of listening to you talk?"

"Why are you so powerful?"

"Been reading your grimoire lately. Found a spell to drain some of your magic." Her smile widened. "And here we are. The apprentice becomes the master."

"Stop this right now!"

Casey cocked her head. "No, don't think I will. Go to sleep."

Raina gasped, and then her head slumped forward as the bands of light disappeared and the witch slid down to the ground. She was unconscious.

The rest of us witnessed this unfold in stunned disbelief. I waited for Raina to shake it off and kick her minion's butt for stepping out of line, but she was currently out for the count.

I glanced toward Thierry, who still stood by the door, watching all of this with a dark expression.

Raina had been our only hope to fix this.

"Now, where were we?" Casey asked, glancing at the rest of us. "Oh, yes. The spirit transference spell. Another one of Raina's useful spells."

"I didn't see anything like that in her grimoire," Heather said in not much more than a whisper. "And I didn't see the other spell, the one to transfer magic."

"I tore out the ones I needed." Casey shrugged. "What can I say? I wasn't near a photocopier."

"Why are you doing this?" I demanded. "What do you want?"

"Just what every girl wants," Casey replied. "True love. A happy life. Absolute power over the entire world." The air remained charged and Casey's hair blew back from her face. "Malik, appear to me. Let me see you."

There was a tingling sensation, like the air before a lightning storm. Then Malik appeared next to her, his black eyes glittering.

"Well done, Casey," he said with a smile.

"Oh, hell no," I whispered. I thought we'd faced the worst with Miranda and her quest for eternal youth thanks to the blood of her unsuspecting vampire victims. Looked like I'd been wrong. "*You're* the witch who's helping him. You're in love with a ghost?"

Casey's red eyes snapped to mine. "What I feel for Malik can't be described as simple love. It's much too epic for that. He's my soul mate. My partner in all things, forever and always. There is nothing I wouldn't do for him."

Malik looked smugly satisfied.

The others—Heather, Todd, Owen, and Rose—all looked on silently. Heather's fingers dug into Owen's hand and her grandmother's on top of the table.

"How did you do it?" Thierry asked from the shadows, his tone holding both malice and curiosity. "How did you convince her? You're nothing more than a ghost."

Malik smiled. "Casey is a gifted witch who needed guidance and confidence. I gave both to her."

Raina didn't stir from her unconscious position on the floor six feet away.

"Did you kill me, Casey?" Owen asked, frowning. "But we didn't even date. I hadn't gotten around to you yet."

"As if I would have bothered with someone meaningless like you, Owen. No, it wasn't me. Who cares who did it? It's done." Casey turned those scary red eyes to me. "Now we need some vampire blood."

"Leave Sarah out of this," Thierry growled. "I'm warning you."

Malik laughed. "As if you could stop anything in your current state. Why don't you wither away now, vampire? You're becoming an annoyance."

It disturbed me how pale Thierry was, how drained. Worry now etched into his expression.

I had to find a way to stall them. At least until Raina woke up. Casey hadn't killed her, although I wasn't sure why. Maybe she wasn't quite strong enough to do a death spell.

Which meant she hadn't killed Owen.

"Miranda was familiar with vampire blood magic, too," I said. "She worked the immortality spell, leaving a few dead vampires in her wake. Did you guys share trade secrets during book club? Or are you all working independently?"

Casey didn't seem particularly shocked by the "dead vampires" comment. "Miranda's a vain, pathetic idiot. I know about the magic she plays with and who suffered because of it. If she doesn't stay out of my way, I'm going to kill her."

"Too late," I said with a shrug, fighting to keep my voice steady. "Raina beat you to it."

Casey's eyes widened a fraction. "Unexpected. But I don't really care one way or the other. She was a nuisance, always thought she was better than me. Little did she know I was the one meant for greatness in our coven. Not her."

"You're doing all of this because you're in love with Malik," Heather managed, her face pale.

"He's the most incredible man I've ever met in my life." She gazed at the witch hunter's spirit.

Meanwhile, I was attempting to have a nonverbal discussion with Thierry.

What do I do? I tried to ask.

Run, he seemed to be urging.

No way. I can't leave everybody here at her mercy.

She means to bleed you, to use your blood in her magic tonight.

Yeah, got the memo. But there has to be another way.

You saw how powerful she is, how focused. Raina isn't waking up anytime soon. Run, Sarah, while you have half a chance.

At least, this was what I assumed he was trying to tell me. And I knew him well enough to think I was pretty darn close.

But I wasn't running. Not yet.

I sent a withering look at Malik. "How many women in town have you been having a ghostly romance with? Just Casey? Or is she just one on a longer list of potential witchy helpers?"

Malik raised an eyebrow. "Jealous, Sarah? I could have added you to my list of helpers if you'd been a little more—"

"Gullible?" I finished. "Sorry, but that's the old me. The new me can see through a womanizing jerk from a mile away. Even the dead ones."

"And yet here we are." He glanced toward Thierry, who had faded even more since he'd first appeared. "And I'm the one with all the power."

"Hold on. I don't understand," Owen murmured, his voice weak. "Who killed me?"

An excellent question.

"I didn't kill him," Casey said bluntly. "Neither did Miranda. She actually liked the idiot and refused to spill even a drop of his blood. Not Raina, either. She bled him every time they were together, then made him forget."

"What?" Owen said, surprised. "I mean, the sex was great, but she was bleeding me, too?"

Malik's expression darkened significantly. "You were sleeping with Raina?"

Owen frowned. "Dude, I sleep with everybody. It's kind of my thing."

I worked it over in my mind. "A witch killed Owen. And if it wasn't Casey, it wasn't Miranda, it wasn't Raina . . ." I shot a look across the table at Heather. "It had to have been you."

Her eyes bugged. "Me? Why would I do that? I was in love with him!"

Todd groaned. "Infatuation, not love. Trust me, there's a difference. Love is eating cat food for two months without complaint."

"Heather didn't kill me!" Owen exclaimed. Then he frowned. "Or did you?"

She shook her head, her face pale. "Of course not!"

"Enough of this," Casey snapped. She drew a dagger from underneath her jacket. Before I could do more than stand up from my chair, she was right in front of me and grabbed hold of my face to direct my gaze to hers. "I need your blood."

"Let her go," Thierry snarled. "Malik, tell your witch to unhand my wife or she will be joining you in death."

Malik just coolly stared at him, unaffected by the dark threat in Thierry's voice. "Just fade away, vampire. It's time for you to be on your way."

"I'm not going anywhere."

Malik snorted. "I'm afraid you're wrong. In fact, I'm surprised you're still hanging on to this mortal coil. Let go, my friend. Find your way to the afterlife."

Thierry's gaze flashed. "I did not die. I will not leave, not unless I get to take you with me."

I didn't like ultimatums like that—not ones that put his existence at risk, even if it might be for the greater good.

Currently, however, I couldn't look anywhere but into Casey's red eyes as she held the dagger to my wrist.

Raina had to wake up. She was the only one I knew who could stop this before it was too late.

"Todd, Owen," Thierry snapped. "Do something."

"Would if I could," Todd replied. "But I . . . um, can't stand up. Damn witches."

"Ditto," Owen said tightly.

"Tell me what to do next, Malik," Casey urged. The blade pressed to my arm, but she hadn't cut me yet. "We need to do this right. You know the spell better than I do."

"You're right, I do know it."

"How much of her blood do we need?"

"None. We have enough vampire blood already."

The blade eased off and a frown creased Casey's forehead. "I don't understand."

"I know." A fresh smile drew the corners of Malik's mouth upward. "You have been very accommodating, my dear. Thank you for your help. I've appreciated your attention to detail."

Her face lit up. "Anything for you, Malik. Anything at all."

"Your services, however, are no longer required."

Bewilderment crossed her expression. "I don't understand."

"Even after stealing some of Raina's magic these last few weeks, you don't have nearly enough to complete this particular spell. But that's all right. My true love will finish up just fine."

I exchanged another confused glance with Thierry.

"Your *true* love?" Owen repeated. "Excuse me?"

Casey's red eyes brightened with anger, and magic crackled in the air. "What are you talking about?"

Malik's smile turned wistful. "She's been with me for so much longer than you have. That kind of loyalty means everything to me."

I sent a wary glance toward Raina on the floor, expecting her to rise to her feet and laugh maniacally about how fabulously she had us all fooled. That she and Malik were still together, and that this had all been a part of her devious plan, three hundred years in the making.

"Who is it?" Casey demanded. "Who is—?"

Her knife flew out of her hand, hovered in front of her in midair for a long, horrible second . . .

And then it plunged directly into her heart.

She gasped, her eyes widening with surprise, pain, and bitter disappointment, before she fell forward onto the table.

I literally yelped with surprise and staggered back from the dead witch.

Heather shot up from her seat as if the spell holding her there had been broken with Casey's death, her chair skittering backward.

"It was you," I managed. "You're helping Malik!"

She just stared back at me, fearful and frantic. "What? What are you talking about?"

"No, Sarah. It wasn't Heather." Thierry wasn't looking at me; his gaze was focused elsewhere. I followed it around the table.

Owen appeared stunned, Todd in utter shock, but then my gaze fell on Rose.

Rose was smiling.

"I've wanted to do that for the last ten minutes." She shook her head. "That girl was a royal pain in the butt."

"Grandma," Heather said shakily. "What's going on? What is this?"

Rose glanced at her. "A love story, darling. One for the ages."

"You were involved with Malik," Thierry said, his voice jarringly hollow and echoey. He'd become even more translucent than before. It hurt to see such strain on his face, as if he was fighting to stay visible. "It was you all along."

"Yes," Rose agreed. "I love him. I have since I was young. Many men used me, left me, but he never did. He taught me, he showed me how to use my powers as much as I could. He introduced me to Raina's hidden grimoire many years ago and the knowledge of vampire blood magic. And here we are."

Rose. It was Rose. The grandmother who'd seemed so helpful, so pleasant, so . . . harmless. The elderly witch who had a grimoire full of gardening and doggy spells. It didn't seem possible, but the proof was right before me. She didn't try to deny it. She seemed happy to finally have it all out in the open.

"Crap," Owen murmured. "Didn't see that coming."

"I gardened with her for two months," Todd said under his breath. "Never had a clue."

Owen glanced at the other guy. "Who are you, again?"

Todd grimaced. "Hoppy."

Owen blinked. "Hoppy the *toad*?"

"My beautiful Rose," Malik said, his expression now peaceful. "It's finally time for us to end my suffering. For me to be reborn."

"In the body of a master vampire," I said, stunned.

Of course. This was the plan all along. To resurrect Malik in Thierry's body. It was all so much clearer now.

I'd figured if anyone, it was Heather—young, pretty, ready for true love, even if it might be with an evil spirit.

But Rose . . .

Eighty years old, but still willing to throw it all away for some incorporeal gigolo.

"I've tried the spell several times before," Rose said with a nod, "but humans are too frail. And vampires . . . they have to be older—very old, in fact, to withstand the pressure of a foreign spirit taking over. Thierry is absolutely perfect for this."

Thierry had drawn closer so he now stood next to me. His gaze moved from Casey's body to me. His gray-eyed gaze didn't overflow with optimism.

Current standings: him a ghost, me a fledgling—against a ghost who could drain a spirit and cause bodily harm to the living, and a witch of indeterminate power.

Not good odds.

Then again, Thierry had always been the glass-half-empty to my glass-half-full. Together, we made a full glass. We balanced each other. Light and dark, fledgling and master. We could figure this out. Because there was no damn way I was giving up his body without a fight.

Rose's revelations did help clear a few things up in my mind.

"You're the one who killed Owen." I said it, not as a question, but as a statement. "But it wasn't a death spell like we thought."

"Owen was a failed experiment." Rose shrugged. "Sorry, Owen."

"You killed me?" Owen just stared at her bleakly. "But I thought you liked me."

"I did. You were a beautiful man. You would have made an excellent host for Malik's spirit. Alas, you weren't old enough—not powerful enough in either body or spirit. When I tried to do the spirit transference spell the other day, you . . . exploded."

Thierry crossed his arms. "Then you were afraid to try the spell again when it involved the man you believe you love."

"I don't *believe* I love him," she snapped, her wrinkled gaze going cold and hard. "I *know*."

"So your next experiment was to put Owen's spirit into *my* body, hoping that I too would not explode." Thierry's lips were tight, which was the only betrayal of his anger toward the woman who had seemed so kind, so harmless, and even flirtatious with him.

He'd been fooled.

So had I.

Rose's eyeballs hadn't given her away. But maybe I hadn't been looking closely enough.

"It worked perfectly," Rose said.

Owen shook his head. "What happened to me is over. I'm dead. But—but you don't want this body. Thierry's thirst is too much for me to handle. You should do yourselves a favor and look elsewhere."

In his own way, I knew he was trying to help us. I sent him a grateful look as I tried to come up with a way to distract Rose long enough for us all to get out of there and hope Raina would wake up sooner rather than later.

Rose didn't seem concerned by Owen's proclamation. "See, the difference is, Owen, that Malik is strong. You are weak. You give in to temptation, whether it's blood or a hussy in a short skirt. Malik has all the patience and control that you lack."

I found myself unable to hold back my steadily rising anger a moment longer. It erupted all at once.

"You bitch," I snapped. "I'm going to kick your geriatric wicked witch ass all the way back to Oz."

"Sarah." Thierry's voice was firm. "Calm yourself."

"Calm myself?" I sputtered. "She tried to steal your body! Your life!"

"She failed."

Rose laughed. "Failed? Wrong. I'm about to succeed beyond my wildest dreams. It's time to finish this."

"Grandma, please don't do this," Heather pleaded.

"Heather's right, Rose," Todd said. "Let's talk about this."

"Be quiet or I'll turn you into a toad permanently," she warned. "Malik, come stand next to me."

As he did so, her eyes turned red and magic so powerful that it raised the fine hair on my arms charged the room. She smiled at my look of shock.

"Vampire blood, dear. I won't be needing yours. Master vampire blood works so much better than fledgling. And I have all I could possibly need."

I stared at her for a moment. "Thierry's body . . . you bled Owen when he was unconscious."

"That would explain how I feel," Owen said with a nod. "Like a thousand leeches have been feasting on me all day."

Rose's smile held. "His wounds healed up so quickly that nobody would have guessed it. But there it is. I'm nearly as powerful as an alpha now. I can do the spell. And this time I'll do it perfectly."

"Raina! Wake up!" I crouched on the ground so I could shake her. She didn't move. I checked her throat for a pulse, relieved to find one. She wasn't dead, just really, really unconscious.

The air charged with magic.

This was it. We'd officially run out of time.

"Owen!" I yelled "Run! Just go!"

He met my gaze and nodded, then, taking whatever energy he still had in reserve, he bolted from his chair and out of the room.

I followed, the others right on my heels. Owen got almost as far as the front door before a blast of magic hit him in his back and sent him sailing into the wall next to the mirror, where he left a big dent.

Rose shoved me out of the way, her strength surprising even me.

I'd wanted Owen to get out of this house and run as far and as fast as he could. Funny how yesterday I'd done everything I could to stop him from doing just that.

Malik stood back, his arms crossed, and watched the show as if fascinated by this culmination of years of planning. He seemed to have every confidence in Rose's abilities. Every confidence that he would walk out of here tonight in a strong, tall, handsome—if slightly ancient and eternally bloodthirsty—vampiric form.

Not if I had anything to say about it.

Thierry's spirit stalked the edges of the room, assessing the situation before him like a caged lion. He had become very translucent now. I wanted to warn him to stay back, to not get too close to Malik. That bastard was dangerous on too many levels to count.

Heather stood on the other side of the room, staring at her grandmother as if she were looking at a stranger. Todd didn't leave her side, still determined to protect her, even though I knew a shape-shifter—even one wearing a snazzy kilt—had no chance against a powerful witch.

"Yes, this will be the perfect vessel," Rose said to Owen, her gaze taking him in from head to foot. "A master vampire, one with hundreds of years of life to make him strong, unbreakable, unstoppable. Immortal. Jonathan Malik will live again, and I will be by his side forever."

"You think so, huh?" I said, disgusted by every word that came out of the old biddy's mouth. "No offense, but do you really think a gorgeous vampire will want much to do with an eighty-year-old grandma?"

Her gaze shot toward me. The next moment I was flying through the air. I hit the coffee table hard, breaking it on contact. The wooden shards stabbed into my skin.

I yanked the splinters out, flinching from the pain, and got back to my feet. I wasn't finished with her.

Across the room, Thierry flickered out and I thought for a horrible moment that he was gone. But a second later he flickered back into view right in front of me.

I gulped hard. "New trick?"

He searched my face. "You need to get Heather and Todd to safety. You can't stop her. All you'll do is get yourself killed if you stay here."

"I already got killed today. Stake through the heart, courtesy of Miranda Collins."

"What?" His gaze raked over my bloody shirt, widening, then snapped back up to my eyes.

"Raina healed me in the nick of time. But all I could think about in those moments was the fact that I'd miss you so much."

His brows drew together. "Sarah . . ."

"I got a second chance and I'm not wasting it. No matter what, Thierry, we're together in this. Either we fix this or we can both be spirits together. Got it?"

He stared at me a moment longer, as if ready to argue, before his gaze hardened. "Got it."

"Good." I turned to see Rose, who had a whirlwind of magic going on now, sparkling circles of power spinning around her like supernatural hula hoops. Her gardening clothes and white hair blew back from her face from a mystically summoned wind.

Malik watched her, naked anticipation and greed on his handsome face—but I saw no love or devotion there. She was only another minion to him, one he'd been able to fool with his lies and promises and empty charm.

"He doesn't love you!" I yelled at Rose. "Stop this! Your granddaughter loves you! You're destroying everything right now!"

She made a flicking motion toward me, and I flew backward again, this time slamming hard into the wall by the bay window. A crack formed on the glass, but it didn't shatter. It knocked the wind out of me for a moment and I gasped for breath.

Rose was beyond reason—beyond sanity. Her world had narrowed to this spell and the ghost she believed loved her.

"It's time to remove the old . . ." Rose twisted her hand. Owen's spirit was sent sailing out of Thierry's body as if she'd just plucked a Kleenex from a box. "And prepare for the new."

Owen scrambled to his feet, looking down at himself with shock. Then he sent a bleak look in my direction. Now spiritless, Thierry's body crumpled to the floor near the bottom of the stairs.

Heather still stood at the opening to the séance room, staring at her grandmother with horror etched on her face.

Okay, my theory about Heather being evil and deceptive and secretly power hungry?

I was wrong. Oops.

The sorcery-wielding granny appeared to be powering up again, since her sparkly hoops were spinning faster and faster. The wind blew through the entire house now, knocking everything in its path to the floor.

"What did she do with your blood?" I asked Thierry. "Is that what she's channeling right now?"

He kept his focus on the witch. "Likely she consumed it while reciting a spell."

My stomach clenched. "Like a magical elixir."

"Exactly. The power is already inside of her, like mercury in a thermometer. It's rising up and when it gets to maximum . . ." His jaw clenched. "I can't stop this, Sarah. But there is someone who can."

Raina told me only an alpha witch could do that time travel spell . . .

"Heather!" I yelled. "You have to stop her!"

She stared at me with confusion. "How?"

"You're an alpha witch!"

Her mouth dropped open and she shook her head. "What are you talking about? Alpha witch? I—I'm barely a witch at all!"

Todd stood solidly at Heather's side, surveying the magic-infused room with shock.

I frantically waved at him. "Todd! Say something to her! She doesn't believe in herself."

He nodded, then pulled her around to face him. She didn't resist, her breath catching as she met his gaze. "Heather, I think you're amazing."

She looked to be on the verge of tears. "No, I'm not. And—why would I believe you? I don't trust anything you say."

"I should have told you the truth long ago. I know that. I'm sorry. But that doesn't mean that you're not amazing. And that I'm madly, passionately in love with you."

"This is adorable, really," I said, sending a furtive look toward Thierry's now vacant and vulnerable body, "but Salem's version of *The Bachelorette* is not going to help right now. Let's focus on the magic, on the confidence. Pretty please?"

"You love me?" Heather stared at Todd with shock. "Are you serious?"

He just nodded. "I've never been more serious. You have so much magic inside of you. But something's held it back all this time. I've always believed in you, Heather. It's time for you to believe in yourself."

Every second that passed was a second lost. Malik stood tall, with an arrogant look on his face. This was his victory day. The first time I saw him in the café he'd told me "soon." This was what he'd meant.

He believed he would soon live again. And soon was now.

Raina didn't burst into the room to wave her magic wand. There was just a white-haired witch who was ready to destroy everything in the name of love, and allow a man who'd killed and tortured women just like her back into the world.

All we had in our corner was a shifter, a vampire, a fading spirit, and an alpha witch who didn't believe in herself and never had.

We were going to lose.

Chapter 20

"I want to help!" Heather cried, twisting her necklace as she watched her grandmother as if looking at a complete stranger, "but I don't know how! I can't do magic without a grimoire."

Heather's mother had had powerful magic inside her. And even though she'd made us believe that her magic had faded through the years, Rose was also an accomplished witch—far beyond simple gardening and doggy spells.

But Heather had always struggled. She didn't have any more magic than what she'd shown us. She'd given me everything she had—and then some. When she tapped too deeply into the magic, her nose bled.

But why?

My gaze moved to her necklace, the one her grandmother had given her after her mother's death.

"Do you ever take that necklace off?" I asked.

She looked down at the piece of jewelry she twisted between her fingers. "Never. Why?"

"Of course, Sarah," Thierry murmured, as if following my line of thinking. "It has to be."

My gaze met Thierry's and held. "Do you think I'm right?"

"Only one way to find out."

I nodded. Then I raced across the room, grabbed hold of Heather's necklace, and ripped it off her neck, breaking the chain.

When the chain broke, the blast of magic sent me flying backward across the room, where I landed again on the broken coffee table.

"Oh, come on." I winced as I pulled a small but painful splinter out of my shoulder. "*So* not fair."

Then, before my eyes, the necklace dangling from my grip turned from gold to black.

Heather gasped. "What is going on?"

I looked up at her grimly. "This necklace worked to dampen your magic, Heather. Rose didn't want you to know you were an alpha."

The evil granny in question ignored us, intent on her task. The hoops of magic circled her arms now, close to her skin. Her hands glowed. She looked as if she were summoning Thor himself to do her thunder-god bidding.

She'd bled Thierry's body a lot for that much blood magic.

The thought only made me angrier.

Heather stood there, her arms out to either side of her, her eyes wide and full of awe. "Sarah, I can feel it inside of me. Why would she keep this from me all this time?"

"Because she didn't want you to be able to stop this," Todd replied before I could. "But you can. Can't you see? You can!"

Heather's eyes were wide. "The magic inside me is like an ocean—so big and wide and . . . Wow. I never knew."

"Suggestion? Jump in that ocean and start swimming!" I urged. "Swim, Heather, swim!"

The magic in the room was so thick I could barely catch my breath.

Out of the corner of my eye I saw Thierry's spiritless body jolt—as if a paramedic had taken electric paddles to it.

Malik's form flickered. "Finish it, Rose, my love, and we can be together always."

I couldn't wait for Heather to take action—not even knowing if she *could* take action. I began moving toward Rose. Before I got there, Malik stepped in front of me.

"Not so fast, vampire." He backhanded me again, but I recovered faster this time. I swiped my fist toward him but caught only cold air.

Thierry moved toward Malik, his gaze predatory.

"Don't get closer to him!" I yelled. "Be careful!"

"*You* telling me to be careful." Thierry shook his head, and despite everything, a smile curled the side of his mouth. "How ironic."

"He's dangerous!"

"So am I." Thierry launched himself at the witch hunter, and they both went tumbling across the room.

"I'll destroy you!" Malik snarled.

"You can try," Thierry snapped back, "but my will to live is stronger now than it's been in centuries. You'll fail."

"Let's put that to the test, shall we?" Malik clutched Thierry's throat, holding him at arm's length. His eyes turned black and he began to inhale deeply. Thierry's form flickered, his face contorting with pain.

"Thierry!" I screamed.

Owen's spirit launched himself across the room and tackled both of them. He plowed his fist into Malik's face and pulled him away from Thierry.

"Thierry and I have never been best buds," he snarled,

"but I'm on his side in this. Your girlfriend killed me for you, you witch-hunting bastard."

"You were only one of many." Malik easily spun away from him, stepping out of both of their reaches.

I allowed myself a brief moment of relief. Owen had saved Thierry before the rest of his energy had been completely devoured. But it had been close, too close.

Despite our difficulties, Owen had just earned a million brownie points in my book.

The inn was charged with magic—every molecule filled with static energy. My hair even began to stand on end.

I spun on my heels. "Heather!"

"I don't know!" Heather yelled over the roar of the swirling wind. "I'm not sure I can stop her. Grandma, please. Don't do this. I love you!"

Rose turned her scary red eyes toward her granddaughter, her gaze serene despite everything. "And I love Malik. There's never been anyone else for me. I would kill for him; I would die for him. So don't get in my way or I'll destroy you, too."

Tears streamed down Heather's cheeks. She raised a hand toward her grandma, and rings of sparkling magic began to circle her as well. No nosebleed this time, just pure magic. Her eyes turned red. "I won't let you hurt anyone else."

"And I won't let you stop me." Rose thrust her arm out and sent a lightning-like charge of magic toward Heather.

"No!" Todd leapt in front of the young witch to block her, taking the force of the blast full on. He crumpled to the ground in a heap.

"Todd, no!" Heather cried. She fell to his side. He didn't move, but his chest showed he was still breathing.

"Damn shifters," Rose snarled. "That wouldn't have been enough to kill him. Let me try again."

Heather turned her red eyes toward her grandmother. They weren't filled with tears; they were filled with outrage.

"Stay back," Rose warned. "The next blast will kill both you and your boyfriend. You might have magic, little girl, but you have no control. I have a lifetime of it. I gave myself over to black magic when your mother died. I haven't looked back."

Black magic must have been what had turned her this way—this deceptive, selfish witch who couldn't see beyond her blinders. Who couldn't see beyond Malik's wishes.

For the briefest second, I felt desperately sorry for her.

"Well, this is quite a sight, isn't it?" The voice made me whip my head toward the séance room with surprise. Raina, hunched over, emerged from the adjoining room, holding on to the walls as she went as if she hadn't gotten her strength fully back.

Weak or not, the witch who'd kidnapped me and tied me up in her dungeon earlier today was a sight for sore eyes.

"Thought you'd never wake up," I said tightly. "But I'm glad you did."

"I can help," she muttered.

"You sure about that?"

"I can try."

"No, stay back," Heather hissed. "She's my grandmother. This is my fight now."

"Sarah," Thierry hissed from nearby. I turned to see him, alarmed by how pale and translucent he was. "Stay back."

"Thierry, what are you—"

"Don't worry about me."

Heather took a step toward her grandmother.

"I don't want to kill you," Rose said, a muscle in her cheek twitching. "Truly, I don't. But I can't let you stop this. I can make you forget. I can make you forget all of this, including your own magic. It's for the best."

The forgetting spell—the same one Raina used on a lesser level for the vampires she bled to maintain her immortality. Miranda didn't have that level of power, which was why she'd had to kill the vampires she bled. But Rose was as powerful as an alpha right now, with all that master vampire blood swirling around inside her—her thermometer heated up to maximum. She could do it.

In fact, she could make *all* of us forget if she wanted to.

"You won't forget I'm your grandmother, dear, but you'll forget everything else. And no one will ever keep me from Malik. *No one.*"

Raina groaned. "She's another witch after you, Malik? This is getting absolutely ridiculous."

I noticed that the two had locked gazes, the witch hunter ghost's attention drawn away from the old woman from the moment Raina entered the room.

He looked at her the way he had at the edge of the forest more than three hundred years ago. As if she was the most beautiful thing he'd ever seen.

"It could have been different, Raina," he said, his voice hoarse now. "I wanted it to be. Do it, Rose. Raina's power has been drained. She can't stop you right now. Take away your granddaughter's memories if you wish to save her life, and then we'll deal with the others."

"Yes, my love."

"Give this up, Malik," Raina warned. "I won't ask again."

His gaze hardened. "Don't you know me by now? I never give up."

Then the floor began to tremble and shake as if there were an earthquake rolling through town.

"Are you doing this?" I asked Raina.

She shook her head, her expression growing worried. "No."

Rose's sparkly magic solidified before her in the shape of an arrow.

Heather stood there, her wild red hair the same color as her eyes. Despite everything, she looked calm. Focused. "I can't believe you kept this magic from me my whole life. I can't forgive you for that."

"What's done is done." Rose sent the arrow hurtling toward Heather.

Just as the arrow would have hit Heather, the air all around her rippled. The arrow bounced off this shielding and flew backward toward Rose, where it hit her squarely in her chest and disappeared. Gold light emanated from her chest, crawling up along the line of her throat, over her jaw, and up her cheeks until her entire head glowed with sparkling golden light.

She gasped, her eyes rolled back into her head, and she slumped down to the floor only feet from where Todd also lay unconscious.

All of this happened in seconds.

Heather's eyes, still red and scary, suddenly lost their serenity. "Oh, my God. Is she dead? Did I kill her?"

Raina moved toward the witch on the ground, crouching down to check the pulse at the old woman's throat. "She's still alive."

"I'm glad you stopped her. She was out of control."

Malik addressed Heather. "Your power is incredible, much greater than anything I've ever seen before."

Heather regarded him with a withering look. "Back off, jerk. This is all your fault."

"Oh, Malik," Raina whispered. She shook her head. "How far you've fallen."

He turned to face her, and their eyes locked. "Without you I'm nothing, my love."

Her harsh expression wavered and I saw that wistfulness in her eyes.

Thierry whispered to me, loud enough for only me to hear. "I don't trust her. If she chooses to help him, they'll need more vampire blood. You're the only one in town now. My body"—he glanced over at it—"it's too weak from the previous bleedings. My blood will also be weak right now. Raina would need it to be as strong as possible in order for Malik to survive the transference. They'll kill you."

I shook my head, determined to stay. "He can't have your body."

"Sarah, look at her. Despite everything, she still loves him. All this time, it's never changed. Can't you see?"

I gazed into his gray eyes. "I do see. I see more than you think I do. Raina still loves him, I agree. But she's changed over the years. He hasn't. I thought he had, but he hasn't. He's nothing like you."

He searched my face. "I don't understand."

"Change is everything. People are capable of changing, no matter who they are and what they might have done in the past. But they have to want to change. They have to want to be better."

I glanced toward Heather, now crouched beside Todd

again. She held his hand in hers and sent a worried look in my direction. Owen stood by the staircase, eyeing all of us with distrust and uncertainty. Rose lay unconscious next to the couch.

And Raina and Malik faced each other as if the rest of us didn't exist.

"It was real between us," she said, her voice quiet. "I know it was."

"It was. The others . . ." He frowned. "You wouldn't help me. I thought you would change your mind eventually, but you never did. I was forced to look elsewhere."

"You seduced them."

"As much as I could with words and promises."

"Women enjoy both."

"So did you. Once. And you once loved me."

Her eyes glistened. "I still do."

Malik took a step closer to her. His form shimmered in the semidarkness of the room. "Push away your uncertainty, your guilt over past misdeeds. Help me live again right here, right now. We can begin a new life together, just the two of us. In my heart it was always you, nobody else. You know that, don't you?"

"I know," she whispered.

"I love you, Raina."

"And I love you." She took a step back from him. "I release the spell I put on you once, so very long ago. I release it and I release you from the bonds that hold your spirit here in Salem."

I watched her, ignoring the sick, sinking feeling I had.

"Sarah . . . ," Thierry growled, "go now."

I shook my head. "Just wait."

Malik jolted forward as if an unseen hand had pushed him. "Excellent, Raina. I'm pleased Casey did not drain you of all your magic. Do the transference spell quickly. My ties to the mortal world are now tenuous at best."

"I release you," she said again, her eyes turning red and her hands stretching out to her sides, palms up. Fresh, pure magic charged the room. "I release you, Jonathan Malik, the man I have loved for more than three centuries. I have learned much in this time, but you have not. You are evil and you continue to hurt those who are innocent. You've never stopped." Her expression remained fierce. "I release you to the judgment that has awaited you all these years."

"Raina!" Malik roared, the reality of what was happening now hitting him. "Don't do this!"

"It's done." She dropped her hands back to her sides. A tear slipped down her cheek. "I'm sorry. Good-bye, my love."

Flames began to lick at Malik's ankles. He stared down at them as if in shock, then sent a dark glare toward her. "Stop this!"

"I can't."

"Damn you!" He yelled it this time, his voice a resonating boom through the entire inn, one that echoed off the walls. The flames rose to cover his entire body, and a moment later, he disappeared in a flash of fire and rage.

Raina staggered backward and fell to the ground, sobbing.

"See?" I whispered to Thierry, the tightness in my chest finally easing off. I would have hated like hell to have been wrong. But I knew it. I *knew* it! "She'd changed, but she finally realized Malik hadn't. I saw it in her eyes . . . I felt it in my gut. And I believed it."

"You are so much wiser than I give you credit for."

There was something in his tone that made me turn

away from the raven-haired witch to meet his eyes. But I could barely see him anymore, only a ghostly outline.

"Oh God, no . . . Thierry . . ." Panic gripped my heart with a clawed hand. "Raina! Do something! Malik fed on Thierry's energy. He's nearly gone!"

Thierry looked nowhere but into my eyes. There was no panic in his gaze, only regret. "I wanted more time with you."

This was not happening. Not after we'd defeated the evil ghost and his witches. Not after I survived a fatal staking today. He wasn't going to fade away. I wouldn't let him. "No, Thierry! Don't you even think about leaving me! You have to fight this!"

His jaw tensed. "I'm trying. I am. But he took it all, Sarah. He wanted to leave just enough so you'd witness me fade away completely."

He flickered, disappearing for a horrible moment, before he reappeared.

"Somebody do something! Help him!" I was frantic by now. "Thierry! Focus on me. Just hold on a minute longer, okay?"

The slightest edge of a smile curled up the side of his mouth. "Never giving up, no matter how bad things get. You are incredible. I was so lucky—"

And then he was gone. Just gone—faded away into oblivion right before my eyes like a horrible switch had been flicked for the last time.

I trembled from head to foot, but I wasn't crying or sobbing. Not yet. No, I was furious. This wasn't how the story ended. Not for us. Not after everything we'd been through.

I whirled around and faced Raina, ready to destroy this town with my bare hands, alpha witches and all, if that's what I needed to do to get him back. "I don't care what you have to do—take my blood. Take as much of it as you need, but you have to get him back here. You have to heal him and make him whole, and then you need to put him back into his body."

Tears still streaked down her face, but she moved closer to me and put her hand on my shoulder. "Sarah, calm down."

I wrenched away from her and turned toward Heather. "There must still be some of Thierry's blood left from before. You can do the time travel spell again. I can go back a little while, possess a body and stop Malik from draining him."

Heather shook her head, her face pale. "I'm sorry, Sarah."

I faced Raina again, but now the witch was blurry from my own tears. "I can't lose him. Not like this. Please, you have to do something."

"He was right about you. You don't give up. Even when all is lost. You really love him, and he loves you." She took a deep breath and let it out slowly. "I admire that. I envy that."

"So do something!"

"I already did."

I blinked. "What?"

She shrugged. "I might be having the worst day I've had in three centuries, but I'm not a total selfish bitch. Just so you know."

It took me a moment to grasp what she was trying to tell me. "The spirit transference spell . . ."

"I know it by heart. So many times I nearly used it for Malik." She exhaled shakily. "Thank God I never did. I feel it's my one saving grace."

My mouth was so dry I could barely speak. "Don't even try messing with me, lady."

"I'm not. However, whether it was successful"—Raina spread her hands—"that's another matter. It's possible I was too late to save him."

My breath caught and held. "Now you're *really* messing with me, aren't you?"

"Yeah," Owen said from his viewpoint at the edge of the room. "She's *so* messing with you."

Without another word, I staggered over to where Thierry's body lay on the floor by the stairs. I collapsed to my knees beside him and grabbed hold of his hands. They were cold, too cold.

"Thierry . . ." I stroked the dark hair back from his forehead. "Are you in there? Did she do it?"

I checked his pulse—he had one. It was very slow, but that was nothing new. Vampires had slower heartbeats than humans, and master vampires had even slower ones. But even a pulse didn't necessarily mean his spirit had been returned.

But then his dark eyelashes began to flicker and his eyes opened. Storm gray eyes met mine.

"So," he said softly, "yet again, I suggest you leave when there's danger and you flatly refuse. I don't know why I bother anymore. You're truly the most stubborn woman I've known in my entire existence."

Relief exploded from me like a volcano of fireworks on July the Fourth. I fell into his arms and kissed him hard and deep.

"I thought that was it," I murmured against his lips. "I thought you were gone forever."

"And I thought *I* was the pessimist in this marriage."

I couldn't help but smile as I held his face between my

hands and inspected him for injury. He looked fine, wonderful, fantastic—if very pale from the blood loss. After a moment, I helped him to his feet. "Are you all right?"

He nodded. "I'll recover."

"I won't," Owen said. "I mean, I'm thrilled that everything turned out okay, but look. I'm still dead."

He didn't seem furious or ready to wreak vengeance. He just looked depressed.

"I'm sorry, Owen," I said, sadness for him darkening my sunbeam of joy.

"Well, there *is* Raina's spell," he said, his gaze thoughtful, "if we can find another suitable body . . ."

"No way." Heather had just helped the recovering Todd to his feet. She kept her arm hooked through the shifter's and leaned against him a little, as if they were both supporting each other now. "I'm sorry, Owen, but that can't happen. You'd be doing exactly what my grandmother tried to do—steal a body, ruin a life. You have to see that that's wrong, don't you?"

Owen opened his mouth as if to argue and then closed it. "Yeah. You're right, of course. It's wrong. But this sucks."

I felt horrible for him. Owen Harper might have been a womanizing opportunist, but he'd helped out when we'd needed him the most. And he hadn't deserved getting killed in the first place.

"I'm sorry it had to end this way for you, Owen," Thierry said.

Owen's brows drew together. "Yeah, well, I'm sorry I tried to steal your body and have sex with your wife."

Thierry's jaw tensed. "Apology accepted."

Owen regarded Thierry for a moment. "How do you deal with that bloodlust, anyway? It's like nothing I've ever experienced before."

I tensed as I waited for his answer. I wasn't sure, either, but now I had confirmation that it was a constant battle for him.

"Practice," Thierry said. He didn't elaborate.

Suddenly Rose stirred on the ground and opened her eyes.

"My goodness," she murmured as she sat up. "I must have taken a spill. What on earth happened?"

"You don't remember?" Heather asked, her voice tense.

"I'm not sure." Rose looked at each of us in turn. "Did I do something wrong?"

All I saw in her eyes was confusion. The memory-erasing spell she'd tried to use on her granddaughter had backfired and hit her instead.

She was damn lucky it hadn't been a death spell.

"The darkness in her is gone," Raina said. "Whether you forgive her or not is up to you, Heather."

"What about her magic?" Heather whispered.

"It's all gone. She's no threat to anyone anymore."

"You took her magic," Thierry said. "As Casey took some of yours. Didn't you?"

Raina raised an eyebrow at my husband's quick deduction. "Consider it payment for services rendered, vampire."

Rose looked at all of us, bewildered. "I don't understand a word of what any of you are saying."

Rose had no more magic; she had no memory of her desire to help Malik. It was as if all the bad had been erased from her like writing on a chalkboard. Was it really that easy?

According to the sad look on Heather's face, it wasn't. This couldn't simply be forgiven, years of holding her back from her rightful magic. Years of lies and deception.

That Rose had wanted to spare her granddaughter was

the only check in the "good" column, in my opinion. Having her memories erased did not forgive her for what she'd done.

And I wasn't the only one to think so.

"Unbelievable. So she kills me and she gets away with it. Just great," Owen said, shaking his head. "So where do I go now? Can anybody answer me that?"

There was silence among us for a moment. Thierry reached down and took my hand in his, his expression grim.

Then there was a popping sound as Lorenzo's head appeared, floating in midair in the middle of the circle we'd created.

"Oh, hello," he said. "Where's Owen Harper? Owen? Are you here?"

Owen blinked. "Um, hi?"

Lorenzo swiveled to face the other ghost, his cheery face falling as he swept his gaze over him. "You insulted my meatballs without tasting them and slept with both of my daughters."

Owen winced. "Sorry?"

Lorenzo pursed his lips. "I forgive you! About the daughters, that is. The meatballs—I need more time. Being dead puts a lot of things in perspective. Anyway, I've been instructed to be your guide."

Owen regarded him, stunned. "My guide to . . ."

"Heaven, of course, my friend. So let's not delay. Nice vampires are welcome there, too, I'm told. Your sordid past is not an issue, apparently."

"I *am* a nice vampire," Owen said, smiling. "Usually, anyway. But I don't know if I'm ready . . ."

"There are many beautiful women who, I'm told, have asked to see you immediately upon your arrival."

"Hmm." Owen looked down at himself and brushed off the sleeve of his shirt. "Then what are we waiting for? Lead the way, disembodied head. Lead the way."

"Follow me." Lorenzo began to fade away until he was completely gone.

Owen also started to fade. "Good-bye, all. Sorry again for any problems I caused. I'll send a postcard if I can . . ."

And then he was gone.

I found I was smiling. Heather wiped away her tears.

Owen was bound for a babe-filled Heaven. It was a fitting end for the vampire. He was no angel, but I hoped he'd be very happy up there.

Meanwhile, Rose had taken a seat on the couch. She reached for her knitting while I watched her warily. She seemed oblivious to anything that had happened.

Raina's gaze moved to Thierry. "So now what?"

Her eyes were blue again; the magic that had charged the air was only a memory now. The house was a mess, there was a crack in the bay window and a dent in the wall, everything that could be broken in this room was broken, but the house still stood, and we were all alive.

"What do you mean?" Thierry asked.

"Will you inform the Ring that I'm living in Salem? That I bleed vampires twice a year so I can stay alive and well? Will you notify the handful of witch hunters who still take pleasure in eliminating threats like me?"

Her words were cold and unemotional again, and that worried me. Thierry's reply might mean the difference between her being a good witch and her being a bad witch.

"The Ring would want to know," Thierry replied. "You are incredibly powerful. And you are one who uses vampire blood to sustain her immortality."

"And I plan to continue to do so for many years to come. So what of it, vampire? Will you share my dark and sordid past with those who would do me harm?"

I bit my tongue, letting him handle this without any input from me.

He glanced down at where I held his hand, his lips curving as he noticed how tightly I now gripped it. "I know you saved Sarah's life today. That is worth more to me than you'll ever know. It's reason enough for me not to tell the Ring of your existence. Apart from that, we all have a past to reckon with, no matter how old we are. It's how we govern ourselves now that makes a difference. I believe in change, even for the worst of us. I believe that the future is not wholly reliant on the past. Personally, I have great hope for that future."

She swallowed hard. "Have you always believed this?"

He shook his head. "It's a recent realization of mine. *Very* recent."

"What convinced you?"

"The woman standing next to me."

I tried very hard to ignore my swelling heart, but that was next to impossible. "Who? I don't see anyone here but little ol' me."

His lips quirked. "I guess she left earlier."

I couldn't help but snort at that. "Always joking around."

"Yes, I'm such a joker." He directed his amused gaze back to Raina. "For what it's worth, I don't plan on telling the Ring or anyone else about *any* alpha witch currently living in Salem. However, I would appreciate it if you choose your future coven with a bit more care."

Raina laughed out loud at this. "I may be powerful, but I've never been the best judge of character." She glanced at Heather. "What about you?"

Heather regarded the alpha witch warily. "What do you mean?"

"The full strength of your magic has been hidden from you for years."

"Oh yes," Rose added absently as her knitting needles clicked together. "Heather's mother was a very powerful witch. I'm sure Heather will take after her eventually. If only she believed in herself!"

Heather glanced toward her grandmother, pain sliding through her gaze. "I believe in myself now."

"Good." Rose nodded, her attention not leaving the colorful afghan. "I'm so happy to hear that."

"If it helps, I believe in you, too." Raina's gaze traveled over both Heather and Todd, who hadn't left her side. "And I want to help you learn, to grow, to make sure that you can handle the gift you've been given."

Heather didn't reply for a very long time. She studied her clasped hands. I wasn't sure what her answer might be—perhaps to deny the magic she had, to go back to when it was safer and simpler. But this experience had changed her, made her stronger, and not just when it came to her hocus-pocus ability.

She did finally believe in herself. The thought made me very happy.

Finally she nodded. "Thank you, Raina. I accept."

"You'll need a familiar," Rose added. "A nice black cat . . . yes, that's a good familiar for any young witch. You'll have to go to the shelter and see what stray animals they have. The best familiars are strays."

Speaking of stray animals . . .

Everyone looked at Todd.

"I should probably go," the shifter said tightly.

Heather finally drew away from him, as if realizing for

the first time how close they'd been during this entire magical showdown. "Yeah, you probably should."

The pain on his face was enough to make my heart hurt, but he didn't say another word as he moved toward the door, looking very much like a sexy, bare-chested, kilt-wearing Highlander torn from the cover of a romance novel.

"Just, um . . . come back tomorrow," Heather called after him, shifting her feet. "When I've had time to process all of this."

He froze, then slowly looked over his shoulder. "You really want me to come back?"

She shrugged. "Tomorrow I'll know if I can ever forgive you and start dating you again now that I know you were my secret guardian toad for two months *without saying a goddamn thing to me while letting me get naked in front of you on a daily basis, you jerk*!"

His mouth fell open. "You are so sexy when you're furious, you know that?"

"Go!" She pointed at the door, which magically swung open.

"I'm going. Bye, everyone!" He gave her a grin. "See you tomorrow, Heather."

When he left, I was about to comment on the whole Todd situation when I heard a buzzing sound. It was Thierry's phone, lying on the floor by the decimated coffee table. Thierry picked it up and glanced at the call display.

"Who is it?" I asked.

His gray eyes flicked to mine. "Markus Reed."

My happiness about defeating the bad guys, solving the mystery, and living to fight another day faded away completely.

The Ring had rung.

Chapter 21

I followed Thierry up to our room, leaving the others downstairs.

He pressed the phone to his ear. "Markus, what is it?" A pause. "I hadn't realized you'd called my phone before this. I haven't been avoiding you. I've been . . . unavoidably detained."

Body stolen and bled nearly dry. Disembodied spirit drained of 99.9 percent of its energy.

"Detained" was a nice way to put it.

He hissed out a sigh. "I know what they're looking for. I don't have it. I never did. They'll have to look elsewhere, since I can be of no further help to them in this matter. And if they have a problem with that, then they can deal with me face-to-face, not by making inquiries over the phone. And I swear, Markus, if you ever try to bully Sarah again behind my back, you will deeply regret it." His expression tensed a moment later. "No, you can't speak to her."

"Thierry. It's okay." I held my hand out for the phone until he finally, grudgingly, gave it to me. "Hey there, Markus. What's up?"

"I've been trying to help both you and Thierry. You see that, don't you?"

My grip on the phone tightened. "Is that what this is? Help?"

"By now, you've deduced that the Ring wants an amulet that your husband spent many years seeking just before his disappearance. The elders believes he knows where it is."

"Well, the elders are going to have to learn to deal with disappointment." I flicked a look at Thierry's tense expression. "I did learn this much while I've been in Salem, Markus—the amulet was allegedly destroyed in 1687. So if the Ring wants it so bad after all this time, I suggest they time travel back to get it."

There was another long moment of silence on the line. "They won't like this answer."

"Tough. Anyway, to quote my smart and gorgeous husband, if they have a problem with that, they can deal with us face-to-face. *Both* of us." I was feeling rather reckless after what happened downstairs. Currently, I couldn't seem to summon up even an ounce of fear toward a shadowy group of old vampires who liked acquiring shiny trinkets to add to their collection.

"I will tell them that."

Thierry held his hand out toward me, requesting the phone back. But I wasn't finished yet. "Markus, do you know what the amulet does?"

"Sarah," Thierry growled. "You don't want the answer to that question."

I glanced at the master vampire as he sternly gestured for me to hand back his phone. "Wrong. I most certainly do. Markus?"

"Are you familiar with djinn?" Markus replied a moment later.

"The alcohol or the genies?"

"Some have called them genies."

Interest piqued. Definitely piqued. "Three wishes, golden lamps, that kind of thing?"

"Yes, very much like that. That, Sarah, is what the amulet does."

"Interesting." To say the very least. "Thank you, Markus."

"You're welcome, Sarah."

I finally placed the phone back in Thierry's outstretched palm. He held it to his ear. "He hung up."

My heart drummed wildly. "A djinn, Thierry? That's what this amulet is all about? You were looking for a genie to grant you three wishes?" I'd dismiss it as fantasy, but I knew by now that everything I once considered fantasy could very likely be true . . . and strolling down any given road in any given city.

His lips thinned. "I liked obtaining rare and dangerous things. This amulet is as rare and dangerous as they come. A djinn . . . it's a kind of demon. One bound to its master's every command."

"Wow." The magnitude of what that could mean to someone who wasn't totally pure of heart staggered me. "Do you really think the amulet was destroyed?"

"I never heard anything more about it, nor learned of any new sightings since. If someone has it in their possession, they've kept it hidden for three centuries."

I raised an eyebrow. "So you really didn't want to use this amulet for yourself, huh? You just wanted to put it on a display shelf, all nice and pretty? Come on, Thierry, admit it. I met the old you. That was a man who might have been tempted by power like this."

His expression turned thoughtful. "Honestly, I'm not sure anymore what I might have done had I gotten my hands on it." His brows drew together with confusion.

"You ask this as if it's vaguely amusing to you now. As if it doesn't disgust or scare you. Why?"

I took his face between my hands. "Like I said before, you're different now. You're better. That guy in the past? Not nearly as hot and amazing as this guy in front of me. My gorgeous, brave, amazing, ancient, cranky, and enigmatic husband, Thierry."

"I was always cranky and enigmatic."

"And the Ring can kiss my ass."

This managed to summon a smile. "Mine too."

I kissed him. Frankly, I'd take him any way I could get him.

The rest of the world be damned.

We stayed at the Booberry Inn that night and got ready to leave first thing the next morning. I could barely believe we'd arrived only three days ago.

I gave Heather a tight hug while Thierry took our suitcases out to the rental car. "You're going to be okay?"

"I sure hope so."

"What about your grandmother?"

Her expression shadowed. "I have an appointment at Salem Acres later today. I—I can't live with her anymore. She doesn't remember anything, but I can't forgive her for this. And I can't live with her under the same roof knowing what she did, what she kept from me all this time."

"I know. I don't blame you a bit." I gave her another hug. "You *are* going to be okay, you know. I have absolutely no doubt about that. And, by the way, I'm *always* right about these things."

"Good to know." She gave me a bright smile as I stepped back from her.

"So what about you and Todd?"

The smile wavered. "Oh, him."

"Yeah, him. He's crazy about you, you know."

"He lied to me for two months. He pretended to be a toad, Sarah. A *toad*."

I shrugged. "He wasn't really pretending. He *was* a toad."

Thierry had come back into the inn and regarded the young witch with curiosity, his arms crossed over the front of his black shirt. "You should give him another chance, Heather."

Her eyebrows went up. "You really think so?"

"He deceived you so he could protect you. While his methods were questionable, I believe he's an honorable man. If you keep an open mind, you might be surprised by what the future could hold."

I hooked my arm through his. "Thierry de Bennicoeur, resident Cupid in the making."

Heather grinned. "Maybe you're right. Maybe it's time to stop hiding from what life has to offer. I want to be fearless from now on—passionate, exciting, and spontaneous. We'll go on one dinner date and see how it goes."

"One dinner date." I nodded. "That sounds passionate, exciting, and spontaneous. Sort of."

"Baby steps, Sarah. I can't totally change overnight, you know." She twisted a finger into her long red hair. "Maybe we'll go to dinner at Lorenzo's tonight."

"Great meatballs."

"Apparently the best in New England." She paced to the entrance to the living room and gazed in at her grandmother sitting on the sofa, quietly knitting. "Raina wanted me to say good-bye to you for her. I'll be seeing her later today for my second magic lesson."

"Second?"

"The first was last night after you both went upstairs. I'm

sure you noticed that Casey's body . . . well, it's not here anymore. It was a bit of a tricky spell, but it was fascinating."

I grimaced. That was probably what Raina had done with Miranda as well. "First lesson of witch club: magically hide the evidence."

The smile crept back onto her face. "Raina also taught me something a little less morally questionable. She wanted me to do a spell for you for a wedding present. One from both of us."

Thierry and I exchanged a look.

"What kind of spell?" he asked.

Heather thrust out her hand. "Give me your wedding rings."

I eyed her palm skeptically. "You're not going to change them into platinum-coated lizards, are you?"

She frowned. "I don't know if that's even possible. But . . . no."

Hesitantly, I took off my ring. Thierry, even more hesitantly, took his off as well. We placed them in the palm of her hand. She covered them with her other hand and closed her eyes. A moment later, a blinding white flash of light emanated from between her fingers.

When she uncovered the rings, they were still there and they looked exactly the same as before.

"All done," she said brightly.

I took my ring from her, expecting it to feel different, but it felt the same. I slipped it back onto my finger. "What did you do to it?"

Her eyes glinted mischievously. "Just a little something."

"Care to share?"

"I'd rather you discover it for yourself."

"That's ominous. And after the last few days, I'm not all that comfortable with ominous."

Heather laughed and followed us to the front door. "So where are you headed now?"

"Good question," I said, and looked at Thierry. "What's next on our jet-setting agenda?"

He raised a dark eyebrow. "Let's just say that there will be sandy beaches. Plenty of shade. And many of those fruity drinks you like with the little paper umbrellas."

My breath caught. "We're going on a honeymoon? A real one?"

He nodded. "I've already informed the Ring that we'll be unavailable for two weeks. Perhaps more."

I gave him a huge grin. "This is the best news I've had in . . . well, it's been quite a while. You're kind of brilliant, you know that?"

His lips curved. "I thought you'd approve."

Thierry opened the door and I enthusiastically dug into my purse to find my sunglasses. It was an incredibly bright day, and I preferred not to be blinded on our drive to the airport if I could help it. I put them on and paused to adjust them, checking myself in the hallway mirror, then swiped my finger along my bottom lip to fix my hastily applied lip gloss from earlier in the—

Wait a minute.

I slowly glanced at Thierry's reflection. He, in a word, looked stunned.

"I can *see* you," I managed, gesturing wildly. "In a mirror. A regular, human *mirror*."

His brows drew together. "And I can see you, too."

I looked back at Heather, my mouth open wide. "You did this, didn't you?"

She could barely hold back her grin as she shrugged. "It was Raina's suggestion. A witch's spell took away a vampire's ability to have a reflection in the first place.

Even an alpha can't change that across the board, but for a couple vamps we can make a bit of an exception. Just don't lose those rings."

Every mirror. Everywhere. No need to avoid reflections for fear of freaking out any nearby humans who could alert vampire hunters.

"Best wedding present ever!" I grabbed her into another tight hug. "Seriously. You are so awesome! Thank you!"

Thierry laughed low in his throat. "You are a very talented witch, Heather."

She grinned. "I know, right? Who knew?"

I wasn't lying. It was a great present, one I appreciated maybe a little too much for someone who didn't consider herself nearly as shallow as she'd (arguably) once been. But really, you don't know how important a reflection is until you've lost it. It wasn't life or death, it wasn't the end of the world *not* to have one, but to have it back—well, I couldn't lie. It rocked.

I studied my hazel eyes for a moment before shifting my gaze to Thierry's stormy gray ones. They were the same eyes I'd looked into when I'd met the younger Thierry—the one who didn't have quite the same maturity, who hadn't learned the right lessons, who hadn't come nearly as far as the one I'd chosen to spend the rest of my life with.

Same eyes, but a much different man existed behind them.

That other Thierry would learn, he'd grow, and one day in his distant future when he least expected it, he'd meet a young brunette with a tendency for sarcasm and a knack for getting herself into deep trouble at the drop of a hat. I wished that other Thierry luck—he was going to need all he could get.

I was perfectly happy with this one, thank you very much.

Read on for a sneak peek of
Michelle Rowen's next
Immortality Bites Mystery,

From Fear to Eternity

Coming from Obsidian in summer 2014

If I wrote the vampire handbook, I'd include the following three tips that every fledgling should remember: First, try not to smile too broadly in public. Fangs have a tendency to freak people out. Second, locate the nearest blood-selling establishment as soon as you arrive in a new city so there are no—*ahem*—accidents. And third, don't get cocky. Just because you're "immortal" now doesn't mean there isn't a long list of people who'd like to challenge that theory.

And some vampires have longer lists than others.

With uneasiness, I eyed the massive mansion at the end of the long, winding driveway as our taxi drove off into darkness.

"I *really* don't feel good about this." My comment earned me the edge of a smile from my husband, Thierry. "What? Why is that funny?"

"Only because you're suddenly the cautious one."

"I'm always cautious."

This earned a full-on look from him. *"Always?"*

"Look 'cautious' up in a dictionary and you'll see my

picture. Also look up 'tentative' and 'wary.' It's a full photo spread. More of a collage, really."

"I think I must have left my real wife back in Hawaii. Who are you and what have you done with the delightfully reckless Sarah Dearly?"

When Thierry got sarcastic, I knew I was in trouble. That was my specialty, not his.

"I guess I'm cautious on the rare occasions that you're not. I mean, what is this place? Who invited us? And, most important, when can we leave?"

"After I get some answers." The humor faded from his face, which was actually a relief. He wasn't sloughing this off as nothing.

This was *so* not nothing. This was very much in the realm of *something.*

I'd just experienced the most divine three weeks of my entire life—in Maui on our honeymoon, which included beautiful beaches viewed from the shade of umbrellas (vampires don't burn up in the sun, but we will get a hell of a sunburn if under its glare for too long), all the fruity cocktails I could stomach (about three times as many as you might guess), a luxurious private house rather than a hotel suite, a plethora of shops to explore, and, especially, spending one-on-one time with my gorgeous if enigmatic husband. I didn't ever want it to end.

But, as the saying goes about all good things . . .

At least I had the pictures to remember it had actually happened.

The most surprising thing about our honeymoon? No drama. No ghosts, no evil witches, no vampires with agendas, no shape-shifters with attitude. Just bliss with a capital *B.*

But then Thierry got the e-mail. It came in late Thursday night from an unknown sender. It was a personal invitation for Thierry to attend an auction tonight in Beverly Hills.

He got a lot of e-mails and a lot of invites to charity functions and other important events, so I wasn't sure why this one had seemed to trouble him so greatly. I looked over his shoulder at it to see that the PDF file looked professional and alluring. And California—well, I'd never been to California before. Swimming pools and movie stars . . . Sign me up.

It wasn't the invitation itself that bothered him. It was the unsigned message that went along with it.

I have something you've wanted for centuries, something you've only recently thought of again. You believe it was destroyed, but it's not. Bid enough on it and it can finally be yours.

It was enough for Thierry to immediately get on the phone and book a flight away from paradise and back to reality.

"You don't have to come with me," he'd said as I started throwing my clothes into my suitcase without even folding them. "You can stay here and I'll return when it's over. I told the elders we wouldn't be taking any new assignments for a month and there's still a week left."

The elders were Thierry's brand-new bosses—the leaders of the vampire council known as the Ring. Thierry had recently taken a job with them as a consultant, a traveling investigator who looked into vampiric problems of all shapes and sizes as they arose—problems the Ring deemed dangerous or unsavory when it came to protecting the secret from the rest of the world that vampires existed and that we very rarely sparkled.

I launched some wadded-up ankle socks into my suitcase like a pair of Angry Birds. "Just what is this *something* you've wanted for centuries that you thought was destroyed . . . ?" I trailed off, my eyes widening. "No way. It couldn't be."

His lips thinned, which translated nicely into: "Why, yes, it most certainly could be."

"The amulet?" I gaped at him. "But . . . that's impossible. We already know it was destroyed. And now it . . . it's miraculously up for auction? That's *way* too much of a coincidence, isn't it?"

"It seems to be, but I don't know for sure. There's only one way to find out."

I began pacing the bedroom and ringing my hands. The floor-to-ceiling window looked out at the beach and the ocean, a view like something from a beautiful postcard. "Somebody wants to kill you. This is the carrot they're dangling in front of you to . . . to lure you into a deadly trap!"

"Paranoia doesn't suit you, Sarah."

"And becoming a big dead puddle of goo doesn't suit you, either."

He stopped me from my frenetic pacing by gently taking me by my shoulders. "It's only an auction. And if by chance it is what I think it is, then I need to acquire it so it can't fall into anyone else's hands. It's that simple."

"Simple, huh? Great." I let out a long, shaky breath. "Three weeks with no problems. I guess that's way more than I'm used to."

"This isn't a problem. It's an opportunity."

"Now you sound like a fortune cookie. And by the way, I'm definitely coming. Unless you tell me in no uncertain terms that you don't want me to, I'm on that flight."

He raised a dark eyebrow. "You hate flying."

I grimaced. "Flying is great. I love flying. Every moment I'm a mile above the ground trapped inside a metal coffin of death is fun times."

Positive thoughts only.

So the plan for tonight was pretty simple. We'd go to the auction, we'd check things out, and we'd scram the moment we got enough information.

At least, that was *my* plan.

I knew practically nothing about this amulet, but what I did know scared the bejesus out of me. There was a time, centuries ago, when my tall, dark, and gorgeous, secretive, well-dressed, charming, delicious, usually non-sarcastic—did I mention secretive?—husband got a bit bored with his immortal life. This was well before he met me, of course. I'm only twenty-eight, sired less than a year ago, and he's pushing seven centuries.

But I digress.

Olden-days Thierry liked collecting expensive, magical, and sometimes deadly objects. I enjoyed collecting Beanie Babies at the height of their popularity. We all have our hobbies.

This particular bauble he sought, however, was a bit more dangerous than any other. It was an amulet that allegedly contained a djinn—that's a genie to anyone not familiar with the clinical term. And a djinn is a kind of demon that will do the bidding of its master. And its master would be anyone who possessed the amulet.

This amulet was rumored to have been destroyed around three hundred years ago, give or take a decade or two.

Destroying demon-filled objects seemed like a good plan to me. But if it might actually still exist?

Bad plan.

Even worse was that glint of distinct interest I saw in Thierry's gray eyes on the taxi ride over here from our hotel when he'd mentioned the amulet again. It was only for a moment, but it was enough to make my stomach do a very unpleasant and uncoordinated hula dance.

Thierry wasn't always quite as awesome as he is now—there was a time when he was power hungry and didn't particularly care who he hurt. And he'd never told me just what he planned to do with that amulet had it ever got into his possession. And, yeah, maybe that did worry me just a smidgeon.

A microscopic smidgeon.

I hooked my arm through his as we entered through the ornate front doors into a house that looked like a cross between *Spartacus* and the Playboy Mansion. Expansive black marble floors. Thick Roman columns. A massive crystal chandelier hanging above our heads. A winding staircase with gold railings that looked like something out of a movie—an expensive one that had no possible chance to recoup its budget.

"Wow," I breathed. "Welcome to Lifestyles of the Rich and Snotty."

"Yes, welcome," a tuxedoed butler said, nodding slightly to acknowledge us. He made me jump, since he seemingly appeared out of nowhere. "Your host will be joining you soon, at which time the auction will begin. Please join the others in the parlor and enjoy some hors d'ouevres and champagne until then."

"And who might our host be?" Thierry's cool, apprais- ing gaze swept the foyer before landing on the butler.

"Your questions will be answered in due time, sir. The parlor is just ahead through those doors. Please, enjoy yourselves and let me or the other servants know if you require anything further."

He moved away without another word.

"Mysterious host," I said. "Ominous mansion. Creepy invitation with dubious intentions. But, hey, at least there's free champagne."

"I knew you'd find the bright side to all of this."

I blew out a shaky breath. "We're leaving the moment we can. Promise me you are not going to do anything crazy."

Thierry gave me a pointed look. "I don't do crazy, Sarah."

That was debatable. But . . . okay.

If the foyer looked like Hugh Hefner visits Rome, the parlor was way more *Downton Abbey*. I swear, it felt as if I'd stepped back in time. Which, since I'd done that fairly recently for real, was a bit disconcerting.

There were at least twenty guests here, milling about and chatting with one another.

As a maid walked by, I snatched a flute of champagne off her tray and took a long sip.

"Sir?" the maid asked. "Would you like one as well?"

"I'd prefer a cranberry juice."

"Of course. I'll be back in a moment." She moved off toward a door at the back of the room.

"No champagne?" I asked.

"Not in the mood."

Due to a rare addiction to blood that brought out his dark side, Thierry avoided the red stuff whenever he could. At his age, he didn't need to drink blood to survive. But he still had a preference for crimson-colored beverages.

"So, here we are," I said, glancing around the group.

"Yes, here we are." His gaze cut across the crowd. "And there are more surprises. I know several people in attendance."

"You do?" Everyone was a stranger to me. But when you were as old as Thierry, your Facebook friend list got a bit long. "Like who?"

"Andrew Myles." He said this only loud enough for me to hear it. His attention was fixed on a dark-haired man on the other side of the room, one with a thick body like a football linebacker and round glasses that magnified his eyeballs to twice their size. "One of the Ring's elders."

A breath caught in my throat. "One of the elders is here?"

"Yes." He didn't sound thrilled about this, but I wasn't all that surprised. There was no love lost between Thierry and his new employers. He hadn't exactly accepted the job because he relished the chance to sign fifty years of his life away—a standard Ring contract—literally in blood. "But, really, I can't be that surprised. Andrew would be the one most interested in acquiring the amulet for himself."

My mouth had gone dry so I took another swig of my champagne. "Will he cause a problem?"

"Undoubtedly."

"Great. More reason for us to skedaddle as soon as inhumanly possible." Another person who stood next to Andrew caught my eye. "Is that . . . No, it couldn't be. Wait—yes it is. Is that Sasha Evans?"

Thierry blinked. "It is."

"Sasha Evans here? I mean, I know this is California, but . . ." Color me starstruck. Sasha Evans was a beautiful, blond, and willowy A-list movie star known for her two Oscars as well as her long list of infamously stormy relationships with some of the hottest actors in Hollywood.

I was a major fan of both her movies and her scandals.

"Sasha's collection rivaled my own at one time. I've seen her at many events like this over the centuries."

I tore my gaze away from the gorgeous blond actress to stare at my husband. "You're telling me she's a vampire?"

"Yes, that's exactly what I'm telling you. Some say she's a witch, too, but that's more from reputation than magical ability."

"A *vampire*. But . . . how is it possible that no one's found out the truth?"

"Well, this is Hollywood. I'd give her a couple more years before she likely stages her own death so no one wonders why cosmetic surgery has preserved her so very well for her rumored age."

Sasha Evans was a vampire. The tabloids would *love* that little piece of gossip.

"I see the Darks are here as well." His words were now coated in a layer of disapproval. "They don't come out very often."

"The Darks?"

"Yes, Anna and Frederic Dark, the couple to your left in the corner looking deeply morose."

I glanced over to where he gestured to see two people with impossibly pale skin and hair so white that I would've guessed they were albinos if it weren't for their black eyes. They wore black from head to toe.

"They're rather . . . dramatic." They were the physical representations of what most people expected when you said "vampire." Very goth, very pale. And they were engaged in some deep conversation as they ignored the rest of the party. "You know, I've seen something like them before. That girl I met in Las Vegas, the one who stayed underground so long that the sun now burns her."

"Yes, the Darks are the same—by choice. Some vampires have taken it upon themselves to become, as they say, *purified*, which to them means avoiding the sunlight completely. But it's a self-fulfilling prophecy. They avoid the sun, so eventually the sun harms them after they lose pigment and their eyes turn permanently black. They take this as a sign that they're evolved—it's like a religion to them. Their faction would like all vampires to behave the same." His expression darkened. "Sometimes this is used as punishment for a vampire, forcing them to remain in darkness until they can no longer walk in the sunlight. It's a very long and painful process to return to normal."

There was something in the way he said it, something that made a chill run down my spine. "You've experienced this personally, haven't you?"

A small, humorless smile touched his lips. "You need another glass of champagne."

I sure did.

The maid returned with a tray of champagne and one highball glass with cranberry juice. Thierry took it from her with thanks and handed me a fresh flute of the bubbly.

"I'll take that as a yes," I said.

"You know I don't like to talk about my past."

"Oh, I know. But sometimes when you say nothing, it tells me everything." I swallowed past the lump that had suddenly appeared in my throat. "It hurts me to know you've been through so much pain in the past."

He smiled and leaned over to softly kiss me. "I've survived. I'm here with you now and all is well, Sarah. Never better, actually."

"I'm glad to hear that."

His gaze moved to something over my shoulder and his expression hardened. "Oh no. *She's* here."

"What? Who's here?" Alarmed, I turned around to see what had coaxed such an unpleasant reaction. "Oh crap."

I promptly swallowed the rest of my champagne in one greedy gulp.

"My dear Sarah! My darling Thierry!" The "she" in question made a beeline toward us and clasped my face between her hands to kiss me noisily on both cheeks. Then she did the same to Thierry. "What a wonderful surprise to see you both. It's been much too long!"

Not nearly long enough in my estimation.

The woman rivaled Sasha for being the most beautiful in the room. Where Sasha was pale elegance, Veronique was raven haired, couture styled, Louboutin pumped, and had the face of an angel and the body of a lingerie model.

And did I mention she was Thierry's ex-wife?

"Veronique." A smile—which looked more like a grimace—drew Thierry's upper lip back from his teeth. "You look lovely, as always."

"I do try." She flashed me a killer smile. "As does your darling little girlfriend."

"Wife," Thierry corrected. "Sarah and I were married a month ago in Las Vegas."

The look of utter shock that slid behind her eyes at this announcement almost made me laugh.

Almost.

Don't get me wrong. I didn't despise Veronique at all. We'd met before, back when Thierry was still married to her, if estranged. She was not only his ex-wife, but had also been the one to turn him into a vampire in the first place. They'd met during the Black Death plague in

Europe six and a half centuries ago and been together on and off ever since.

Well, until he met me.

I still didn't think Veronique had gotten over her shock that her ex-husband's little "fling" had turned into something way more than either of us could have anticipated. Not that she cared either way. If there had been any real love in their marriage, it had died around the same time as Shakespeare. Or, you know, somebody really old.

"Well," she said, clearly flustered by this announcement. "Congratulations to both of you. How wonderful."

"Thank you," Thierry said. He slid his arm around my waist. "We're very happy."

"Happy?" She raised a perfectly waxed eyebrow. "I had no idea you were capable of that particular emotion, Thierry."

"No," he said. "You wouldn't."

"Veronique," I interjected before the tension got any thicker. "Wow, it's great to see you again. And it hasn't been *that* long. Only a few months."

"Long enough for major life-altering events to occur. Goodness, my dear. Married! To my husband—"

"*Ex*-husband," I reminded her. "No sister wives need apply."

"Quite." Her red-glossed lips curved. "You're still as amusing as always."

"I do my best."

"Jacob, please join us," she called to a man in an expensive dark blue suit. "I'd like you to meet a couple dear friends of mine."

The man approached, grinning broadly. "Veronique, my sweet, any friends of yours are certainly friends of mine."

"This is Sarah Dearly and my former husband, Thierry de Bennicoeur. Sarah and Thierry, this is Jacob Johansson, my beau."

Her beau? How cute.

"Charmed, charmed." Jacob clasped both of our hands in turn. "Are you looking forward to the auction?"

"I am," Thierry said. "Although I'm not sure who invited me."

"The invitation came to Veronique."

"And I have no idea who it might be, either," she said. "Not that it really matters. We're here and it is set to be a lovely evening."

Debatable. Definitely debatable.

"Show them the book," Jacob suggested gleefully.

"Oh, darling, I don't want to brag."

"You have every reason to brag, my sweet. It's incredible. You're incredible and everyone should know it."

I exchanged a wry look with Thierry. He looked desperately uncomfortable in the midst of this cocktail party from hell, especially faced with this woman.

While I couldn't help but envy Veronique's seemingly effortless perfection, I had no real worries about Thierry's ever returning to her. He might have a lot of secrets he'd prefer I didn't know, but a lingering desire for his ex-wife was not one of them.

"What book?" I asked.

"Veronique's novel," Jacob said. "It came out yesterday, and with the preorders and Internet buzz, I have every confidence that it will make a very strong showing on the *Times* list next week."

"You wrote a novel?" Thierry sounded deeply surprised. "I didn't even know you *read* novels."

"There are many things you don't know about me,

Thierry. Perhaps this is only one of them." Veronique elegantly shrugged a bare shoulder. "What can I say? I was inspired to tell a fictional story. It came out of me in a rush of creative magic, if you will. And before I knew it I had a book. All I needed then was a publisher."

"And that's where I came in," Jacob said proudly. "Little did I know when I met her three months ago that this beautiful woman had penned a page-turner that I had to get on the shelves in record time. And we succeeded, didn't we, my sweet?"

"We certainly did." Veronique fished into her purse and drew out a slim hardcover novel, which she handed to me.

I stared at the title. "*The Erotic Memoirs of a Vampire Vixen*?"

"Yes."

"Catchy, isn't it?" Jacob grinned. "I was going to rename it *Fifty Shades of Slay*, but why chase the market? This stands fully on its own. Brilliant from cover to cover. And hot like you've never read before. My fingers are still singed from it! Whew!"

"And this is a *novel*, you said?" Thierry took the book from me to glance warily at the back cover.

Jacob laughed. "Well, it's not a *real* memoir. After all, there are no such things as vampires."

Veronique hooked her arm through his. "Of course there aren't."

He was adorably clueless, wasn't he?

I reached for the book again, only to find that Thierry was not letting it go without a small fight. Finally I yanked it out of his grip and glanced at the back cover description. This "novel" was about a seven-centuries-old vampiress and her sexual adventures, including those with her equally ancient husband, a dour but passionate and sexy man.

"Does this actually say 'tall, dark and fangsome'?" I asked. "Like, seriously?"

"You can have that copy," Veronique said. "With my compliments, my dear. I'll sign it for you later. Happy reading."

"Thanks," I managed, then desperately scanned the room for the maid. "I need some ice for my drink. Very, very badly. If you'll excuse me."

Thierry didn't try to stop me as I slipped away from them, tucked the book under my arm, and pursued the tray-carrying maid as if my life depended on it.

I needed to cool down. Literally. That woman . . . She drove me seriously batty.

The Erotic Memoirs of a Vampire Vixen. Ugh.

"Excuse me!" I called after the maid, but she slipped through another door. Following her, I found myself in a huge, stainless-steel sea of a kitchen.

At least I was away from the party. I pressed my back against the wall and stared at the cover of the book again.

"Let it go, Sarah," I whispered. "This does not bother you one bit."

I knew one thing for sure. I was never going to read this book. Like, ever.

Since I'd come in to get ice, I might as well follow through with that plan. I moved toward a large refrigerator and opened up the freezer portion.

It took me a moment to realize exactly what I was looking at.

Instead of ice cubes, the severed head of a man looked out at me.

My empty champagne glass shattered against the ceramic tiles and I clamped my hand against my mouth to keep from screaming.

A severed head. In the freezer.

And that wasn't even the freakiest thing about it.

A second later his eyes popped open.

"You!" he blurted out. "You need to help me! I've been murdered!"

Also available from

Michelle Rowen

Blood, Bath & Beyond

An Immortality Bites Mystery

Being engaged to a centuries-old master vampire can be challenging—especially when he takes a job with the Ring. Thierry's in for fifty years of nonstop travel and deadly risk. It's enough to make any woman reconsider the wedding... any woman except Sarah, that is.

Traveling to Las Vegas for his first assignment, they encounter a child beauty pageant contestant from hell, as well as a vampire serial killer leaving victims drained of blood, potentially exposing the existence of vampires to the whole world. But when Thierry's truly ancient history comes back to haunt him, and he's accused of a crime he didn't commit, it's up to Sarah to clear his name before their immortal lives come to an end.

"Sharp, witty and does not disappoint."
—Night Owl Reviews